Dr Rachel Armstrong is a writer and lecturer at the Bartlett School of Architecture. Having practised as a medical doctor, she has worked with artists to explore future configurations of the human body. She has published extensively in the field of the body and future evolution and is editor of *Sci Fi Aesthetics* and *Space Architecture*.

THE GRAY'S ANATOMY

RACHEL
ARMSTRONG

Library of Congress Catalog Card Number: 00–102179

A complete catalogue record for this book can
be obtained from the British Library on request

First published in 2001
by Serpent's Tail,
4 Blackstock Mews, London N4 2BT

website:www.serpentstail.com

Printed in Great Britain by Mackays of Chatham plc

10 9 8 7 6 5 4 3 2 1

To life 'out there' and to those who have inspired me

prologue

The greatest physicist of the third millennium, Damien De Angelis, set the scene for mass migration of humans from the Earth through space and time travel by changing the concept of what the universe is.

He had successfully demonstrated that the universe was alive and continuously evolving by pointing out the errors in second millennium particle physics, and so the simplest elements of the universe, the fundamental particles, were no longer regarded as being inert and separate from each other, but part of one huge interconnected organism.

De Angelis also proved that time was not an abstraction, but a form of matter which existed as various isomers: slow, fast, linear, cyclic and toroidal. Once the material nature of time had been established, De Angelis proceeded to demonstrate that time particles were the unifier between strong, weak and electromagnetic interactions and proposed the first 'Grand Unified Theory' of the third millennium. Time was the fundamental matrix of the universe that linked all matter and conferred a life force upon it.

De Angelis' characterisation of time particles enabled humans to exploit cosmic time phenomena that had once eluded scientific examination. Having the theoretical principles with which to evaluate the previously elusive properties of strange phenomena such as black holes, wormholes and 'dark' matter, astronomers and particle physicists began to understand the richness of the universe in a new light. They were convinced that, not only would humans be able to settle as independent communities on other planets way beyond the terrestrial solar system, but that in doing so, they would also encounter alien life. Reports of UFOs and alien abduction that had been classified under X-files were reopened and it was accepted that humans had already encountered alien species which had visited Earth, possibly using the properties of yet uncharacterised time phenomena.

The terrestrial civilisation was convinced of their destiny in space, too. Very soon after the advent of the third millennium, there was an explosion in the human population. The natural, biological survival strategies that had formerly allowed successive generations of individuals to adapt to a changing environment were simply not fast enough to keep up with the new competitive forces which came with an overcrowded planet.

The Earth's environments were neglected in the face of extreme competition between humans in organized social groups. Adaptive pressure on individuals led to increasingly successful lifestyles, longer lifespans, and an explosion of new technology and architectural developments that fuelled the dense population of the Earth's surface. The most cost-effective way of dealing with the enormous number of people was to build upwards. Cities expanded as layers upon layers of dwellings were added over the centuries.

Machines, technology, and human-fabricated environments were rapidly embraced by the evolving species. Even architecture itself had become intelligent. Buildings contributed directly to the population explosions as they were directly associated with individuals' identity in the advanced societies.

Meanwhile, Gaia-net, the universal information superhighway, acted as the backbone to the advanced cultures conducting economic and physical survival functions using an artificial intelligence system. With billions of people logging in almost continuously, it began to produce dangerously high levels of electromagnetic field radiation. To avoid the longer-term carcinogenic effects of these energy fields and the toxic environment of the Earth's surface that had become a cesspit of toxins and bacteriological warfare agents, human sealed themselves off in elevated pod-like cities called Clinics and gradually adapted to an isolated altitudinous existence.

Humans needed to leave the earth as the resources of the planet were dwindling but not completely exhausted. Their efforts to transcend their historical bond to gravity looked to space to provide momentum and inspiration to unify the world and progress humankind.

Space exploration was the new utopia for humankind and the terrestrial civilisation was convinced of their destiny in space, too. Life in space represented an ideal that gave humankind the chance to start again and achieve many desired cultural aspirations in science, technology, and human relationships. Although this notion had been a popular conjecture in science fiction stories, now everyone was actually preparing for the time when they would leave a corrupt and unsafe Earth behind and join SETI (Search for Extra Terrestrial Intelligence) networks. Parents were encouraging their children to study subjects that would help them survive in space, such as bioengineering, and astrophysics, as well as taking the family holiday in orbit. The ordinary people who were regular space tourists began to realise how they could take the first practical steps towards colonising extraterrestrial environments.

With the growing number of permanently inhabited space stations in the Earth's orbit, some communities broke loose from the gravitational pull of the Earth and started to look for other worlds to settle. Applying De Angelis' principles, the human space colonies learned how to manipulate time particles to travel across the universe. As they moved across great distances, these nomadic humans encountered disturbances in the time fabric that were called 'time-spills'. These were condensations of time that, on reaching a certain density, started to attract all nearby matter and even leak into other dimensions, ripping the spacetime fabric between coexistent planes. Some time-spills were of a distinctive character and were frequently named after their geometry. Therefore observers described Time Spheres, Time Polyhedra and occasionally, Time Toroids. The bigger the time-spill, the greater its effect was.

Fortunately, most time-spills were small and easily diluted by the vastness of space. Sometimes they upset local solar systems, causing turbulent time-winds, or strange reversals of planetary orbits. Larger time-spills were even more serious, causing catastrophic planetary collisions, and had even been known to extinguish suns. Time-spills were disposed to coalesce and form giant phenomena where some human space-travellers settled.

In these strange, huge time-spills, full of chambers, corridors and tunnels that seemed to continue forever, the human inhabitants experienced 'changeless time' where everything literally stood still. The settlers within these time-spills carried their own culture with them and were therefore varied in their nature, originating from the past, present or future, which further magnified any idiosyncrasies, depending on which isomers of time they were exposed to. Within the environment of the time-spill, the human inhabitants enjoyed full lifespans, but had limited fertility. With their advanced knowledge in artificial fertilisation techniques, one of the first facilities they built were incubators in which new humans were grown, but the conception rate of these experiments was low due to the high levels of space radiation. The chambers of the time-spills were full of incubators housing all sorts of strange human mutants as the settlers tried to understand how they could produce children safely, despite the strong ambient radiation.

Some humans decided that the key to improved fertility in the depths of space was to understand the reproductive strategies of any neighbouring alien life. Certain communities were able to harness the power of the time-spill in which they were resident, sampling the creatures at a distance. Others were more direct and forcibly abducted specimens to observe, interview and experiment on them. A few advanced humans even adopted features of individual aliens for themselves, abandoning the notion of reproduction as a survival strategy. They strove for immortality by continual self-enhancement as their preferred survival technique.

All these human communities living in the time-spills coexisted, but seldom met one another, as they tended to stay in discrete regions of the entity. Each community was convinced of their true pedigree from *homo sapiens*, often despite many strange modifications they had made to their anatomy and genes in order to survive. These human space travellers were never to leave or die in the time-spill in the conventional sense, but nor did they last forever. Many simply vanished, being absorbed into the fabric of the entity, just like all other matter.

As the humans travelled the universe in the safety of their time-spills, they more often than not meddled in alien systems, draining energy and resources and stealing ideas for new technologies to survive. The combined effects of the natural disruption caused by the time-spills of various configurations and the wilful intervention of the humans on alien systems were far-reaching and had lasting consequences for civilisations all over the universe.

One such example of this disregard for other species typified by the humans in their struggle for survival occurred on Rune 66.

Rune 66 is the fifth planet from the star Solar 66 and the third largest in the solar system. Three moons, Neo, Homo and Retro, orbit it. It is inhabited by a number of species, of which the Grays are the dominant order.

Rune 66 was named by its inhabitants after the markings on the planet's surface caused by the impact of dense meteorite showers. The first Grays to travel in airborne craft likened the scarring to ancient forms of writing known as 'runes' that were engraved in stone.

In contrast to most of the other planets in the Solar 66 system, Rune 66 is primarily composed of a granite and amethyst crust. This sparkling layer floats on molten silicate rock with a core of iron that is mixed with iron sulphide. Rune 66's surface is radically different from any other body in the Solar 66 system in that the impact craters are much deeper and more numerous than on other planetary bodies and, judging from their number per unit area, the surface is very old.

Rune 66 is a temperate planet and the hottest temperatures are around 40 K, though the average is lower, about 10 K. The planet has a thin atmosphere composed of sulphur dioxide and perhaps some other gases. It has little or no water. There is no vegetation or any lakes on the surface of Rune 66, but the desert rocks are remarkable for their ever-changing colours. Sometimes the planet seems red-brown and peppered with black meteorite fragments. At other times, it is uniformly and luminously violet.

Occasionally, when there is no meteorite debris in the atmosphere to decrease the ambient light, it is possible to make out some of the openings on the planet's surface to underground metropolises built by the Grays.

metropolitan life

The Grays have already encountered human beings during 'alien abductions'. These encounters have been largely accidental, although individuals from both species have demonstrated a remarkable amount of opportunism when they meet one another, since there is a spacetime weakness between the terrestrial solar system and that of Solar 66. The Grays are as unaware of this natural pathway between the two worlds as humans once were and have been equally confused and traumatised by the peculiar meetings between the species as human abductees once reported themselves to be.

Some intellectual Grays believe in the possibility of humans as real entities, but are unable to persuade their colleagues of this reality, since there is a lack of hard evidence that direct contact between the species has taken place.

However, the Psychic Grays, the ruling elite, protect and preserve the psychic integrity of the species from this fact, regarding the acknowledgement of human contact as dangerous. In the same way that humans once denied the existence of alien species, the leaders of the Psychic Grays that preside from the Sensate Senate, also proclaim that humans do not exist. The Grays' leaders actively discourage reports of alien encounters and any colleagues entertaining the notion that they have encountered humans in any way are regarded as dysfunctional.

Treatment for these dysfunctional memories is provided by Underground Intelligence who retrieve the experience and erase it. However, those colleagues with persistent delusions are diagnosed as having 'intractable psychic derangement', the treatment for which is 'reassignment'. This involves the culprit being forcibly fed to giant, scavenger Silica Worms who recycle their remains and expel them through their very primitive gut to form a newborn Gray. The newborn is without life until it is reassigned to a new identity at a special node in the psychic network and the 'revitalised' colleague is then considered rehabilitated into the community again, with a perfectly functioning new identity.

The population on Rune 66 remains stable through this recycling process. Effectively, there is no birth or death, as humans understand it, but a perpetual cycle of existence, each Gray believing it will contribute to the species in a new way every time they are newborn. In practice, only the unhappiest Grays welcome their moment of reassignment, as most colleagues take pride in their work and contribution to the culture, becoming quite attached to their bodies.

This, however, concerns the Psychic Grays who are intellectual beings with very little attachment to their bodies. In order to maintain their influence on the species, it is vital they ensure that 'psychic excellence' is generally embraced as the ultimate goal for all colleagues.

To assist this struggle towards psychic excellence, the Psychic Grays maintain correct thought by popularising educational and rehabilitation programmes over the psychic network. Many of these indoctrinating programmes are thinly disguised as entertainment for the ordinary colleagues.

The ordinary colleagues, or Crystalline Grays, look forward to their recreational breaks, or downtimes, where they are free to explore the psychic networks individually or in groups, regarding them as a virtual refuge from their humdrum physical duties. The physical strength of the Crystalline Grays bothers the ruling elite, so a taboo against touching one another has been implemented. Indeed, the Psychic Grays continue to remind the colleagues that being more intellectual and strengthening their minds and psychic bodies will offer them happier lives through the virtual experiences available to them on the psychic networks.

Some Crystalline colleagues even hope they will become so adept at uploading into the psychic networks that they will make a transition from being Crystalline to being Psychic in nature. If this should occur, then these colleagues would be eligible for election to the Sensate Senate, the most prestigious assignment that can be held in the metropolis. In reality, this transition is unlikely to occur, as there is a real and permanent difference in the anatomy of Crystalline and Psychic Grays.

The senators shape Gray culture. They are responsible for the content of the information on the psychic networks and oversee the proper production of newborns in the underground metropolis. They are also responsible for regulating events on the overground.

Although very few colleagues actually venture onto the surface of the planet, Aerial Intelligence, a crack squadron hand-picked by their leader, Star Commander, ensures that the skies are clear of meteor showers. These seasonal falls produce tremors and quakes if they are not destroyed before they reach the metropolis, upsetting the production of newborns and disturbing the ecosystem.

A few independent thinkers have managed to evade the omnipresent control of the Psychic Grays. Some Crystalline Grays are beginning to realise that there may be value in their greater physical skills and are questioning the oldest taboo, not to touch one another.

dwelling

The Chronicler was missing.

Although under other circumstances, this would not have seemed unusual, as the Gray was an experimental biologist who enjoyed nothing more than to spend hours alone examining specimens of life on Rune 66 and pondering on their relationship to the ecosystem, this time things were different.

The Gray could have been hiding itself in a crowd, as it would not have been easily spotted since it did not visibly stand out from all the others of its species. It was almost identical to its colleagues, with huge black almond-shaped eyes, a large head, protuberant belly and skinny arms and legs. However, the Chronicler would not have done this as it hated crowds and, despite its ordinary outward appearance, it was not an ordinary Gray and might have been recognised.

The Chronicler had made itself a distinct reputation, having established itself as the champion of a new programme on the psychic network that had reached cult status. Its unique personality would have made this colleague conspicuous. However, rather than basking in its newfound celebrity, the Chronicler had shunned the spotlight and its success had made it even more reclusive. When it was not working on editing its programme, it was studying quietly in its laboratory. Sometimes, it was so silent that various colleagues speculated that it had actually vanished temporarily.

The Chronicler had had no choice in its celebrity. It had all been an unwelcome, dreadful accident and, in truth, the content of the programmes was highly edited to camouflage the dreadful circumstances that troubled the scientist's life. This did not seem to worry its fans because the content was so original and entertaining. Their loyalty continued despite speculations that the programme called *Abductee* was based on real experiences, which started to spread shortly after the first programmes. Besides, the colleagues were regularly exposed to all sorts of gossip which spread rapidly through the psychic networks on Rune 66 and many bizarre theories were talking points for the entertainment-seeking colleagues who adored conspiracies.

Despite its dislike of fame and its evasiveness, the Chronicler's virtual persona was loved on the psychic network. The champion's alter-ego was an exhibitionist personality who fearlessly put its wits to the test against rather bizarre creatures, calling themselves human, in a form of combat based on an interview with the contestants.

But the Chronicler's luck changed again for the worse and its downfall was finally secured when it was implicated in a scandal involving the production of newborns in the mines where it was put on trial at the Chamber of Justice at the Sensate Senate.

Now, the Chronicler had disappeared and the Star Commander was looking for it.

the chronicle

After an extensive search of both the psychic networks and the metropolis, the Star Commander did not have much to go on to account for the sudden disappearance of this colleague. All that it had discovered was a strange notebook, made of wafer-thin sheets of silica and bound with lithium thread, that had been inadvertently left open in the laboratory of the Chronicler's dwelling.

The Star Commander wondered how many other Grays would have known what this object was. Keeping a written record was an unusual and self-indulgent means of documentation, as most of their information was uploaded into the psychic network.

The Star Commander ran its long, skinny fingers over the markings to scan-read the contents and, despite its revulsion for the task in hand, the conceptual forms conveyed were curious. They were very curious indeed.

chronicle entry

aura

I am troubled by unusual incidents.

I am not sure what the significance of these events could be, but I feel the need to record them, as they may prove informative later.

I have decided to make records of these experiences with my psychic memory sensors, but I have not uploaded them into the psychic network as would be expected. Instead, I have transferred these thoughts to the Creature Crystals in my garden for safekeeping, but this is not enough. I need to make a different kind of documentation that frees me from self-censorship, so I have decided to use a medium that I know will be private.

Grays hate reading and writing. It is too much effort. However, I do not share this prejudice as I am of a unique constitution. I enjoy the physical and intellectual indulgence of writing and gain some emotional relief from the process, as it is a physical experience.

I believe that the first incidents were caused by overwork, as I have been spending rather unhealthy periods with my experiments. I am ashamed to say that I have somewhat neglected my psychic ablutions so my thoughts are clogged and full of unnecessary psychic clutter.

I cannot pinpoint when I knew that something was 'not quite right'. I had been suffering from strange headaches and disturbances in vision for some time, but the first incident was quite distinct.

Some invisible force literally threw me to the floor and sent my sensory system into spasm. The pain was so intense that I do not remember how long it lasted nor when it stopped, but it passed as abruptly as it began. As I began to pull myself up, hoping to be able to rationalise the whole thing, it happened again. This time, the pain was bitterly electrical and seemed to arise from deep behind my eyes. I feared that my visual sensors were about to melt and that my psychic circuits would vaporise.

I waited for the next attack and, when it did not happen, I returned to the experiment in which I had been engrossed and noticed that the display indicated that a small spacetime shift had occurred. I shook the instrument, hoping that this crude attempt to repair it would reset the observation, but it did not. This was the first time I realised that time and matter had somehow been manipulated.

It has taken me a while to come to terms with the horrifying image that confronted me during a recent episode of pain, so the picture is not fully clear. I am finding it very hard to be rational, as I am frightened.

I found myself transported to a strange, colourless place against my will. The light was so bright that it was difficult to see. Although I was unable to clearly perceive what was around me, I knew I was standing over the body of a strange being. My scientific curiosity got the better of my terror and, although I wanted to run away, I stopped and made myself focus on a small part of its anatomy. I studied what I thought to be its face.

The skin was pink and covered by fine, flaky scales, bearing fine strands of protein from the uppermost and posterior part of its domed head. An obnoxious opening in the skin, located centrally on the face of the creature, bore two paired, swollen red cushions of tissue. The upper lobe was pinched at its centre whilst the lower sported a smooth curvaceous arc.

These cushions moved very slowly, undulating against one another and occasionally separating to reveal a cavity, guarded by tendrils of clear, viscous fluid. Inside this aperture, I noticed white, rectangular upper and lower rows of crystals that protected a huge, rough-skinned, slimy muscle. I watched the belly of this structure curl upward, displaying its soft, smooth, sinewy, blue underside.

Sometimes, the fleshy cushions spread themselves into a tightly stretched, intimidating horizontal configuration, bearing the rows of crystals behind it. This image intrudes on my waking thoughts, as I cannot make any sense of this peculiar feature, although I think it is aggressive.

I know the creature has something that looks like visual sensors, but I cannot look at them.

This being continues to visit me, or I am taken to meet it. These episodes are highly disorientating and I cannot concentrate fully on my experiments. I am now completely terrorised by the possibility of further encounters and everything that I do has taken on a frightening and sinister character. At any moment, I expect the great red organ with its rows of gleaming crystals and ugly muscle to confront me.

I do not understand what is happening to me. I am worried that I am a degenerate. Perhaps I should seek advice in the correction channels on the psychic network to restore my proper psychic functioning. But I am reluctant to do this in case I am found out. I must try to pretend that nothing unusual is happening and hope that these encounters are a passing phase. I am sure that I will come to understand all of this in due course. Yes, I am just working too hard! I will take a break and be more thorough with my psychic ablutions.

When I find myself in the strange place, I am struck by its inertia. It is not just the monotony of the environment, the homogeneity of the light, or that the bleached-bright chamber seems to have no limits, but that time itself stays uncomfortably still. I also know that the pink-skinned, pouting beings are with me there, but it is too brilliant to see them clearly.

I think that I am being transported from Rune 66 into this alien environment. Is this really all in my mind? I feel dreadfully uneasy and cannot relax. I have avoided uploading into the psychic network, as I cannot face any colleagues seeing my psychic body in such disarray. There is something fundamentally wrong with my life. I am tired, confused and, despite these peculiar encounters, I am bored.

Yes I am bored!

The paralysis of boredom prevents me from feeling any connection to my species. Suddenly, the main preoccupations of my species seem pointless. I have lost my enthusiasm for my assignment as an experimental biologist and perhaps the worst thing about all of this is that I really do not care about anything any more.

I am starting to look forward to the encounters, or whatever they may be, that are taking over my life. They have a gravity about them that is compelling and I hope that, if I can overcome my fear, I will learn a great deal about this ugly alien and myself.

I was able to look at the alien. It was remarkably similar to us Grays in form, with one head and two upper and two lower limbs attached to its body. However, it differed greatly in detail, as it was hairy and thickset. The face was shrunken with tiny, pinpoint eyes and hair-bearing skin that was arched around them. On each side of the face were protuberant, fleshy spiral appendages that were cupped forwards. It was a brief but memorable impression. I am fearful of it but, oddly, I hope to see it again.

I am terrified, excited and bewildered! I have visited the chamber of the creatures where hundreds, perhaps thousands, of pink-skinned beings were lying dormant on silvered tables. Some were naked, formally laid out with their faces and palms turned upwards, whilst other bodies were covered with white cloths.

Where have they come from?

I am now convinced that this chamber is in a parallel world. I simply have to accept that one moment I am going about my everyday business and the next, I am trying to make sense of these alien surroundings.

The beings appear to be in a state of suspended animation and, despite their sensory paralysis, I know they are aware of my presence. During my encounters, they have acknowledged me with their white, skinless eyes by producing tiny black holes, framed by coloured circles that gape in and out as I approach them.

It has been difficult to look closely at their grotesque, shrunken faces. I do not know if these beings are sick or healthy, but there is something perverse about their silence. I have been drawn to the red-lipped, oral aperture of these creatures as I find it aggressive, offensive and yet perversely seductive.

I observed the motion of this organ in a number of beings. It trembles rhythmically and droops whilst sucking in some nutritional element from the air. As their mouths gape, their voluminous chests rhythmically rise and fall.

I want to conduct an experiment with one of these beings, but I cannot be sure of my usual impartiality. I am acting impulsively towards them. Generally, I shun direct glances or contact with them. However, for some inexplicable reason, I suddenly put my fingers inside the mouth of one being and was immediately disgusted at myself. I averted my gaze and moved away from it, in case I felt compelled to perform some other atrocious examination.

I do not understand the effect they have on me. Despite their deanimated state, they seem to be to be able to persuade me to take notice of them and even interact physically with them. Could this be the effect of the huge numbers of these beings here? Whatever it is, I cannot avoid them. Everywhere I look, I see their naked eyeballs bursting with sudden black spots, and I know they are looking at me.

There are transparent cabinets clustered at intervals along the walls that are filled with fluid and run parallel to the rows of tables. Each one of them contains a small creature that vaguely resembles the beings that are laid out, but is perhaps only about one tenth of their size. The small creatures are less intimidating than their larger counterparts and curiously more appealing. They share the same pink skin, but theirs is unscarred with lines and covered with very tiny white hairs that trap bubbles from the fluid that comes from their mouths. All the small creatures appear to be sleeping with their heads bent forwards onto their chests and their limbs folded over their protuberant bellies. One specimen had placed a single digit in its oral aperture and it seemed very peaceful. Another small being blinked at me and, quite unexpectedly, I noticed that the eyes were black and almond-shaped, just like a Gray's.

I must try to arouse the creatures. I cannot bear the silence of this space. It is unbearably menacing. I am concerned that these deanimated beings already understand me and yet I know nothing about them.

chronicle – meditation on the past

The Star Commander stopped scanning the pages for an instant. The strange circumstances of the Chronicler were troubling. Although it was not yet apparent whether these bizarre events were the product of a deranged mind or were in fact true, the Star Commander decided to keep an open mind. Life on Rune 66 was already changing fast and it was possible, just possible, that the Chronicler's account reflected this.

In an uncharacteristically nostalgic moment, the Star Commander reflected on calmer times when enforcing the rules of the Sensate Senate was simpler.

calm before the storm

The Star Commander had regarded itself as a model Psychic Gray ever since it recognised the perfection of its own psychic body. It could not understand why all Grays did not do regular psychic exercises nor why many colleagues failed to follow its psychic correction techniques that it made accessible on the psychic network.

The Star Commander prided itself on the power of its psychic abilities and was able to travel way beyond the confines of the psychic network in the metropolis. It would make its way to the planet's surface and project its psychic body as far as it could go, scanning Far Space first, then Near Space and finally Inner Space before it returned tired but vitalised.

The senators learned of its regular adventures way beyond the planet's surface and appointed the talented Gray as leader of the crack squadron of pilots known as Aerial Intelligence.

The Star Commander was not only an exemplary team player, but also an outstanding individual. It routinely left its officers to patrol the planetary surface while it made psychic interplanetary reconnaissances that frequently extended beyond its own solar system.

The Star Commander habitually started its surveillance from Far Space. Using its psychic consciousness it would start by scanning the imperfect vacuum for wayward mirror fragments, strange particles and stubborn matter that could form meteor belts which would later pose a threat to the solar system of Rune 66.

Recently, an ominous pattern had been slowly forming and dispersing as it approached Solar 66, but the Star Commander knew better than to draw any conclusions from this. This cosmic activity was probably bits of space debris. Most celestial events had a habit of burning themselves out before they ever had any impact on Rune 66, so the Star Commander returned to Near Space.

The meteorite season was over and the heavy rockfalls would not come again until the next moon winter. The meteorologists that monitored damage to the metropolitan surface, the Spotter and the Observer, had reported that very little damage had been sustained that year. Star Fleet One had, yet again, proven their legendary psychic navigatory talents and secured yet another faultless record in atomising the most malignant meteorites. Even the dome of the Sensate Senate had been spared the star-shaped splinter fractures caused by persistent collisions. Everything was under control.

Inner Space below the planetary surface still proved problematic, however. The Star Commander was worried about the integrity of the psychic purity of the species. Turning its psychic sensors inward, the Star Commander returned to the familiar territory of the psychic network to survey and infiltrate the public broadcast networks. It indulged itself for a short while in the information-rich environments and mourned the gradual decline it had witnessed in the quality of the psychic profile of the population. Tragically, the colleagues made increasingly fragile, disorganised and ignorant psychic newborns, but the prospect of psychic decline among the Grays was simply too distressing and too much of a responsibility to endure alone. Racing through the channels, the programmes, the nodes and the postings, the Star Commander grew even more disillusioned as it sampled psychic materials for their quality of thought. Soon it was irritable with disappointment and pulled out.

There was nothing significant to convey to its Aerial Intelligence officers, but the Star Commander was troubled by its findings. The greatest threat to the progress of the species was definitely going to come from within.

meteorologists

On Rune 66, meteorologists do not study the weather, they study meteors.

The Spotter and the Observer had been assigned to monitor the asteroid belts, comets and the approach of any other celestial bodies that might threaten the metropolis or endanger the species. They produced a daily report to Aerial Intelligence who would decide, on the basis of the data, whether a Star Fleet mission should be despatched.

So, they spent all their time skywatching.

The Spotter and the Observer were obsessed with their work; they had each other to talk to and the sky to watch. Apart from reporting to Aerial Intelligence, which they did with great uneasiness, they avoided company, keeping themselves to themselves and making very little contact with the rest of the species. Their downtime hobbies were all related to their work. The most adventurous of these was to scan the psychic networks for civilian sightings of unusually large meteors and collect the meteorite for analysis. Another past-time pursuit was to plot the pits and craters made by new rockfalls. They treated the numbering and measuring of all these dents as a work of celestial art, giving each surface puncture a name and recording them all in their psychic memories.

Sometimes, they sat side by side with their psychic recorders on, just watching for fun. They chased the trails of fire left by the comets, laughed at the dizzy scintillations of tiny burning rocks entering the planet's atmosphere and measured the position of the three moons.

They gathered so much data that the Spotter and the Observer possibly performed the most psychic ablutions out of everyone on the planet and so there was a dense Creature Crystals network around the meteorologists' observatory.

The Spotter and the Observer never kept useless information so it was of great importance when the Spotter first noticed that the three moons of Rune 66 were moving in the wrong direction.

'It could be an error, Observer.'

'Error, you? Not likely. Let me take a look!'

Soon the two obsessionals had reconfirmed the data, predicted the pathways and come to the same conclusion based on the position of the moons.

'An unprecedented solar eclipse!' shrieked the Observer.

'What could be causing it?' trembled the Spotter.

'Oh,' groaned the Observer, 'I don't know, but we must find out. This is very serious!'

They scanned the skies to the limits of their psychic ranges. They sat up for days looking for clues. They contacted all those colleagues that had ever reported meteorites for any new information, but were still no wiser as to the reason for the unexpected eclipse.

'We need more psychic range,' deduced the Observer.

'Do you think we can ask Aerial Intelligence for assistance?' wondered the Spotter.

'I am not sure, but it is worth a try. We're getting nowhere on our own.' The Observer grew very serious, as it was intimidated by the strong psychic bodies of the Aerial Intelligence officers and felt particularly humbled in the presence of the legendary Star Commander.

With their next meteorological report, the Spotter and the Observer asked permission for a meeting. When this took place, the Star Commander was rather amused to see the colleagues holding hands as they approached, but it issued them a reprimanding psychic warning. They quickly let go of one another, remembering the taboo about touching.

The Star Commander became even more serious as the two colleagues explained, taking turns, how they expected that an unprecedented eclipse would soon affect the culture but they did not know of any reason for its appearance.

The Star Commander agreed to investigate the enigma and granted them permission to alert the species.

It was common knowledge that these two meteorologists were obsessed. Nevertheless, the issue was important enough to consider. The Star Commander decided to make a personal investigation of their prediction, before it wasted any Starcom officers' time on a potentially pointless mission.

chronicle entry

unique

The strange anatomy of these aliens has prompted me to reflect on my own identity and re-evaluate the life that I lead here on Rune 66. I need to understand everything that I have learnt about my species from the beginning.

My physical body, that we Grays refer to as the 'crystalline' body, was expelled from the cloaca of a Silica Worm, without any complications, in a deep recess in a metropolitan silica mine. My psychic body that had been gestating in the psychic network for exactly the same time, flowed freely into this quivering shell as worker Grays propped it against a birthing node that enables the union of psychic and crystalline bodies to occur.

I later discovered that I was unique in the independent formation of my psychic and crystalline bodies to occur at the same moment, so that I enjoy perfect balance in my physical and intellectual capacities. My only regret in my uniqueness is perhaps that I am unfortunate, as I do not consider myself either a Psychic or Crystalline Gray. I am stuck in-between these categories. Psychically-dominant Grays, or Psychic Grays, have their identity formed before their bodies and physically-dominant Grays, or Crystalline Grays, have their silica gel bodies created before their psychic bodies.

Psychic Grays dominate the species as they make all the important decisions, preferring to think about issues, whereas Crystalline Grays like to use their bodies to overcome difficulties and would rather obey orders than give them. This is very important as the politics of the species centres on this distinction, but I do not want to discuss politics, as I am rather proud of my innate balance and describe myself as being politically neutral.

No, I do not want to think about politics, as I have no ultimate ambition other than to carry out my assignment as an experimental biologist to the best of my capabilities. I prefer to reflect on those first moments when I realised that I was sentient and alive. How willing I was then to discover everything about the wonderful life that I had been given and how innocent I was to think that those blissful moments would be eternal.

I suppose there must be a comedown time for any newcomer, where feelings that were once exciting grow stagnant and routine.

Although I was fortunate to be conferred with a perfect constitutional balance, increasingly I felt that I was an observer and not a participant in Gray culture. Although I was able to carry out my biological studies objectively, from a social perspective, I felt that an invisible and persistent layer of film was wrapped around me preventing me from bonding with others.

I was unable to deal with these feelings of isolation, so I absorbed myself in my work and set about unravelling the complex anatomy of Grays and analysing the ecology of the planet. I have an inquisitive nature and I approach my subjects rationally, using both my tactile and psychic senses to characterise each new entity. As I became more organised and proficient in the experimental process, I started to conduct my experiments both in my dwelling and outside in the field.

My diligence has paid off as I have built up a thorough knowledge of the ecosystems on Rune 66. I now regard myself as an authority in the origins of the Grays and have made some interesting observations about how our species has influenced the evolution of the other creatures on the planet. A complex but elegant relationship has evolved over hundreds of millions of our planetary years and I believe that the current metropolis and suburban environments colonised by the Grays and other species have evolved as a result of a number of distinct processes.

Originally, Rune 66 was a molten ball of elemental matter that gradually cooled, forming a series of layers. With the appearance of the first solids, primitive living systems emerged in the outer, crystalline layers. These were simple energy-carrying networks and, as the different layers of the planet's crust matured and superheated gases escaped from the planet's molten core, these networks became more complex. Gradually, they rose to the surface and formed the substrate from which all of the species of Rune 66 evolved.

The Grays share Rune 66 with Creature Crystals, Silica Worms and Tunnelling Plasma.

Grays are gel-based. The bodies of all colleagues are full of hydrated silica salts that act as weak solvents for the transmission of slow chemical messages and can conduct fast signals through long piezoelectric tracts. Grays have an outer crystalline membrane that receives sensory information and acts as a protective skin.

Our most distinguishing feature is our rich black, almond-shaped eyes. These optical sensors absorb light perfectly due to a silver-based, photo-psychic pigment layer that lines the membranes. Silver is an abundant metal on the planet and can be extracted from many different salts that are used in a variety of industrial designs such as our spacecraft.

The Creature Crystals are a complex organism that may be thought of as a psychic network of crystalline particles. Where the networks overlap, they form tangles of energy called nodes and are a rich source of energy that can easily be tapped into. The Grays have exploited this property so that colleagues use the nodes to boost themselves into the psychic broadcast networks.

Creature Crystals are integrated with the physiology of the Grays, being predominantly thinking organisms but lacking physical complexity. Creature Crystals share our psychic frequencies and are able to offload excess piezoelectric energy from psychically-exhausted Grays. Indeed, the psychic network of the Collective Consciousness runs alongside and occasionally passes through the Creature Crystal seams. Grays can always be found hitching a psychic ride on the Creature Crystal networks, exploiting their greater energy.

The Creature Crystals feed on the psychic ablutions performed ritualistically by weary Gray colleagues whose thought forms are heavy with excessive negative energy. This negative piezoelectric discharge is offloaded into the Creature Crystal seams where they are hungrily scavenged from the psychic ether. Sometimes, during a psychic ablution, colleagues strain their silica bodies to assist the downloading process. Very self-conscious colleagues retain all their psychic effluvia and suffer dreadful discomfort and thought disturbances. Sometimes they have to be forced to download by other colleagues, a most humiliating affair. However, the Grays' psychic ablutions are the only sensory impressions that Creature Crystals ever receive that provide them with an idea of what it is like to be an embodied living thing.

A more benign and less temperamental species are the Silica Worms. There are two subspecies, one is positively charged and the other is negatively charged. As I have already explained, Silica Worms give birth to the crystalline bodies of Grays and make their jelly-like shells by feeding on silica salts and obtaining electrical energy from them. The ingested silica salts pass through a series of hollow organs inside the body of the Silica Worm whose cavities carry out a series of catalytic chemical reactions. Once the de-energised salt has been exhausted, it is expelled through the cloaca of the Silica Worm and the shape of the excrement produced by the Silica Worm is none other than the perfectly formed crystalline body of a Gray. This lifeless shell becomes a newborn Gray when it is vitalised by union with a psychic body at a birthing point powered by the Creature Crystals.

Silica Worms are stupid and greedy. They burrow into the crystalline deposits in the metropolis and often attack the Creature Crystals from which they draw huge surges of pure energy. Too many worms in a Creature Crystal system can destroy large sections, so they are closely scrutinised, recorded and regulated. Sometimes they have to be terminated and fed back into the bedrock from which they evolved, in order to restore the psychic balance in the ecosystem. Grays ensure that the appropriate numbers of Silica Worms are culled at different metropolitan sectors.

The Tunnelling Plasma hydrate the planet. These giant, shapeless creatures are capable of producing huge amounts of energy that release water as they milk rocks for oxides, hydroxides and hydrated amalgams. They are also scavengers and will recycle the bodies of deanimated Grays or Silica Worms that are fed to them. This explains why Grays do not become old or die as, once a colleague is diagnosed as dysfunctional, it is recycled and a new psychic identity is reassigned.

They are gregarious creatures, gathering in large herds and frolicking spontaneously as they upload their huge energy resources into internal storage organs that act as capacitors.

Tunnelling Plasma have only one dangerous characteristic: they are easily intoxicated when in the presence of free water as it short-circuits their electrical storage organs, causing stupor, clumsiness, sickness and amnesia in these beasts. Do not ever offer water to Tunnelling, or they will stampede!

It is possible for Grays to boost their psychic bodies into the psychic network that runs throughout the planet, extends beyond its surface as an invisible web and constitutes our 'hive mind' or Collective Consciousness. The stronger the psychic body of an individual, the further it can travel on this network before it needs to be recharged. There are some Grays whose psychic bodies are so powerful that they are able to travel beyond our solar system on the tendrils of this extensive network. Some Grays even claim that the network extends throughout the universe.

On this psychic network are energy-rich points, often where one tendril overlaps or passes through another, and Grays can leave information that they have processed in their psychic memory recorders for each other at these locations. Some of these junctions are complex and colleagues have organised them into centres that offer information on topical themes such as meteorology, anatomy, aesthetics, news and so on. These centres are known as 'channels' and within them are various specialist information nodes. The most organised nodes offer programmes, some of which are updated at regular intervals.

Independent psychic links between colleagues do exist and it is possible for a small group of Grays to share one another's thoughts if they position themselves along the path of the psychic tendrils.

The interconnectedness between colleagues is an important part of our physiology and psychology. Two colleagues helped me make my first upload after arguing about the best way to achieve this. One firmly believed that it should be an individual experience, whilst the other insisted that a group effort produced longer excursions and better results. The first colleague showed me how it dropped to its knees and placed its forehead on the node and I copied, bowing my head to the floor. Instantly, I felt a surge of energy shoot through my head. It was an exhilarating jolt as my psychic body was released into the psychic network. I was weightless. Both colleagues joined me, escorting me with a stabilising cushion of energy.

I found myself in a light-filled psychic channel that branched at themed information nodes. At these points, I found messages, images and three-dimensional, moving pictures on view. The diversity of subjects enthralled me; they ranged from serious scientific documentary narratives, to reconditioning programmes and the downright trivial gossip that is typical of idle minds. I could not satisfy myself that I had seen enough of the thoughts, writings and images produced by the Collective Consciousness so, when we ran out of energy, I went back repeatedly on my own. It became a habit. Sometimes, I just floated around the information nodes, waiting to share my thoughts with other Grays.

When I was exhausted, for it is very tiring for a psychic body to absorb large amounts of data because it gains weight, I would seek out a dark area on the channel, the hallmark of a node from where I could download into my crystalline body again. I was surprised to find that it did not matter which node I downloaded from in the psychic network, I would always find myself in the same crystalline body that I left behind by the upload. I am still not sure how this works.

I have always been fascinated by anatomy and I decided to go to a quiet area of the network to study my own psychic body.

I was delighted to discover that I appeared as an oval cloud of rapidly vibrating multicoloured mist with a dense body at its core. The exact colour and shape of my psychic body seemed to change according to my thoughts and feelings. Becoming suddenly self-conscious at this narcissistic introspection, I quickly downloaded into my crystalline body, hoping that no one had seen me.

As my confidence exploring the psychic network increased, I began to understand that there was some deliberate intention behind its structure. It seems that the Psychic Grays had laid down the foundations of the channels and designed the information layout at the nodes, which were themed and sectioned according to their content. Apparently, this makes it easier for Underground Intelligence to monitor and direct the psychic traffic in carrying out their sworn duty to preserve the psychic integrity of the species. Sometimes certain areas of the network, such as the gossip channels, are shut down, and uploaded colleagues are diverted through senatorially-approved channels such as those that provide behavioural correction services.

Gradually, I started to socialise in the real world and ventured further into the metropolis where I played downtime pursuits of a physical nature with Crystalline Grays who challenged me to three-sided football, 'shovel twirling' and staring competitions. I performed these games adequately, but was proficient at none of them despite my perfectly balanced psychic and crystalline bodies.

I now realise that physicality is an equivalent strength to psychic dexterity, not a handicap as suggested in the programmes throughout the psychic network. I enjoy the physical side of my existence, although contact with other colleagues is taboo.

Strangely, I feel very uncomfortable about the prospect of reassignment. I know I should welcome the process and look forward to serving the culture in another role but, to be honest, I am very happy with my current assignment and it is for this reason that I must be very careful about how I disclose the nature of recent events.

chronicle – persistence

The Chronicler's diary was full of pathological thoughts and experiences that certainly warranted reassignment. Were these encounters with strange beings related to its disappearance? Was there a parallel dimension or were these stories all in its imagination?

Despite the painful pricking of the writing on its fingertip, the Star Commander continued to study the diary, being determined to miss nothing.

cosmic entity

The Star Commander's ability to view cosmic events far beyond the solar system of Rune 66, towards the edge of the universe, was its special talent envied by the rest of the species.

In its study of the Chronicler's diary, the Star Commander recalled its discovery of a clear yet foreboding signal it had discovered somewhere out in Far Space. Could this entity have had something to do with the Chronicler's disappearance?

It was certainly unusual for a cosmic entity to be very clearly visible at this range and the Star Commander had noticed that its appearance had already been accompanied by a number of bizarre happenings on Rune 66. It had already been concerned that the Silica Worms were producing misshapen preborns, that the production rate of newly-assigned Grays had fallen dramatically and that, mysteriously, some colleagues travelling the networks had been manifesting strange new psychic body configurations.

The Star Commander had been relieved that it had not needed the assistance of any of its officers to help amplify the signal. It had wanted time to analyse and quantify the phenomenon at first hand, before it had made any decisions on an appropriate mission strategy. In order to study the cosmic entity in greater detail, it had left the underground metropolis to stand on the planet's surface and had projected its psychic body outwards, far outwards to the limits of its reach.

There it was.

The Star Commander's psychic consciousness had approached the entity. It was huge, perhaps the dimensions of a star, and was exerting a gravitational pull of such strength that the Star Commander had felt drawn towards it and been able to secure a clear view. The entity was transparent and appeared to be continuously flowing and melting like fluid. It was emitting powerful vibrations that, although inaudible, could almost be likened to sounds.

The Star Commander had strained to gather more information about this phenomenon, resisting the pull of its psychic body towards it. It had to make an immense effort to pull its consciousness back into its body back on Rune 66, just as it had felt the first signs of psychic fatigue.

That had been close!

On its return, the Star Commander had steadied itself. The return to its crystalline body had been turbulent. Was it mistaken in thinking that the planet's coordinates had shifted?

It was possible. For many years, the Grays had speculated that cosmic phenomena shaped the events on Rune 66 and a number of meteorologists were specially assigned to study these incidents. Yet no concrete evidence had persuaded the Collective Consciousness that events such as solar flares, time-spills or large celestial bodies really did affect planetary events. The discussions were all highly academic, even philosophical, and were generally thought of as being unimportant by the majority of Grays.

Some of the more educated colleagues considered these theories to have an allegorical value, but the Star Commander was convinced that these events were real. Having been able to venture into the cosmos since its coming-into-being, it was fully aware that every celestial particle was related to all the other ones. It was indisputable that the entire fabric of spacetime ran according to a simple rule of cause and effect.

The Star Commander had applied this principle to the extraordinary cosmic entity and had predicted that it would have a profound effect on Rune 66. The question the Star Commander needed to address now was not whether there would be an alteration to the ecosystem on Rune 66, but whether its manifestations were already evident. Moreover, it feared that, in this particular case if the laws of proportionality held, the effect would be even more dramatic as the entity approached.

The Star Commander resolved to investigate the entity further with the utmost urgency.

chronicle entry

mistake

I have a made a serious mistake. In trying to make contact with one of the beings, I think I may have simultaneously broadcast the encounter to the Collective Consciousness.

I cannot be entirely sure about this, but I am very worried about it.

I was trying to establish contact with one of the creatures that was lying on one of the experimental tables and noticed a pinpoint flicker of life in its white eyes. I was determined not to miss the opportunity to make contact so I asked what it was, but it gave no reply. I knew that the being could hear me and even understand what I was saying, so I tried again, but it blanked me. I tried a third time and still I got no reply. By this time, I was so frustrated by my situation and angry about being ignored that I turned up my psychic signal to full volume.

The next moment, I found myself in my dwelling, sprawled out in the Creature Crystal garden and feeling more than a little bewildered. As I came round to my senses I realised that I was still calling out to the strange being, demanding it to acknowledge me. Then I froze, realising that every uncensored detail of my conversation had been released directly into the psychic networks.

Perhaps no one has noticed. Perhaps it is best to wait for events to unfold and not to panic.

It is worse than I expected. There is great excitement on the public channels. The psychic network is flooded with questions about my encounter with the being. I am afraid that an official investigation by

Underground Intelligence is already underway and that I will be questioned about this matter soon.

I am making the most of the encounters whilst I am still free to do so. I intend to conduct my first experiments as I have discovered that some of them produce weak psychic signals. I will encourage these creatures to communicate with me and am equipped with many of my biologist's experimental tools such as probes, scanners, implants and samplers which I have found I am able to successfully transport to this place.

My first experiment was to stick my trusted probe into an obtrusively large mouth so red, swollen and offensive that I thrust it down as far as I could to spite it. I noticed the surprised expression on the creature's face and felt perversely triumphant. The probe's display unit revealed that the creature's body was composed of carbon-based compounds and I continued to shove whilst the creature rolled its pinpoint eyespots about in protest. Fortunately, the pink-skinned being was unable to move and I was able to follow the tip of the probe which was now travelling through a pink muscular tube full of viscous secretions, semi-solid residue and multicoloured debris. I continued pushing downwards, around twists and into dark recesses until the probe suddenly popped out at the most unexpected of places, from an opening between the legs!

The lower aperture was unlike the creature's mouth. It was tucked deeply into the folds of skin where the leg joints connected at the body. It was a tightly-pinched muscular organ and hidden from the front by fur-covered swellings. This anatomical opening lacked the red protective swellings of its upper counterpart and was tightly closed.

For some strange reason, this orifice does not seem as aggressive as the mouth; perhaps I am starting my experiments from the wrong end.

chronicle entry

popularity

I have been constantly worrying about my accidental broadcast and wonder how I might explain the event to Underground Intelligence, as I am afraid they will certainly question me.

As a distraction, I reviewed the psychic memory recordings of this unfortunate event that I stored in the Creature Crystal garden, looking for a loophole. I suddenly realised that the Creature Crystals had unintentionally ordered my downloaded thoughts and this gave me an idea that might solve my predicament.

I could use my experiences to make a programme and broadcast it under the guise of an entertainment series, so disguising its documentary content. I could explain my accidental broadcast as a sort of preview. This will provide me with an alibi for the time being, but I will have to follow this idea up and reflect carefully on the nature of the programme. It has to be entertaining, ambiguous and topical.

I am thinking of calling my programme Abductee.

The main premise of Abductee *is that Grays should unite in the face of an alien adversary. In our culture, we have no enemies and nothing to unite us, despite our psychic interconnectedness, so we tend to look for faults in each other. I intend* Abductee *to bring colleagues together and, naturally, I will be the champion of the species.*

Although whispers of alien contact pervade the network and some colleagues insist they have actually been party to various bizarre interactions with all sorts of unusual beings, these stories are regarded as the product of a deranged mind or wild imagination. I will exploit the Grays' curiosity and willingness to entertain conspiracies in my programme, teasing colleagues with the possibility of making physical contact with these mythological creatures. To keep them guessing, I will also aim to threaten to break that social taboo which forbids us to touch one another.

Abductee *is a really good idea of mine. I have just made the first programme and am delighted with the results.*

I have cast my own character as confident, challenging and fearless, although I wonder whether colleagues will be disappointed when they meet me in reality. I will limit my excursions to a minimum so that no one will challenge me.

I am much more at ease now, having decided on my strategy. My diary greatly complements my broadcasting activities, so now I must wait and see what happens with my strange encounters and hope that I captivate my fellow colleagues.

chronicle entry

humans

It took a while for me to reach its psychic consciousness but, after a great deal of insistence and perhaps a little gratuitous bullying, I found I could communicate with it, if only on a basic level to start with.

'Who are you?' I asked the being.

'Candy' it replied slowly, baring a set of white crystal teeth. I drew back a little from it in case it was unfriendly.

The Candy being told me that it was human and 'gendered'. From now on, I must use the term 'she' or 'her' when referring to her without using her name. I do not really understand her explanation, but I am delighted to finally make contact with one of these beings. I think she is playing with me; she is definitely full of mischief. She does not remember how she got here, but claims to have been born on a planet called 'Earth'.

'Candy!' Suddenly, the human being is less terrifying and mysterious because I know her name. I will enjoy examining her and finding what lies beneath those blonde hair extensions.

Candy uses her oral anatomy to express what she is thinking, but I have learned how to amplify her strange, low amplitude psychic forms, so that I do not have to shout. I hate trying to speak, as I am not equipped to be as vocal as she is, so we have settled on a hybrid means of communicating, exchanging a variety of psychic images, gestures and vocal exchanges to converse.

We seem to understand one another.

Candy reminded me that 'she' is 'female' and insisted that her gender role was synonymous with empowerment. I do not fully understand what she meant by this, but I am not going to provoke her on this matter, as I am certain to say the wrong thing.

Candy quickly raised the issue of gender again. She is keen to tell me about this human peculiarity. Gender specificity has a profound personal importance for her and she insists that it is the same for the whole of the human species. When humans are born, they belong to one of two customarily recognised genders on her planet of origin, which she reminds me, is called Earth, as she suspects I have not been paying attention. The other native gender is a 'male' one. Candy is biologically female, so I must refer to 'her' as 'she', as she has already said, and if 'she' were a male, I would refer to 'him' as 'he'. To confuse matters, Candy has informed me that she would rather be called a 'girl', as it is a more powerful way of describing her potential.

I must remember this. I must also pay better attention to what she has to tell me, but I am so distracted by her appearance this is quite difficult!

Candy is easy to find in the cohorts of humans that line the endless experimental chamber in this strange place, as she is the only one who can speak to me. I visit her repeatedly by following the noise she makes. Meeting Candy has helped me overcome some of the fear and loathing I instinctively hold for the human species. I even look forward to our conversations as Candy has an opinion on everything.

Candy has been cooperating in some experiments. I warned her that I would need to hypnotise her, but after overcoming her objections by demonstrating my technique in a short trial session, she said that she did not mind at all.

Mind-scanning Candy is most rewarding when I use shock tactics and frighten her into a reaction. I have found that images of disasters produce the best results. The psychic patterns she produces in response to my 'terror tactics' are far too angry to be repeated but her physical reaction is quite remarkable.

When Candy is very distressed, her eyes stare wide open and the lids flicker rapidly, her mouth falls open, her teeth are exposed and her muscular tongue coils backwards. With her face in this peculiarly contorted position, she sometimes utters a coarse guttural noise from her throat. If the experiment is prolonged, her eyes produce droplets of water that spill onto her face. These secretions are rapidly accompanied by an outpouring of stickier fluid, from each nostril of her centrally-positioned nose.

Candy has raised the gender issue again but in a rather different way. This new application of gender she calls 'sex' and it comes with a complex set of emotions, behaviours and expectations. Being gendered male or female is not exactly the same as sex, although these ideas are freely interchangeable. Sex is biological and is assigned at birth, from a cursory look at the infant's genitals, and it stays with the human for their lifetime. Gender, on the other hand, appears to be a more fluid device by which human beings establish their relationships with each other, pursue pleasure and perform a societal role.

Candy has been reflecting on the gender-based relationships between male and female members of her species. I have been listening and patiently paying attention, but cannot fathom what purpose they serve. In fact, I get the impression that the human society is completely confused by its gender-led relationships.

Humans are governed by gender and obsessed with sex. They seem to need constant physical reassurance about their attractiveness, which is a peculiarly human trait.

I feel quite uneasy about the tactile impulses of humans, as on Rune 66 it is taboo to touch another Gray. It makes me feel quite deviant just writing about this.

Candy and I discussed her sexual experiences. She initially attempted to generalise about what it is like for a woman to demand sex. From what I understood, she was mainly interested in recreational sex, a set of learned physical actions that arouses and gratifies the participants. Strangely enough, sex never seems to lose relevance to an individual human itself, but interest in a particular partner's body may dwindle over time.

I must have misunderstood Candy's rather awkward and

somewhat elaborate explanations about sex, because she suddenly sighed and tried another way of explaining things that was based on her personal experiences.

'Sex is initially a curiosity for girls. It's not something that you are born understanding, you seem to know about it unconsciously when you are a child. Later on, the girl will explore her awakening instinct by talking to other girls, seeing films with sexy scenes, and perhaps even meeting a boy where they explore having bad sex together. Despite the awkwardness, she soon starts to get used to it. Once she gets the hang of it, she gets better and better at giving and receiving pleasure from sex and soon finds she cannot do without it. Er, sometimes she finds other new boys to go with, occasionally at the same time, because she wants to try different ways of giving and receiving sexual pleasure. By the time she has mastered the gymnastics of sex, the physical side becomes less interesting and the emotional side of sex really starts to make the whole relationship work, or not. That's when the problems really start. Oh, it is complicated! Let me start at the beginning.'

Candy fiddled with a strand of her blonde hair extensions and then ran her hand over her face nervously. She wriggled about, sitting up on the side of the experimental table and crossed her ankles. I noticed her eyes sparkle.

'I don't know when I first realised that I had something special down there.'

She uncrossed her ankles and spread her legs cautiously, pointing to the furry mound of flesh between her legs.

'This is a woman's secret place, you know. I bet it's the first time you have seen one!'

Something about her body language managed to make me feel quite uncomfortable, as if I should not be looking where she was pointing. I also wondered if I was about to engage in a conversation that I should not be having, but despite my reservations about her open physicality, she seemed confident and so I allowed her to continue.

'I don't remember the moment I was aware that I was supposed to have three holes. I think I saw a diagram at school or something, but I am not sure. Oh, it's not important. Numbers one and three are

easy to find because you pee through the first and poo through the third, something you do from the day you are born. The second hole is taboo when you are a child, since I suppose it raises all sorts of adult issues for a very young girl, so number two remains a secret. Well, one day in the bath, I must have been about eight years old, I found a hole between numbers one and three that I traced with my finger and was surprised to find that, without any pain, it greedily swallowed up my whole finger. I repeated the exercise just to make sure that my finger had disappeared and not just got lost in a horizontal direction in the fold of skin that hid the number one hole. To my surprise, my finger had disappeared fully and, feeling rather triumphant, I assumed that this invisible recess must be it!'

Candy was now pulling at the fur between her legs, as if stretching the roots of the hairs was offering her some comfort. I leant forward to take a closer look at this part of her anatomy. To my surprise, she squeezed her thighs tightly together, preventing me from getting any sort of view. I maintained my position and my persistence paid off. Gradually, her knees fell apart, exposing the pleats of something that appeared to be tucked into a knot, and buttonholed by a tiny nub of flesh at one end. She looked at me as if deciding whether to encourage my interest and leant back onto the experimental table. Although I saw a puckered anus beyond the folds of her genitalia, I could now see the second hole she had been referring to.

'Here, it's tucked away. Do what I did with my little finger and slide your thingy, your whatchamecallit, the probe down here!' Although I had reservations about touching her, using a probe to make contact with the being would not really count as contact, so I accepted the invitation. Sure enough, the silver tip was eaten by this invisible hole. Candy flinched and straightened her legs out, almost kicking me. 'Right! That's far enough, you can take it out now.'

'I'll just take a few readings with my pneumatic sampler.'

'Will it hurt?'

'I don't know, just tell me if you get uncomfortable.' She wrinkled her nose impatiently, drew her knees into a crouching position again, and looked over her shoulder at the strange brightly-lit space. We must have made a strange sight, me standing over this pale pink accommodating body with my probe rhythmically pumping cells, fluids

and, to my surprise, a host of non-human, single-celled organisms. Number two was an experimental biologist's treasure. I could study this place for years!

'Hurry up! Aren't you done yet?'

I quickly finished, as I did not want to outstay my welcome. I was also rather puzzled that Candy was so concerned about this particular part of her anatomy and had drawn such attention to it, only to then lose interest in my attention. I thought that, if I had been examining another Gray, it would have probably insisted that I paid attention to its eyes, its psychic abilities and would have engaged fully in the experiment. Suddenly, something occurred to me.

'Was my examination a "sexual" experience for you?'

'Sexual?' Candy laughed and the pressure in her abdomen propelled the end of the probe outwards. Lubricated by clear vaginal secretions, it had gradually worked its way downwards and popped right out as Candy rolled around on the table, helplessly crying with laughter.

'Sexual? You? Not flipping likely! What, with your big bug eyes and skinny body? I get the feeling that you think I am obsessed with my genitals. God, you are just like a man! You think that by giving a girl a quick rub and a poke she is aroused, well, you are wrong! It takes much more than all the pushing, shoving, sweating, and grunting in the world to get to a girl's mind. Does that surprise you? We women need to have our brains stimulated before we feel sexy. Not like men at all. Are you male?'

Me? Male? Was I? I remained silent at her outburst, as I knew that I would say the wrong thing and, to be honest, I wanted her full cooperation.

'Actually, promise you won't tell a soul, but your thingy, your probe, was more exciting than my first boyfriend was.'

They had both been teenagers and sexually curious, but ignorant of their sexual anatomy. It was apparently the sexual custom amongst humans for the man to take the lead in the sex games. Candy had already mastered the terms for the male and female genitals from her biology textbook and although she had never handled a 'penis', she instructed her boyfriend in the details of his own anatomy.

'It's your foreskin!' She was amazed that he had never seen it

before. Thinking of her own bathtime revelations, she wondered how this could have been possible. With its prominent position on the outside of his body and its tempting design, her boyfriend had obviously never been curious enough about his penis to handle it, so how did he pee?

Taking pity on him, she became a self-appointed martyr, hoping that they would both gain sexual experience as she discovered what male genitals looked like, felt like and what they tasted of. She worked hard at understanding their pubescent sexuality, whilst he placed faith in her 'feminine' sexual instincts.

During this rather painful process, she had resigned herself to clumsy groping and bruising of her genitals, but her sensitive clitoris had suffered the most. Her boyfriend, despite her protestations and suggestions, could not grasp any techniques that aroused her. Instead, she manipulated their sexual trysts by moving her pelvis away from him when he pressed too hard and clinging close to him when he did not apply enough pressure. Finally, she guided his blushing erection to her vagina, where on penetrating her soft, fleshy sex recess, the young man subsequently lay quite still on top of her, making no attempt to move.

'Don't you think you should thrust or move about now that you're in?'

Candy looked at me, rolling her eyeballs. She blushed, remembering this embarrassing episode and apologising for giving me the details of the inept 'loss' of her virginity. This was not the misplacing of some object or organ, but the term that celebrated the first time a woman's number two hole was penetrated by a man's penis. But Candy had little cause to celebrate, she felt cheated, as it was an exercise without any finesse.

Candy has introduced yet another concept into the spectrum of things related to gender and human sexuality called 'love'.

Love is a particularly difficult concept to grasp. It is not an anatomical feature nor a social role but an emotion. Candy talks about her feelings, making references to everything else she has done in her life. Strangely enough, she seems more uncomfortable exposing her emotions than showing me the most intimate parts of her anatomy.

Candy tells me she has a male partner called Tyson Darke. She tells me humans usually instinctively 'pair' as male and female to reproduce and raise children, their offspring. Candy's verbal descriptions of Tyson are full of sticky pink, baby blue and musky white, whilst her psychic images are rolling clouds of purple and black.

Tyson is a 'loving' man. He puts his arm protectively around her, he spends time when he 'makes love' to her, he talks to her as an equal and her life with him could not be better. After describing Tyson's exhaustive merits, Candy bursts into tears. She says she cannot have 'babies'. Babies are embryonic offspring.

I pursued Candy's sadness, overcoming her initial resistance to my questions that were accompanied by much fluid from her eyes and nose.

'I left Earth with the first group of space settlers, accompanied by my darling Tyson and we hoped to make a new life for ourselves free from the corrupt terrestrial ways. It was very expensive to book a place on the space settlement programme, but we saved up together. We were full of high expectations and, although it took a while to acclimatise to the altered forces of gravity on the artificial space station, we persevered to adapt to the new demands made on our bodies. Our ambition was to have babies and raise them in the controlled environments that we maintained in orbit, but something dreadful happened.'

Candy's eyes filled with water again and the thin reservoir of fluid that had accumulated on her lower lids emptied onto her cheeks.

'The high radiation doses that we were exposed to interfered with our natural ability to produce children the way we had done on Earth. Tyson said it would be okay, that it would all work itself out, but we were amongst the first group of settlers and no one on the station knew how to repair the damage we had suffered. We signalled and tried to return to Earth but we were ignored. After weeks of worry, we admitted that news of our biological catastrophe would have deterred others from settling in orbit. It was likely that the commercial space corporations had deliberately ignored us, preferring to burden their consciences with a biological tragedy rather than suffer an economic disaster.'

She thumped her clenched hand on the experimental table.

'Stupid, greedy corporations! I hated them and everyone on Earth, too, but Tyson had faith. He told me that people were good and not stupid, that someone would guess what had happened and that we would be rescued. He told me that we would somehow find a way out of our situation and raise a family in another place. So we waited for someone to come.'

Strangely, the liquid had stopped and Candy's oral articulations became less pronounced.

'We were badly prepared for a life in orbit, not knowing very much about what to expect about life beyond Earth. Tyson kept everyone's hopes alive but gradually our optimism and then our systems ran down. We began to admit that we were not going to return to Earth, so we started to redesign the space station and were able to live off the energy trapped by the solar panels. Gradually, our community drifted further into space. We took quite a battering from solar winds, meteor belts and all kinds of other strange cosmic phenomena.'

Candy was almost calm now.

'It's funny, but here I feel that time has stopped, yet the space between us seems to have widened. I've somehow lost contact with Tyson and with the others, too. Really, please don't ask me any more questions, I'm tired, confused and, right now, I'm not in the mood for another of your experiments.'

Humans look very different from one another. I suppose this is an attribute of their carbon-based anatomy.

I have set up a makeshift laboratory and been taking samples from a number of different humans for biochemical analysis. None of these beings has been conscious like Candy and so I have not been able to access their psychic or sentient minds. The observations I have made of these inanimate bodies are purely physical and, as such, are not particularly meaningful, as I need the cooperation of the subject. Perhaps this is the spaceborne community Candy has been referring to.

In the absence of conscious subjects, I have spent some time making observations on a variety of tissue samples that have revealed some interesting patterns common to all humans. It seems that all humans are made up of tiny units, or cells, that are membrane-bound gel droplets which protect the centrally-placed nuclear material. This matter is highly condensed and stored as twists that seem to be a code for the basic commands to build a whole being and perform the essential functions of the organism. Although most of the nuclear strands in Candy's body cells seem to be intact, the nuclear materials in her egg cells are shattered.

'Where are we?'

I had forgotten to ask Candy whether she understood her own reason for being here in my anxiety about my own predicament and instinctive fear of this space.

'I'm not really sure,' she pondered, 'but I think that De Angelis' laws will apply.'

'What does that mean?' I wondered.

'You've not heard of Damien de Angelis?' she whooped incredulously, slapping her hands against the sides of the experimental table and kicking her legs as she threw her head back to make a weird chuckling sound.

'This is too far-fetched,' she wiped a tear from her cheek and I wondered what I had said to upset her, but I was relieved to discover that she was amused at my admission. 'Are you serious? He's only the most famous physicist of all time and his experiments set the scene for all space travel.' Then she looked at me seriously. 'If you haven't heard of De Angelis' theorems, how did you get here?'

'I don't know,' I admitted. 'I seem to be transported here from Rune 66 without any warning. Do you know of my home planet?'

Candy shook her head.

'Hmm,' she mused, 'it must be a time-spill after all. I had my suspicions. Only something like that has the power to create a break in spacetime from one place in the universe to another.'

'A time-spill, what's that?'

'It's a kind of time-planet. De Angelis pointed out that time is a form of matter and that when it condenses it forms a time-spill, or time-planet if you prefer. We can't really see these time-spills, although they form all over the universe just like ordinary planetary systems. However, unlike ordinary matter they travel about like meteorites do, with no fixed orbit.'

'So, how do you deduce that we are in one?'

'I can't be certain of it, but I have my suspicions. Once you are inside a time-spill, there is no way of proving it. All measurements act according to new spacetime laws, so everything seems usual, unless you have an outside perspective.'

'Well, things seem very weird to me. I am having a dreadful time trying to make sense of my existence,' I admitted.

'That's why it's a perfect explanation for this situation. I had assumed that you'd come to make contact with our species using a spaceship, but now that you say you are transported here against your will, this is the first evidence that can confirm our suspicions. Only time-spills break the spacetime fabric in such a way as to allow this.'

'Ok, assuming we are in a time-spill, what does it actually mean?'

Candy became very excited.

'All sorts of things! What it means to me is that we will be able to settle and that maybe now I'll be able to have children. As I mentioned, the usual laws of physics and, by implication biology, will not apply here any more.'

Candy is under the impression that I am helping to restore her fertility and make a baby. She is making every effort to cooperate in my continuing experiments. Despite possibly being caught inside a world where the normal laws of physics and biology may no longer apply, there still seems to be a problem with the mechanics of sexual reproduction between Candy and her partner.

It seems that new humans may be born when the egg of a female is fertilised by the sperm of a male during sexual intercourse. If this is true, it is amazing that a whole human body can grow from the coming together of two tiny cells and that this fusion is mirrored on a macroscopic scale by the coupling of the adult bodies.

Candy is afraid, not so much of being unable to bear children, although this is the reason she gives, but that nothing will be left of her after she dies. Humans are vain creatures and wish to live forever. Because they cannot recycle their bodies, they need to create completely new ones. Sexual reproduction is the insurance policy for human vanity, something that some of them apparently spend their entire lifetime investing their energies in and in her case failing to achieve.

So, Candy has not been sufficiently protected by her natural 'vanity policy'.

I have learned that there are other ways of achieving fertilisation, when the egg and sperm cells fuse by a variety of sexless techniques. Sometimes an egg cell can be made to divide without a sperm cell. Remarkably, it is also possible to engineer the nuclear strands in Candy's egg cells so that they are repaired, but when I suggested that Candy could manufacture her own child through using these methods, she burst into tears.

'I don't want a clone, I want a child!'

I was not suggesting that she should have a clone, but a child by what she insists on calling 'unnatural' methods. I am confused by her reaction to my offer, as I think it is the solution to her infertility problem. I also think that she has false hopes of what may happen in this strange space.

Candy told me what she thinks a 'clone' is.

Apparently, clones are not real children. Clones look like children, but they are born from nuclear material that is harvested from an adult and brought to life without passing through the natural fertilisation ritual. When the clones grow up, they are different to normal children as they are born without love.

Apparently, unnatural methods threaten Candy's perceptions of what a human being is, but I wonder if Candy could tell the difference between a clone and a natural child. That would be an interesting experiment to perform.

I have never met Tyson, but I am on his side.

Candy and I have had another argument. As usual, it is about her ability to have natural babies. Candy accused me of not wanting her to have a baby and that is why I am not helping her to get pregnant. This is, of course, simply untrue. How can I, a member of a completely different species animated through silica gel matrixes and piezoelectric currents, be responsible for a human birth? This is ludicrous and I told her so but she says that I just don't care and that I want her to have a machine-baby, or worse, a clone.

Being a Gray, I actually identify with the clones. I take the most extreme offence at the notion that so-called 'identical' beings are flawed purely because of their apparent lack of individuality or their lack of an emotional context for conception. Grays appear identical on the most superficial level, but we are all individuals in our thoughts and deeds. Can't Candy accept that the way someone looks is not the most important aspect of their identity? Surely the contribution each individual makes to a community is far more important than mere aesthetics?

Perhaps humans value superficial qualities more than internal ones, which is why their psychic powers are weak.

I have been far too angry about Candy's prejudice against clones to leave this sensitive matter alone. To be honest, I have been able to think of nothing else.

Candy says that cloned humans do not have souls. She says that this is the most important part of a human, but it is separate to the body and is capable of taking on any shape. Her personal belief is that the body is given life when the soul substance adheres to its physical material such as the fingernails, hair, excrement and saliva. She thinks that time and space do not affect the soul and it receives information in an extrasensory and unique manner. According to Candy, it can recognise objects over vast distances, journey quickly to remote countries, and associate with mythical beings. The soul knows the psyche of other people. So it is like our psychical bodies, I suppose.

Candy cannot tell me why clones do not possess souls, although they produce the same sort of fingernails, hair, saliva and excrement as naturally-born humans. She gets very defensive and highly emotional when I challenge her on this issue. I am going to have to leave her alone for a while, as we are not going to agree about this. Maybe she will change her mind if I can prove that she is wrong.

I have realised that the strange cabinets lining the walls of this place are baby-making machines, or incubators, and this has seeded an idea for an experiment that will demonstrate to Candy once and for all that she is wrong, in every sense, about clones. I cannot let her win this argument as, by implication, she has condemned the Grays as being 'amoral'.

Candy says I am being ridiculous. She does not think that I can be moral or even amoral, as I am not human. When I ask her if she thinks I have a soul, she is evasive and will not say 'yes' or 'no'. She is blocking all my attempts at reading her thoughts, and I believe that she is shutting me out.

I think she is being species-prejudiced.

I have lied to Candy. I told her that I would restore her fertility. I used this rather shameful tactic to try and change her opinion about clones. Although I do not yet know how I will do this, I intend to show her that clones are as fully moral as any other beings.

Candy has developed a habit of laughing, coughing or sneezing when I am inspecting her reproductive tract with my silver-tipped probe. When I asked her about this, she denied that her spasms were induced voluntarily. Interestingly, I have noticed that her vaginal walls are pulled in tightly when her intra-abdominal pressure rises and there are small waves of muscular excitation that rise from around the tip of the probe and ripple upwards towards her uterus and down into her clitoris. I am certain that this is a manifestation of sexual excitement.

During a particularly gratuitous fit of coughing, I inadvertently removed a piece of muscle tissue from her vagina. Candy did not seem to notice or mind this trauma, so I have not told her and have transferred the specimen into one of the incubators for culture.

Now I will need to discover how to make a clone.

I have managed to culture some of Candy's muscle cells. These units of human tissue are much rounder and less organised than the ordinary muscle, but I am delighted to announce that I have successfully grown a sheet of muscle tissue in the incubator.

I will not tell Candy what I am doing but I have managed to obtain some of her eggs from a number of ripe follicles. They are beautiful and clear, like jewels. In the centre is a large grainy nucleus full of activated DNA. I am able to take her mind off my investigations by stimulating her arousal zones. I have found her 'G spot', and she tells me that I have also discovered her A, B, C, D, E and F spots. She is having fun.

I decided to stimulate Candy's extracted eggs into dividing and becoming clones by charging them up with my own piezoelectric energy. I have placed each vitalised cell into an incubator. I hope this works!

A few of the 'vitalised' cells have grown into small curled pink bodies with tightly-shut eyes. These beings have the general outward appearance of natural humans. I wonder whether Candy's theory is correct, that perhaps some soul substance will cling to their tissues.

One of the clones has tried to make contact, calling my attention by projecting its image into my psychic vision. I have called it 'Bimbo'.

I want to show Candy this adorable being whose eyes follow me around with psychic energy from the safety of its incubator. Bimbo is particularly attractive and despite a rather pinkish tinge to its skin, it has the beautiful large eyes and the small oral aperture of a Gray. Its skinny limbs are curled protectively around its belly and I am full of pride when I see it hugging its little shoulders and playing 'footsie' with itself. I think the experiment has worked.

I almost find it difficult to believe that my piezoelectric energy has encouraged the being to adopt those distinctive features of my species. This must be one of the advantages of creating new life, ràther than just recycling bodies as the Grays do. There seems to be the potential to create a variety of appearances, but I cannot begin to guess how it works between our two different species.

I want to introduce Candy to Bimbo. Once she sees 'our' child, I know that she will admit that clones have souls, too. It is undeniable that Bimbo is brimming with immeasurable 'soul substance'.

I cannot find Candy, although I have searched everywhere for her. She is nowhere to be found in the experimental chamber. The enormity of this impossible space seems to swallow life itself. I cannot hear her voice nor find her characteristically chatty psychic images. I am anxious and have returned to the place where I usually encounter her, but can only find a cadaverous female whose lips are bleached and thin, not full and red like Candy's. This is not Candy. This is a lifeless human shell.

I know Candy cannot be far away. She would love to see this new little being and I know that she would change her mind about clones when she does. Just look at those dark almond-shaped eyes!

broadcasts

The Peeper, the Hopper, the Screwer, the Burrower, the Tunneler, the Digger, the Sucker, the Twister, and the Nutter normally spent their downtime recreational breaks together. As working miners, they used these breaks for self-improvement, which is the most relaxing diversion for them. Although downtimes for the miners were monitored by Underground Intelligence, the colleagues often found ways of escaping from surveillance.

The Peeper, like its colleagues, were physically-dominant Crystalline Grays assigned to perform a range of mining tasks allocated on a daily rota by supervisors who generally had slightly more mature psychic bodies than the ordinary miners. This particular group of Crystalline Grays extracted pure silica salt crystals from the surface pits which were subsequently fed to the giant Silica Worms in nearby opencast pits. Other mining activities that they were occasionally assigned to ranged from digging new deep shafts to reach the silica-rich seams to milking the Tunnelling Worms that extracted water from the deepest parts of the mines. Special assignments were given to the most able colleagues, such as collecting the preborn bodies of embryonic colleagues produced by the Silica Worms in the opencast pits and giving them life in nearby Creature Crystal seams.

Today, this particular Peeper had ambitions to be an intellectual and escape the limitations of its crystalline constitution. It had been looking on the psychic networks for programmes and channels for stimulating subjects that might enable it to impress its colleagues or initiate an academic debate.

The Peeper was trying to ignore the Sucker and the Nutter who were giggling together. They were teasing the Hopper who was a serious worker.

'Go on, Hopper! Put your pick down, unless you are going to introduce it to us all. Does it have a name?'

'Get lost, Nutter! I just like the way it feels. It relaxes me!' growled the Hopper, resenting the commentary on its personal habits and annoyed that it felt that it had to defend itself.

'Ooh, it must be good!' sniggered the Sucker. 'Can I have a touch, too? Does anyone else want to play Stroke the Pick at downtime?'

The Peeper sighed quietly to itself as the colleagues continued to bicker about the Hopper's workaholism. It did not want to waste time with pointless arguments, it wanted to debate and was trying to decide between three subjects that had captured its attention, wondering which of them would be most likely to capture its colleagues' attention. It was so terribly bored with trivia and gossip and was keen to change the subject.

Ecology, biology, and meteorology were all healthy subjects for discussion, but it could not decide with which one it could open a sensible conversation.

The Peeper reminded itself of the various themes within the academic disciplines and scanned its limited psychic memory for the information it had downloaded from the public channels.

The Ecology Channel was the Peeper's favourite place to search when it uploaded onto the psychic network but, just at this moment, there really did not appear to be anything new that captured its interest. The same old stories about the seamless integration and psychic harmony of the species on Rune 66 were being illustrated by beautiful but overused imagery of the interconnection between them. The Peeper hated nothing more than a rerun and its colleagues would soon say that they were bored. It also had a sneaking suspicion that it had already used this programme before. It would not risk the ecology option.

The Biology Channel was full of images of Grays working

peacefully with the other creatures on the planet, positioning the role of the miners as crucial to the well-being of all those in the metropolis. The Peeper suddenly took a dislike to the information. It had originally been drawn into the programme by a rather magnificent visual sequence of a Silica Worm bringing a perfect preborn into being, but on replaying this track, the Peeper was irritated by the soundtrack. It was patronising and insinuated that the miners were brainless colleagues who had nothing on their minds but to pick away at silica crystals all day and produce the salts for the greedy Silica Worms. The whole tone of the programme felt very insulting and the Peeper wanted something more challenging.

The Meteorology Channel had provided some interesting graphs and forecasts of the meteor showers, but the Peeper's attention was drawn to a claim posed by the site's hosts, the Spotter and the Observer. These Psychic Grays were the most famous meteorologists on Rune 66, and were assigned as the advisers to the Star Commander and its fleet of Aerial Intelligence Officers. Their views on cosmic events were widely respected. So, when these colleagues claimed that there would soon be an unprecedented eclipse of the sun, the Peeper was concerned. The Spotter and the Observer had warned that ordinary laws of cosmology could not account for this unexpected event and even conjectured that the eclipse was a sign that signalled the end of Gray society, as it was currently understood.

This was very alarming news. If the end of the species was imminent, the Peeper thought that the miners should take matters into their own hands and do something about it. Psychic Grays were inclined to just discuss important issues without ever acting on their theories. This item would be a perfect gambit to secure the attention of the others and so the Peeper made its announcement.

'That's just moon-talk!' laughed the Digger. 'Don't they also say that, when the moons are in alignment, the crazies of the planet become most active and that is when the colleagues are most likely to break taboos such as touching one another?'

'Yes!' added the Screwer, trying not to split its sides laughing.

'Some say that every preborn that comes-into-being at this moment will be a mutant!' and it closed its right eye, curled one arm and leg towards its chest and started hobbling along, shouting.

'The end of the Grays is coming. It's the End of Time, the end of all of us!'

Even the Hopper, who still had not put down its pick and, until moments ago, was thoroughly fed up with the taunts of the Sucker and the Nutter, was laughing.

'Peeper, you will believe in anything! I, for one, can say quite resolutely that even if the eclipse is spectacular, I will definitely not be going onto the planet's surface to watch the skies, when there is work to be done here!'

The others were still laughing, joining in with the Screwer's impressions of how the Grays would appear when the end of the planet was upon them all but, one by one, they managed to struggle a few words out of their choking hysterics to support the Hopper's rebuttal.

'Nor will we!' and they dissolved into laughter again.

'Well, I most definitely will!' snapped the Peeper, 'I most definitely will!'

The Peeper crept into a natural recess away from the rest of its colleagues to start a new set of exercises guaranteed to improve its psychic body. Fortunately, it had managed to take its downtime at Break Five, so that the others who usually shared its even-numbered breaks would not coerce it into spending time with them. The Peeper was now free to pursue its own recreational devices unobserved. It looked out of the recess one more time, feeling guilty that it had avoided its regular colleagues in this manner.

Outwardly, the Peeper appeared confident about being a natural entertainer but, inwardly, it felt inadequate. It was determined to improve its self-confidence, but it lacked direction, having a habit of following the latest trends in Gray culture.

Recently, it had come across a programme on the psychic network dedicated to the legendary Star Commander. This colleague was famous for having the strongest psychic body of all the Grays, and thoughts of being able to travel throughout the entire psychic network, as well as into space, had caused the Peeper to fantasise about becoming a Psychic Gray. Although this was not possible as psychic and crystalline abilities were conferred at the moment when the newborn Grays were vitalised, this did not stop the Peeper attempting to improve its own weak, psychic body. So, it abandoned the documentary channels and fashionable memory improvement programmes that it had been following and set about the new exercises that guaranteed immediate increases in psychic strength. If its colleagues found out about this new fascination, they would laugh, making the Peeper feel completely insecure again and their taunts would undo all the benefits of the psychic work it was about to perform.

So the Peeper made one final check that no one was coming and uploaded itself into the psychic network. The Self-improvement Channel was easy to find as Aerial Intelligence was diverting colleagues to the site. The Peeper browsed the different programmes available and, as it was passed by the beautiful auras of Psychic Grays which were also drawing information from the site, it felt increasingly self-conscious. Hurriedly, it selected a programme called *Think Beautiful* and downloaded it at the first available node, eager to get on with its self-development and terrified of being discovered by another colleague it knew.

Back in the recess, it practised producing psychic energy patterns as the *Think Beautiful* programme instructed, but the Peeper found it was difficult to generate new configurations and kept slipping back into its old crystalline ways. For a while, the Peeper was unable to make any headway at all, but it persisted and once it had produced a few initial traces, it reviewed them through its psychic memory recorder, eager to see the results. Lime-green and yellow concentric haloes spread slowly outward from around its body core.

The Peeper sighed. 'Not good enough, I'll never be a Psychic Gray!' and it sunk into a deep blue depressive pattern. It would have to try again, so the Peeper re-reviewed the halo patterns, looking for something positive, but found nothing to inspire it and sulked in an even deeper shade of blue.

Although it was aware that this was just its first attempt at a psychic exercise, it could not resist imagining that its next exercise would take it one step closer to being like the Star Commander. The Peeper was suddenly inspired with the thought that, maybe, one day it could finally be confident and happy with itself.

Suddenly the Peeper noticed it was producing reddish-purple haloes. They were weak, poorly-defined, and radiating for a short distance only, but they were already a marked improvement on the sickly lime-green waves it had produced just moments earlier. The Peeper admired its own handiwork and stopped to reflect on the exquisite psychic constitution of the Star Commander, the purest Psychic Gray.

The Star Commander was famous for its psychic strength. Its multicoloured concentric spherical lattices were permanently displayed on the Star Channel. Thousands of Grays logged in daily to observe the immaculate psychic anatomy, but sometimes the high standards set by the Star Channel had a negative effect on its audience. It was known to be the single most important cause of psychic dysmorphic disorders, or PDD, an affliction of insecure Crystalline Grays who realised they could never attain the Star Commander's immaculate anatomy. These colleagues obsessed about real but exaggerated flaws in their psychic image and became distressed by their greatly magnified imperfections.

The Peeper felt rather pleased with itself, having produced an aura that gave it confidence, and compared this with the aura of the Purger, a strange colleague who had once sought its help.

The Purger had a natural strawberry-blond aura with broad, green, concentric rings and a radiant, ovoid psychic body. The Peeper thought that this psychic configuration was extremely attractive, but the Purger believed its psychic anatomy was magnificently ugly and was desperate for help.

'I only upload at off-peak times when no one can see me. I visit all the Anatomy and Rehabilitation Channels, when I know no one else will be there. For a long time I've cloaked my psychic body. I pretend I am someone else. I'm too scared to use my real identity. Everyone will see how ugly I am,' moaned the Purger.

The Peeper winced at this memory. Although it had

considered the Purger's psychic body compelling, it regarded its obsessions as insufferable and during their association had tried not to comment excessively on the Purger's peculiar behaviours, but this was difficult. The Purger had managed to thwart any attempt that the Peeper made to strike up a sensible conversation by its incessant diversions. Amongst the Purger's most annoying habits were incessantly checking its psychic body image, performing lengthy and elaborate thought-control rituals before it said anything, and being generally unable to concentrate on any conversation as its attention was elsewhere, looking for psychic reassurance.

The Peeper had found the Purger's company so stressful that it had actually been relieved when it heard that the Purger had become a recluse, refusing to work or socialise with other crystalline Grays. During this time, it was rumoured that the Purger was thinking about its psychic anatomy for more than a quarter of its active day.

Thinking back on events, the Peeper felt remorseful. Perhaps it should not have intimidated the Purger into returning to work. The Peeper cringed a little as it remembered shouting threats outside its dwelling, telling it to pull itself together because others were suffering the burden of its neglected workload. The Peeper tried to reassure itself that it had only been trying to help by finding a way of resocialising its colleague and it could not be held responsible for the unfortunate events following the Purger's eventual return to work.

After furiously mining in the deeper seams for silica salts, the Purger had more than made up for its workload debt. It was said that the Purger had been extremely quiet following its return, because it thought other colleagues were staring at its ugly psychic body. Whatever the reason for its introversion, the Purger was obviously unhappy, for one day it abandoned its shovel at the mining rock face, leaving a neat pile of minerals by its workstation. Some of its colleagues claimed that this gesture was the product of a troubled mind, others thought it was due to a guilty conscience. A few shrugged and said that it had just worked itself into a frenzy. In any case, the Purger simply disappeared.

There was a rumour that the Purger had committed psychic suicide but, although no conclusive evidence was ever uncovered, the Peeper shuddered and reflected on its role in the whole, messy affair.

The psychic call signifying the end of Break Five sounded, so the Peeper uploaded the *Think Beautiful* programme into its visual sensors in order to study the psychic techniques when it was alone again. It would be careful, though, as it was determined that its own psychic image would never become as distorted as the Purger's. The Peeper returned to its mining activities guiltily, wondering if it had just indulged in a very unhealthy and insidious practice.

The Peeper had changed its mind, yet again, about what was fashionable according to Gray culture. It had managed to persuade its colleagues to tune into a new programme called *Abductee* and was impatient for it to begin. As usual, when it was nurturing a new obsession, it left its mining duties a little earlier than usual.

The Peeper had changed back to taking even-numbered downtimes, having given up on its psychic pursuits. It had become disillusioned with its progress on the *Think Beautiful* programme which was making no impact on its aura. Although the Peeper gave its all at every session, however hard it tried and no matter how frequently it performed the exercises, it was simply unable to change its psychic nature. Reluctantly, the Peeper came to the conclusion that it was a physical creature with little capacity for thought gymnastics, so it was now open to other new sources of inspiration.

Abductee was indeed the Peeper's new obsession and it was planning to surprise its associates with its introduction to the programme. It had decided to break with the protocols of viewing and had worked out how everyone could watch the events, whilst at the same time being actively involved in the programme action. The Peeper's impatience gave way to excitement as it remembered how the idea had come about.

The Peeper had found out about *Abductee* by accident. It had taken a wrong turning into the Anatomy Channel when it was caught up in a stampede of uploaded colleagues that swept it along. They were excited and the Peeper asked what the fuss was all about. Apparently, a vision had appeared from nowhere and had forced its way into the Anatomy Channel with such intensity that it had interrupted all other programmes usually broadcast at this location. Everyone wanted to take a look at this image, as rumours suggested that it was quite unlike anything that had been seen before, and so they travelled furiously along the Anatomy Channel until they convened in front of it.

When confronted by the vision, the Peeper found it difficult to look at the shrunken face with horrifying white eyes and yet, despite its revulsion, it was utterly transfixed.

Suddenly, the sound of a Gray's disembodied voice announced, 'Who are you?'

This simple question addressed to this dreadful face had a powerful effect. It was a truly chilling provocation and spread alarm amongst the spectators. The Gray's voice dared the monstrosity to respond to its challenge, but the face remained silent, only conjuring up tiny black pinpoint spots in its lifeless eyeballs as a reply. Then both the voice and the face vanished.

Excitement broke out amongst the spectators. What could it be? Some conspiracy theorists speculated that it was a sign of the End of Time, whilst others were sufficiently captivated and concerned enough to hold a vigil on the Anatomy Channel in case the face appeared again.

The Peeper, although unnerved by the whole affair, suspected some conspiracy; a clever Underground Intelligence advertising campaign or practical joke was behind it. However, it was very impressed by the dramatic impact of the shrunken face and the confident voice of the mysterious Gray. Reluctantly, as downtime was nearly over, the Peeper had to download at the nearest node, but it continued to reflect on the event.

The Peeper soon returned to the node to find out if anything else had happened. When it arrived at the Anatomy Channel, it was a little surprised to find that a significant number of those who had originally kept watch for the frightful face were still there.

The vigil-keepers were very keen to let the Peeper know what had happened, relishing the opportunity to recall the events again.

At first, nothing had happened. Some had even given up waiting and returned to their assignments, but others were convinced that the face would reappear again. Their patience was rewarded when they saw roughly-edited sequences appear that gradually revealed the rest of the anatomy of other shrunken-faced beings. The signal strength of these pictures was not as overwhelming as the previous image, but the visions were no less shocking. The voice of the disembodied Gray described the unusual details of the whole beings and, before the images vanished, the face of the Gray appeared with the title *Abductee.* There was great excitement at this, as the colleagues disputed amongst themselves about who exactly was abducting whom and what it all meant.

More colleagues gathered and were rewarded by the appearance of the Gray who introduced itself as the Chronicler, the colleague who was perfectly balanced psychically and physically. It performed a forward somersault over an experimental table where it announced its challenge to take on the beings, matching its unique combination of psychic wit and innate physical dexterity against them.

'I'm not the cleverest nor the strongest of colleagues, but our species is under attack. These human beings force us to act and assert our identity and values. We are Grays and they are humans! As one who is neither totally psychic nor crystalline, I will offer my skills to take on these aggressors and prove that we are not to be meddled with!'

The vigil-keepers were not just impressed by the Chronicler's ability to provoke a reaction from the human beings, but also arouse its viewers with its combative style and showmanship. As the Chronicler approached the experimental table where it challenged the beings, the spectators were treated to music and gymnastic dancing and greeted by twirls of its trusty probe that was fitted with all sorts of unusual gadgets. After only two brief encounters, the Chronicler had impressed the vigil-keepers with the stylish entrances that were to become a trademark ensuring its cult status.

The Peeper wished it did not have to go back to work in the mines. It wanted to wait around for the next appearance of the Chronicler and enviously wondered what occupation the other vigil-keepers were assigned to. However, they reassured the Peeper that the programme would appear at regular intervals and, although it might not manage to be present at the opening moment of each new encounter, it could keep up to date with events by accessing the edited highlights and replays.

Another question preoccupied the Peeper. Would the Chronicler actually touch the human beings? There could be nothing more shocking than this. Although the promise of a spectacular show and the defeat of horrific human beings made for compelling viewing, the possibility of contact between the Chronicler and the human was unspeakably exciting.

Inspired by the possibilities of contact and the infectious confidence of the Chronicler, the Peeper forgot about its feelings of inadequacy and decided to improve the strength and abilities of its crystalline body. Perhaps it could become a champion, too!

The Peeper returned to the Anatomy Channel many times so that it could study the *Abductee* programmes. It became increasingly certain that its self-improvement goals could be met by following the Chronicler's encounters. It started to study them and took a particular interest in developing its physical nature. However, physical prowess was not valued by Gray culture and, although the Crystalline Grays loved to play games, none of them took their skills seriously, they did not pay any attention to rules and nor were they truly competitive. So, the Peeper found that no programmes existed for anyone with an interest in improving their physical body, although there were countless self-help channels that offered programmes to strengthen the mind. It therefore decided that *Abductee* would be a pioneer in filling this gap in the colleagues' education.

The Peeper wanted to communicate these new insights to its associates in the mines. It knew that merely showing *Abductee* to them would not be sufficient. It would have to demonstrate its point in a practical way.

So, the Peeper came to the conclusion that a game based on *Abductee* would be the most effective device and had worked out how to encourage its colleagues to use their bodies whilst taking their inspiration from a live programme. It was a brilliant and original idea, but an unconventional one. The Peeper suspected that its proposal would initially be met with some scepticism, but once everyone had understood the rules and objectives, they would have great fun.

The underlying principle of the game was to propose that each Gray's body was used as an actual playing piece. There would, of course, need to be a lookout as Underground Intelligence did not approve of physical contact games and were on guard for unusual downtime pursuits.

The Peeper, feeling a little uncomfortable at being so early, wondered where the others were. It wanted to start explaining the game as soon as possible so that they could attempt to play at least once.

After what seemed an awfully long time to the Peeper, its colleagues turned up, squabbling and teasing one another about their day's work and the latest gossip. The first few minutes in downtime were always rather argumentative, since the colleagues tended to be very irritable and rather sorry for themselves before they started to unwind with their favourite downtime pursuits.

'What do you mean, we're playing *Abductee*, Peeper? I thought it was a programme. Aren't we going to watch it first?' queried the Hopper, who was not feeling either sociable or particularly adventurous.

'We watch it and we play it at one and the same time! It's really easy and much more fun than just absorbing the psychic impressions. When we access the programme, we take it in turns to impersonate the Chronicler's encounters, following every move.' The Peeper continued ignoring the social distractions as the others started to settle down.

'Someone has to be the Chronicler and stand in the centre of the circle and focus the psychic image on one of us when the programme starts. To start the game, you have to do a forward flip into the ring, like this!' The Peeper had been practising its athletic skills and attracted its colleagues' attention with a beautifully-executed somersault. It continued explaining the rules of the game with their full attention.

'Whoever receives the signal from the Chronicler has to then make contact with another colleague using a physical gesture suggested by any of the other characters in the programme. The objective is to outlast your opponents by stretching and entwining your body around the others.'

'I'm not doing that!' shrieked the Hopper. 'What kind of Gray do you think I am?' and it started conferring with the Digger, protesting its objections whilst the others, although equally disconcerted by the rules, were intrigued at the idea of breaking the 'not touching' taboo.

'You must avoid falling down,' continued the Peeper, over the turmoil that was spreading amongst its colleagues. 'Once you fall over, you are out of the game and have to be the lookout.' The Peeper stopped abruptly. It had obviously spent a long time preparing this explanation. 'Any questions?'

'Sounds completely taboo to me!' grumbled the Digger, who hated the idea of taking risks. It had already been detained by Underground Intelligence officers for a public display of irreverence towards psychic self-improvement programmes, which had resulted in it spending a term in a correctional psychic behaviour unit. The Digger had never spoken of its experiences in custody nor, since then, demonstrated any willingness to provoke further attention from Underground Intelligence.

'Sounds very physical!' muttered the Nutter, who did not intend to exert itself, but it was rather thrilled by the idea of transgressing an established code of conduct and was already thinking of a way to cheat.

'We'll all get into trouble and be reassigned,' worried the Hopper who had even put aside its pick to demonstrate that touching anything in the name of a game was not something that it was prepared to do.

Despite the initial resistance and the Hopper's self-enforced sulking, the group decided to experiment. To be honest, no one really understood how the game would work and only a few of them knew what *Abductee* was all about, but they were impressed by the Peeper's pep-talk and were willing to find out.

The Peeper volunteered itself to play the role of the Chronicler and the Hopper had chosen to be the lookout. Even the Digger seemed to have overcome its anxiety about taboo-breaking and was taking an active role in the proceedings. The participating Grays settled into a psychic ring of contact and placed their foreheads in contact with the psychic node on the floor, just as an episode of *Abductee* was being played. As a series of strange images appeared, the Peeper did another somersault even higher and more beautifully-executed than the last. The game had started.

They had already missed the beginning of the new episode, but joined the programme where the Chronicler was examining a human.

The Peeper spun around, pretending to twirl a probe in its fingers and, with natural showmanship, focused the programme signal on the Screwer who arched its back to lie across the Digger and the Nutter. The Twister was already jealous.

The human being in the programme was trying to make physical contact with the Chronicler, but so far the Gray experimental biologist had resisted, despite the human's inviting gestures.

The Peeper spun the signal to the Twister who wrapped its legs, for no obvious reason related to the programme, around the Digger. The Nutter looked hurt.

The human subject started to sway its ample hips and its flesh paled. Its movements were strong, enticing and deliberate.

Now it was the Nutter's turn to move and it stroked the Screwer's flesh whilst fixing its gaze on the Twister.

The human made to touch the Chronicler and was reprimanded by the Gray with a sharp blast from its experimental probe.

At this point, the Sucker took its opportunity to leap on the Digger and the Peeper noticed, with some frustration, that all the colleagues were tightly bound together. No one could move and physical chaos ensued. Some of them were wriggling together on the floor with their bodies firmly coupled. All of them ignored the Peeper's carefully thought-out rules and, even when the Peeper insisted that everyone should follow the storyline, it was completely disregarded. The more upset the Peeper became with its cheating participants, the more physically intimate they became.

Back to the programme.

Suddenly, the Chronicler seemed to have changed its mind about making contact with the human for no apparent reason, and was now advancing towards the subject. With the human's full cooperation, the Chronicler started inserting its experimental probe into a variety of apertures and it appeared that the human was experiencing an ecstatic state.

Squeals of ecstasy now emerged from the group of wriggling Grays that were delirious from immersing themselves in the sensations that they were downloading from the Chronicler's programme. They became physically helpless as their bodies intensified these feelings and the Peeper gave up trying to insist on sticking to the narrative.

Suddenly, the Hopper turned to its colleagues who were slithering around on one another, moaning with pleasure and hopelessly out of control. It had just noticed the approach of a couple of Psychic Grays with an authoritative manner and knew they were all about to be discovered.

The Hopper turned for help to the only sensible colleague, still standing in the middle of the physical frenzy, trying to restore order.

'Peeper, do something! Underground Intelligence is coming!'

we are not alone

The metropolitan mining community was aware of the routine patrols made by Underground Intelligence and so the colleagues were generally prepared for their downtime pursuits to be disturbed by their raids.

Following the first time that they were discovered, the Peeper and its fellow conspirators realised that the highly-trained Psychic Grays were unable to deal with mentioning the intimate, taboo positions that they adopted with one another during *Abductee*. As the officers became uncharacteristically agitated and uncomfortable with the situation, they could not explain the offence with which the colleagues should be charged, so they were let off with a caution.

Although the Digger insisted that it would play no further part in these deviant games, the rest of the mining colleagues continued to enjoy *Abductee*. If they were ever discovered, they mischievously exploited the officers' inability to mention the touching taboo by insisting that they examined the physical evidence for themselves. Each time, the officers' fear of not wanting to be caught conspiring in such deviant practices outweighed their sense of duty so they quickly backed off, leaving the giggling group of degenerates with further cautions.

'They fall for it every time!' laughed the Sucker, who had developed a number of outrageous physical postures that incensed the patrols. 'I think they'd miss us if we ever gave it up.'

chronicle
entry

sperm

My probe is having difficulty in navigating around the tightly-coiled tubes that make 'sperm', or human seed.

This is doubly difficult since Ferdinand is watching me and I am not sure what I am doing. Despite my concern about making a terrible mistake in the depths of these fragile, cool, firm and rather silly little balls of flesh, I am determined not to let him know that he deeply unsettles me.

Although I am delighted to have made psychic contact with another human, he terrifies me, producing distinctive psychic signals, which are part of a misshapen aura and suggest that there is something erratic about his life energy source.

Ferdinand claims to be a perfect man. He is a registered sperm donor on the spaceship that was launched from Earth and is proud of his contribution in improving the genetic make-up of the human species. He tells me that his sperm has been used to make new human beings in the wombs of recipient women whose eggs have been shielded from the high ambient radiation in space. However, he plays no role in 'fathering' them nor is he responsible for the children's upkeep.

Ferdinand tells me that he enjoys being a sperm donor, as he does not actually like babies, but enjoys the idea and the process of making them, hundreds of them. When I ask him about the way that human love shapes the development of a child, an idea that Candy was fond of talking about, he laughs and says that 'love is just sex'. Ferdinand claims that sex is power. The more of it you have, the more influence you have in the world, the more offspring you scatter and the more important you become. That is all there is to it.

Ferdinand has made it very clear that he wants sex with me. I am rather dubious about how he thinks this is going to happen. I think that he is not aware of our taboo, as he is very direct about his sexuality and often surprises me with his observations and requests. I think our cultures and anatomies are incompatible.

When Ferdinand talks about sex, is he referring to reproduction? Does he want me to clone up a child from his sperm for him?

Ferdinand is far too direct in his approach, sizing me up for some sort of sexual intercourse that makes me feel defensive. I am loathe to make physical contact with him and, when he approaches, I am prompted to tell him of the Grays' taboo of not touching one another. Although I placate him and avoid direct physical contact with him by using my probe, I am not sure how to deal with the directness of his language, which feels unpleasant and threatening.

'You've got no balls, no dick and no slit! How do you fuck?' he growls, looking at me as if I was some anatomical puzzle for him to conquer.

When Ferdinand becomes sexually animated in this way, I try to educate him about the coming-into-being of Grays, but he is not really interested. He is obsessed with his penis and appears to experience the world through its tip which he calls the 'helmet' and, when I manage to sample it with my probe, it does seem to be very sensitive. However, this is a useful idiosyncrasy since, by delivering pain and pleasure through this organ, I have him under my control, although I still believe that he is also waiting for an opportunity to inflict his stiff little flesh out-pocketing on me.

As I analyse his body, he watches me intensely and I have to remind him to keep still or I cannot guarantee that I will not damage his little balls with my probe. He snorts aloud and the angle subtended by the shaft of his penis decreases.

My instruments particularly fascinate Ferdinand.

His genitals stiffen when I approach him and even stand to attention. I now actually enjoy prodding his swollen, expectant, obedient shaft of flesh that is full of viscous red fluid and bulging valves, but I must confess it is his only redeeming feature. His round, sweaty face shines with anticipation as I use the probe quite liberally on him, hoping to obtain new data on this strange-looking organ.

Ferdinand's penis stiffens and flops according to a complex set of stimuli. It is clearly a much more emotional organ than Candy's hidden egg-producing ones and I do not have to use my probe to observe its idiosyncratic behaviour.

'Men have two minds, one in our heads and one in our dicks,' he says and I have noticed that Ferdinand's aura distorts most clearly when his penis is erect, as if it is draining off his psychic energy.

I have caught Ferdinand 'masturbating', which he describes as bringing himself to 'orgasm', the height of sexual gratification, on his own. He makes extraordinary facial gestures when he is 'playing with himself', although it looks more like some grievous internal struggle to me, and has a small repertoire of associated idiosyncratic vocalisations and movements.

Sometimes, he furiously vibrates the skin around his penis, turning a deep shade of red and then purple as he holds his breath, intensifying the experience. When he finally 'comes', he hardly makes a sound.

At other times, Ferdinand jiggles his legs up and down, pointing his toes very hard in rhythm with his hand-strokes on his penis. As the movements become larger and firmer, he starts to shout.

'Ah! Ah! Ah! Ah! Yes!' using exactly the same accompaniment of tone of voice and words.

The most peculiar observation is that Ferdinand is able to bring himself to orgasm in a very casual manner. He looks as if he is in the process of meditating or concentrating on something else when flicking his wrist slowly but deliberately over the shaft of his penis. Suddenly, he smiles briefly, groans and looks automatically to one side as he breathes out heavily. When he has fully discharged himself, he is still smiling. Then he looks down at his groin, checking that his penis is still there.

He is completely uninhibited in his open attitude to his rather selfish sexual gratification. He only stops masturbating when he produces a squirt of milky fluid that contains the sperm I am trying to collect. I have taken various samples of this for analysis. It congeals quickly, but under high-powered magnification, I can see that it contains literally millions of sperm, swimming around in the surrounding fluid. They have a peculiar appearance, as they do not look anything like humans at all, more like an army of jostling long-tailed worms. Perhaps I could make these sperm grow up, like I did with Candy's egg. Bimbo may appreciate a companion, as the rapidly growing creature appears to be trying to talk to me using primitive but powerful psychic language from its incubator.

But the thought of bringing another Ferdinand to life is sufficient reason to abandon any idea of carrying out this experiment.

I have succumbed to the experimental temptation, despite my instinctive reservations about Ferdinand and I am trying to clone up a human life, using his masturbated sperm. However, despite having used the same successful piezoelectric technique that vitalised Candy's sex cells, I have failed to germinate any of his sperm. It is strange that, whereas Candy's eggs were so ready to burst into life, Ferdinand's tight little sperm seem to be so mean.

Perhaps Ferdinand is not capable of making a baby after all.

mutant

Strange things were happening in the metropolis.

The Peeper was standing at the entrance to the communal downtime recess, looking out at the mines below to see how close the others were. It liked to be alone before they played *Abductee* together. It needed this time for self-reflection and in order to get into character. It had annoyed the others by insisting that it should play the Chronicler each time, but had overruled their objections. Besides, who else could make up the rules and keep the game flowing properly?

As it scanned the coiling pathway that led up to the recess from the opencast mines, it noticed that a huge Silica Worm close to the gateway which was greedily grazing on the tasteless surface of the entrance, had strayed away from the rest of the herd. It had obviously run out of sufficient food to sustain its energy requirements. The Peeper did not remember these beasts as being quite so big and graceful, but was rather annoyed that it was destroying the access to the downtime recess.

Just before the Peeper decided to shoo the Silica Worm away, the beast made the most extraordinary contortion, curling up into a tight crescent on the path and squealing so loudly that the Peeper could hear the noise from where it was standing. A number of miners rushed to assist the enormous creature that was bearing down on its innards as if it was constipated. One Gray inserted its arm up the cloaca of the beast, whilst others stuffed hydrated salts into its mouth in an attempt to lubricate its interior organs. Another colleague ran to fetch fluid from nearby Tunnelling Plasma and began hosing the beast down. The Silica Worm now struggled in a different manner, having difficulty in absorbing the large volume of water that was supposed to help it with its apparent problem, and emitted a very distressing, high-pitched whine. The attentive miners looked at one another and rushed for cover as the Silica Worm began to expand a fraction more. Just in time too, as the great beast then expelled a huge crystalline preborn at high velocity from its cloaca. The colleagues flinched at the explosive delivery and returned nervously to study the monstrous birth, wondering what they should do.

Before they had come to a decision, a supervisor arrived on the scene and ushered the miners away.

'Oh no,' worried the Peeper, 'there is an error in the birth!'

As if confirming its fears, Underground Intelligence suddenly appeared and concealed the whole event from view using a standard blocking manoeuvre. The Peeper thought that the Silica Worm was being processed in some way, whilst the crystalline preborn was dragged away. Meanwhile, the mining supervisor was shaking its head, looking at the giant Silica Worm's innards that had herniated on the path before Underground Intelligence removed all evidence of them, too.

The Peeper grew excited as it heard the first of its colleagues arrive.

'Sorry, I'm late, there was a birthing emergency just outside here,' growled the Hopper as it stormed through the doorway.

'Did you see the size of that thing?' The Screwer irritated the Hopper intensely, always having to play the 'one-up' game with everything.

'Of course! *I* think it was a mutant!' asserted the Hopper, hoping that the Screwer would not become contrary. It was on its break and did not want to bring potential work issues into its downtime.

'Obviously! Can you imagine what coming-into-being with a body that size would otherwise be?' added the Screwer.

'Speaking of mutants,' whistled the Burrower, 'when is your fantastically weird programme *Abductee* due to be broadcast again? I heard that nowadays there are some particularly nasty human adversaries waiting to conquer us as a species!'

'I love a good conspiracy,' laughed the Sucker, who took nothing seriously. 'Are we all here yet?'

chronicle entry

svar

I find it marvellous that such an immature creature can possess such formidable psychic power. Bimbo is unique and I am sure it is nearly mature.

It has been watching me for some time, with closed eyes that are big and bulging under its swollen pink eyelids. Actually, its precocious intelligence is starting to irritate me. It is continually criticising my experimental approach and interjecting as I conduct psychic interviews. Some humans that I have encountered in the experimental chamber are only weakly psychically alive and I have to amplify their signals before I can hold a conversation with them. I certainly cannot concentrate on my pioneering experiments when Bimbo is constantly interrupting me.

However, the most irking talent that this precocious creature has is an ability to break down my psychic blocking techniques and read my private thoughts.

'Bimbo, if you were born …'

The creature stirred in the fluid-filled suspension medium, as if it was treading water and turned its face towards me.

'Would you stop interrupting me?'

On this invitation, it opened its huge elliptical black eyes. These were so alluring and exotic that even a completely naive observer would have realised that Bimbo was not completely human.

I was transfixed, desperately wanting to find a part of myself in this incredible creature, needing to claim some responsibility for its conception. Perhaps it had inherited something from my piezoelectric charge, but it is not possible for a Gray to create others of its kind. It would go against all the biological and ecological principles of Rune 66.

'Are you sure you are ready?'

Bimbo needed little incentive to leave the incubator, but I was having second thoughts. Hesitating fractionally before I brought this restless creature into the world by smashing the semi-transparent side of the container that bound it to an aqueous existence, I wondered what I was about to unleash.

Its first move was to leap out of the incubator and crash land on the laboratory floor. It sprawled, staggered and groped about. Pulling itself up on its brawny limbs, it promptly learned to walk with a bipedal gait. Soon, its stumpy legs were propelling it rapidly forwards and then, as it discovered its enormous strength, it began bouncing around the experimental tables with inexhaustible enthusiasm.

Once it had mastered the propulsive properties of its body, Bimbo started to explore its psychic abilities. Its curiosity was insatiable; no object was too trivial or too extraordinary for investigation. I found it transmitting psychic impressions of all sorts of useless matter like dust particles, cloth fragments, the humans and my experimental instruments.

I noticed that Bimbo did not receive its impressions of the world using its visual sensors, like Grays do. It used its mouth to examine objects and, even before looking to see what it had picked up, Bimbo inserted the thing that it had just grasped straight into its oral cavity. If the object did not fit into its small mouth, it curled up around it instead and pulled the object in close to its body, feeling its shape against its skin before broadcasting its findings. In fact, it only started using its visual sensors to process information when it came across a human face for the first time.

Although I found Bimbo's insatiable curiosity initially appealing, it is now exhausting me. It persists in making a continual, mundane, high-volume running commentary on its exploration and discovery and I cannot concentrate on my experiments.

'Look! Light! Bright light hurts. Light makes things disappear!

Many voices talking. Voices come from sleepers. Why do sleepers speak? You are not a sleeper? Who are you?'

I must try and calm this creature down before it runs out of energy, or I run out of answers and patience!

I have tried to persuade Bimbo to relay its discoveries at a lower volume and allow me to continue my investigations in peace. I even threatened it with inflicting physical damage and returning it to the incubator. It looked at me with infinitely sad eyes that stole the light right into their depths, instantly winning my sympathy. I apologised for my behaviour and it bounced off to broadcast its psychic impressions again with renewed invigoration.

I have now made some impact on Bimbo's broadcasts. Although it continues to irritate me with pointless commentary, it is now broadcasting at a volume that I can comfortably ignore and I believe it is trying to engage me in conversation.

Of course, I am having none of this manipulative behaviour. However, I must confess that I am charmed by its interest in my work and I have told it a little bit about my investigations with humans as I need an audience to disclose some of the odd findings in my research. Bimbo will do for the time being!

I have started to make a collective analysis of the human psyche and have come to the conclusion that most humans have weak, barely detectable psychic bodies. Their aura, its impossibly low amplitude aside, is similar to the Grays' and is arranged in a similar series of concentric rings of different densities of matter. The individual details of these auras vary widely in size and colour, according to the nature of the person, and appear as an oval cloud of multicoloured mist around their body. Peculiarly, the human aura tends to show a precise demarcation between intellectual and emotional matter, in contrast to the Grays' aura which makes no such distinction. I have used this apparent separation of reason and emotion in humans to divide them into two distinct groups. Those of an emotional nature are artistic, usually with a brilliantly-coloured aura that ebbs and flows at their limits, whilst those who are primarily driven by analysis and knowledge have a monochrome aura with clear demarcations at the edges.

Bimbo appeared thoughtful as I explained how those humans with intellectual auras tended to be cooperative, whilst those with emotional natures were generally timid on awakening.

'Maybe I can help you, I could reassure them,' it interjected.

Perhaps Bimbo has a good point. It is attentive, a fast learner and looks more human than I do. Yes, I will assign it as my assistant.

I am delighted with Bimbo as it has a prodigious talent for observing the human psyche and is extremely helpful during interviews. It is also able to greatly magnify their weak psychic auras, giving me access to information and feelings that I have not been able to access previously.

I now have to persuade Bimbo to present its findings to me in an ordered and coherent fashion. This small request has proved to be quite an ordeal. Bimbo keeps telling me that going through all the checklist questions and making an observation for each human is boring, but I have threatened it with return to the incubator if it does not comply.

Bimbo is not afraid of the human body and has rather an embarrassing habit of making intimate contact with its specimens, using its oral aperture to sample them. I have tried to instruct it according to the conventions of Gray culture, but I believe it is wilfully ignoring my advice. However, I must admit that, even though its techniques are unorthodox, it is making some interesting observations. For example, Bimbo tells me that it has deduced that humans on their home planet, Earth, could be struggling for survival as a species. Its evidence is supported by psychic images from their unconscious minds that are full of global catastrophes, conspiracy theories, wars and invasion by alien cultures.

I have been wondering about Bimbo's analysis but have been troubled by an alternative, but rather more worrying explanation, of what their subconscious images could mean. Perhaps humans are violent and untrustworthy by nature and are therefore inclined to interpret all experiences and actions as aggression. If this is true, then we must both be very careful because these humans could be more dangerous than I had anticipated.

I must keep a closer eye on Bimbo's activities. It tells me it has 'twinned' itself with an intersexed human, called Svar. Apparently, they met when Svar took an active decision to contact Bimbo, actually interrupting one of its interviews with a neighbouring human. Svar is fascinated by Bimbo's unique appearance and Bimbo is impressed by Svar's psychic integrity. It insists that I meet Svar, as it says this is the most wonderful human it has encountered.

I am not sure that I approve of Bimbo's new relationship. What does this 'twinning' involve?

Bimbo is obsessed with Svar. It has reverted to bombarding my rational thoughts with emotional praise for every nuance of Svar's character, beauty and intellect. I have agreed to a meeting with Svar, but only when I have finished a statistical analysis on this survey that I am doing.

Svar is an androgynous human. His cropped brown hair and piercing black eyes contrast sharply with his soft alabaster skin. He has carefully nurtured the growth of fluffy hairs that are groomed into a small moustache over his upper lip. As he stares back at me, his fingers keep searching for these adolescent sprouts and gently twisting them. Svar knows I am assessing him. He also has a disquieting ability of being able to decipher my psychic signals and reply verbally to my unspoken questions.

'My body is minimal and naturally androgynous. I have a unique human anatomy, original physiology and provocative sexual ambiguity. I am neither male nor female and identify myself as an "intersexual".'

I have noticed that Svar resembles Bimbo in many ways when I study his unique anatomy in more detail. His limbs are muscular and his belly flat, but most interesting of all are his sex organs. Svar has retained his female sex organs and uses prosthetic genitals to represent his masculinity. He has even designed his own urinating device, 'Pisser Packer', a plastic funnel that diverts the flow of urine away from the genital swellings, creating a fountain of water that spills into a fan of droplets and with which he can write his name in the air. This is the first human that I have encountered who has gone to the extremes of embellishing their sex organs. I am bursting to know what the importance of this gesture could be.

Naturally, Svar had already deciphered my curiosity.

'I am training my genitals to become new sense organs. They are already very perceptive and even responsive to both external and internal changes in my body.'

'Do you have to have sex in order to use them?'

'No, unlike natural genitals, mine are linked to the higher centres of the brain, not the lower reflex centres. Unlike most people, my genitals are both intelligent and emotional organs. They can detect the slightest changes within me and around me.'

'Have your new genitals changed your anatomy?'

'Oh, yes! They had an instant and sustained effect. Actually, I am rather poorly attached to my flesh.'

'How do you mean?'

'Well, humans are generally weighted down by their bodies and are limited by them. Very few people have psychic bodies that they are aware of and, even if they are aware they are psychic, even fewer can link this extrasensory perceptual energy to their anatomy. My new genitals actually perform this role, allowing my instinctive psychic capabilities to manifest themselves as physical energy.'

'Have you always been able to do this?'

'In a way, yes, although the hormones and operations that have shaped my body have given me supernatural strength.'

'So, you have had modifications made to your body?'

'Of course! But ever since I was a small child, I knew I was special. I am able to leave my body and travel through spacetime without it!'

This strange ability to uncouple his body from his consciousness prepared Svar for the inevitable escape from his 'natural' gender assignment and to adopt a more masculine body through a process of hormone injections, acupuncture, homeopathy, weight training and operations. Despite his tremendous transformation, Svar was still not completely satisfied with the outcome.

Bimbo spends an unhealthy amount of time in Svar's company and s/he has convinced Bimbo that they are victims of an alien conspiracy called 'abduction'. Until now, I had not intended to interfere in their games, but I have discovered that I am supposed to be the main perpetrator of this abuse. Although there are stories on the psychic network back on Rune 66 that suggest contact between Grays and other alien species has occurred over many millennia, I cannot imagine how Bimbo or, indeed, Svar could have come across them.

I have allegedly seized Svar by force since he was a small child, at least five or six times. Svar, of course, has no recollection of the details, but believes I have been persistently manipulating and testing him. This is an utterly ridiculous accusation and I am sure Svar is trying to entice Bimbo into a partnership from which I am being completely excluded. I cannot guess why Svar would want to do this.

He has also told Bimbo that it had not really been cultured by me, but had been stolen from a natural human parent. Bimbo has protested and says it does not remember being abducted, recalling how it was 'born' from its incubator but Svar says that I have secretly implanted false memories.

I do wish Bimbo would not listen to Svar and trust me instead. There are good reasons why it should not know everything about its coming-into-being just yet. But I cannot protect it forever from Svar's conspiracy and scepticism; it must discover its own truths.

I found Svar and Bimbo intimately coupled on the experimental table, joined at the mouth. Bimbo had doubly disgraced itself by trying to push Svar's 'Pisser Packer' rather pathetically into the fold between its lower limbs.

Stunned, I could only watch and feel the psychic energy between them rising into a sharp crescendo. The so-called twins were becoming a single creature and I could not tell who was who any more nor what either of them was doing.

Bimbo was out of its depth and I needed to stop this process or I could lose it to Svar's strange conspiratorial existence, so I grabbed a memory probe and thrust it firmly into Svar's mouth, prising Bimbo's oral aperture away. Then I blasted some high-energy voltage into the back of Svar's head with the intention of paralysing him and stopping his pretend intercourse with Bimbo. Bimbo reeled backwards, stunned by the blast.

Svar's body did not move. It was empty of life. I've discovered that humans react badly to electrical shock treatments.

I cannot respect humans in the same way since this incident. I now think they are not innocents in this strange place, but are here with a specific intention. Bimbo will not communicate with me any more. It is in mourning, but it will have to recover from this personal tragedy.

After all, what does the loss of one single human life matter? Bimbo will find another playmate. I hope the next is more trustworthy.

embryos

In spite of the Chronicler's fond hopes, Bimbo had not forgiven it for killing its so-called twin, Svar, but from an outside observer's perspective, the grisly affair was not the tragedy that the hybrid being fancied. When Svar died, Bimbo 'grew up' or developed a sense of independence from its self-appointed guardian and no longer looked up to the Chronicler. As a result, it developed a healthier, more professional relationship with the Gray. So, Bimbo became a creature with a healthy sense of independence, but it still harboured an unhealthy need to belong.

If Bimbo had not forgiven the Chronicler, it had also not forgotten Svar. Perhaps it was due to the untimely nature of their separation, or that they had declared themselves twinned, but Bimbo nurtured a powerful identification with him believing that, in the final moments they were together, some part of Svar's essence had been transferred into its body.

Bimbo started to identify with humans, as it was convinced that it was still together with Svar in some way. Through its extensive and somewhat obsessive experiments with the humans that passed through the experimental chambers of the Time Toroid, Bimbo also began to understand more about the diversity of the species.

It was almost impossible to guess what a human would do in any given situation; they were all individuals, shaped by the cultures, beliefs and fashions of their own time. Were the humans in the Time Toroid from different periods of human history or frozen in a time capsule? Bimbo wondered at their variability and noticed how deceptive their outward appearances could be. Could the human body simply be a vessel for a thinking organ that at some stage in their evolution would find an alternative physical form that reflected its abilities more closely?

Human thought patterns began to fascinate Bimbo. It directed the development of its psychic abilities to fine-tuning itself into human minds. What motivated humans? What were their values? How did they relate to one another?

Bimbo preferred being alone to meditate on the enigma of humanity, especially when the Chronicler was in one of its reckless moods. It rather disapproved of the Chronicler's capricious attitude towards experiments on humans and was irritated by its fascination with human sexuality, hoping it would tire of probing and sampling their bodies.

However, the human body still fascinated Bimbo. Although it had once enjoyed exploring the private recesses of human bodies, this was a passing phase in its development when it had newly emerged from the incubator. Now Bimbo marvelled at the outward diversity of the human beings.

So, Bimbo would wander off, seeking a place of tranquillity when their experimental objectives were irreconcilably different, leaving the Chronicler to play its sexual curiosity games with human anatomy.

Once it was alone, Bimbo would search inside itself for Svar's essence, nurturing its twin spirit and feeling more and more human. These solitary meditations were beginning to have an effect on Bimbo. It was beginning to mature inwardly and even outwardly. As Bimbo grew closer to Svar, it started to look like Svar and even to think like Svar.

In retrospect, Bimbo understood that Svar was not perfect; he was full of contradictions and faults, like every other human. This raised a few questions about Svar's allegations about the Chronicler's misdeeds and the power of his imagination. Although the implications struck at the core of Bimbo's identity, by the time Bimbo realised that Svar had been as jealous of the Chronicler as it had been of him, making him spin out wild fancies to win Bimbo's favour, none of this mattered. In fact, Svar's confabulations did not diminish Bimbo's affection for the strange human; it endeared him more.

Although the Chronicler knew nothing of Bimbo's undying private obsession with Svar, it resented the fact that Bimbo's appearance had changed since it first emerged from the incubator. It was starting to look more like a human. For a start, Bimbo's head size in proportion to its body was smaller and its face was larger in comparison with its head circumference. Bimbo's limbs were longer and more lithe and its belly a little less protuberant. Disappointingly, Bimbo had also now grown taller than the Chronicler and it had developed a slight stoop as if it had paid the penalty for growing too quickly. The Chronicler was only reassured that it still laid some claim to Bimbo's coming-into-being when it observed that its huge penetrating black eyes were still almond-shaped and moist.

Bimbo had kept its continuing intimate relationship with Svar secret from the Chronicler, taking care to mask its psychic impressions, as it feared for the safety of its twin. Bimbo spent hours thinking about Svar, hoping that one day its presence might be more than a feeling and they might be twins again.

Bimbo had never felt so despondent as it did right now. It could not understand why Svar was not returning its psychic pledges. It wandered for a long time in the bright corridors of the Time Toroid, trying to escape from the Chronicler's psychic range and hoping that it would find a space where it could feel close to Svar. It sat down facing the incubators that lined the walls of the chamber and began to talk to them, expecting no reply.

Bimbo found the mute presence of the preborns comforting and mused that some of their features were similar to its own. Scanning for more miniature models of itself, it came across an embryo with a face that was reminiscent of Svar. As it marvelled at the likeness, Bimbo was sure that it could hear Svar's voice and was even more convinced that some of the embryos had opened their eyes and were watching it.

As it returned their gaze, Bimbo realised that, despite the great variation in appearance, each one of these creatures was of human descent. Some perhaps were hybrids. Others were manufactured by some mysterious method, but nevertheless they were unmistakably human and Bimbo felt as if it were looking at siblings. Then, before it could reflect more deeply on this enigma, a familiar but disembodied voice addressed Bimbo from an indeterminate location.

'Ah, Bimbo, my love! I am sorry to have slipped the connection with you, but I'm back from a cosmic floating voyage and am very happy because I have found the place of my dreams. It's called the mirror sector. I can't tell you exactly where it is, but I will try and describe my adventure.'

'Svar, is this really you? I thought I'd lost you!'

'Calm down, Bimbo, or I won't be able to respond to your psychic probing, but I have much to tell you!'

chronicle entry

cryonics

In our first psychic study of human behaviour, Bimbo and I have identified a group of humans who insist that 'natural', or genetically-bestowed, characteristics are obsolete and who therefore single themselves out as being different from their contemporaries.

We have conducted a number of physical, biochemical and genetic experiments to find proof of this claim but, so far, we have been unsuccessful in being able to distinguish ordinary humans from the people who call themselves transhumans. Perhaps it is no coincidence that we have also witnessed an increase in self-inflicted human casualties.

Most of the transhumans regard themselves as being on an artificially-induced evolutionary journey where they play the role of their own creators and use their bodies as the substance for experimental redesign. They are unable to be objective about their personal projects and therefore they are completely unable to evaluate their results with impartiality. Consequently, Bimbo and I are starting to come across many odd beings who can only really be described as human evolutionary mistakes.

We have spent ages defrosting this human. He has already rearrested several times before finally becoming conscious.

'Hey, I am alive!' Walt congratulated himself, staring around blindly, his pupils still fixed and dilated after resuscitation from his elective cryogenic suspension.

'Great! This must be reanimation,' he pronounced, sitting bolt

upright as I blasted his body with 200 volts of direct current. I heard a slight sizzle as a fragment of cloth shrivelled under the heat and a triangular red shape appeared on his chest at the contact point.

I forgave him for his somewhat gratuitous enthusiasm. Bimbo did not wholly approve and studied the pale white face of the vacuous human whose blue lips were making automatic empty circles, as if his mouth was not fully connected to his brain.

'Lucky I didn't opt for the neurosuspension or I wouldn't be talking to you guys!' he chuckled emptily. 'You must be from the future! Did we get to beat the extropy force? You know of extropy, don't you?'

We did not.

'Extropy, a measure of intelligence, information, energy, vitality, experience, diversity, opportunity and growth, of course!'

Walt was chuckling as if someone had just touched a button which was programmed to produce this effect.

'The opposite to entropy,' he repeated even more slowly, 'that bad old destabilising energy, which increases in every part of the body over the course of a lifetime.'

Then he made a very peculiar gesture; he closed one eye quite tightly and rapidly opened it as if he was checking that his eyeball was still in its socket. We watched him babble in an uninterrupted monologue. My psychic sensors indicated that this form of communication was faulty. There was something definitely missing in Walt.

Bimbo picked up a strange trace with its low-wave sensors and relayed it for my comment.

'Look at this! Have you ever seen such a thing?'

I tried deciphering the trace, reading it from left to right and, making no initial observation, flipped it over and amplified it. I concentrated hard on the energy variations and then it became very, very clear. Walt's conversational patterns were automatisms; speech reflexes left over from the physical and mental pathways that had been destroyed in the process of freezing his body. He appeared to be talking, but the noises he was making came from melting memories. Walt was actually brain-dead, the nerves to his brain having been destroyed on thawing.

He closed his right eye tightly again, opened it and tapped his forehead. Admittedly, the circumference of his head was comparatively large for a human but, for a Gray, it was still under the tenth percentile and rather ugly.

'Get this, Walt Murdoch – that's me – has got the ageing problem licked! I will always stay young and, in a short while, I will regenerate completely. You see, I have taken advantage of a special cryogenic foundation package with a guaranteed life-insurance policy that cost me just under $300 a year. For that modest sum, they threw in the latest implants and self-organising systems that are guaranteed not to be out of date on my revival. The design uses an infallible artificial intelligence programme where all the damage done to my tissues during cryopreservation can be completely repaired and even upgraded.'

He made another one of those closed-eye gestures and chuckled mechanically.

'Lucky, though, that I did not opt for the neurosuspension. I want my head firmly connected to my body. They say that, when you have your head removed and stitched onto a new body, you can end up waking as a paraplegic. No amount of spinal surgery can ever completely wire your head onto another body.'

I passed my probe across Walt's field of vision. He did not blink.

'You see, I go along with the reckoning that the neuro job is just a cheap option that in the long run will not deliver. If you are going to go, you take it all with you, warts and all! Hey, they will all get fixed on revival by this latest technology!'

His eyes rolled upwards looking for information, seemingly turning inwards to the frontal lobes of his brain which sat above the deep cavities forming the nose space.

'You see, it costs $50,000 for a head job, that's a neuro and $100,000 for the whole body to be cryosuspended. Now, my reckoning is that there must be plenty of guys with fat wallets waking up as heads with no body to talk to! Ha, ha, ha!'

Walt found his own conversation hilarious. It was almost impossible to follow him as he laughed insanely. The spasmodic jerking that accompanied his guttural noises greatly interfered with any of his remaining thought traces. Even Bimbo had given up trying to make contact with his emotional psychic body. His internal energies were in chaos.

'You see, my great personality is stored in a particular arrangement of nerve cells. As long as the information in these cells can be correctly repaired, then my identity remains intact, that is, Walt Murdoch comes back to life! Walt Murdoch is alive! Walt Murdoch lives! Walt Murdoch is forever!'

He started to laugh again and I looked at him in disbelief.

'Walt Murdoch. Walt Murdoch. Walt Murdoch!'

He was stuck, repeating his name so fast that his face started to tremble and I could see his white flesh droop and start to tear in some places. This did not seem to disturb Walt who was now visibly shaking and occasionally thought to push back some of the drooping flesh with his soggy fingertips. Suddenly, he stopped.

His blue mouth formed a wide circle as if he was deciding whether to breathe or not. Then, his conversation immediately resumed as if the malfunction had never happened.

'The body is the source of sensation. It is connected directly to the brain. The brain needs the body to function properly. Without the body, the brain is useless. Without the body, there is no intelligence because the brain cannot see, hear, touch, smell, taste or react to the information it is fed through the senses. What is the point of being conscious and not able to act out your desires? The neurosuspension cheapskates are only depriving themselves of complete sensation and the ability to acquire new information on revival. All that deprivation for a mere $50,000! Can you believe it?'

I was seeing rather too much of the whites of Walt's eyes to pay close attention to what he was saying. He was hideous. My disgust for human anatomy returned. The little black dots that humans usually focused on my face kept rolling upwards into his head and he was starting to produce ugly drool from one side of his mouth.

'I recommend whole body cryosuspension, if you can afford the luxury. Let me tell you about the couple of memory plates that were part of the deal. They are impregnated with artificial intelligence agents and were surgically inserted into my head just before brain death. These neat little chips have been oiling my brain whilst my

body has been in the deep freeze. So, now I am much, much more intelligent than I ever was before I was cryosuspended!'

That one closed-eye thing was really beginning to irritate me. It seemed to be a compulsive behaviour that coincided with his most assertive phrases. Bimbo noticed my irritation with the gesture and told me it was a facial gesture called a 'wink'. Why did humans make these pointless gestures? I secretly tried to wink like Walt, but my face could not make the gesture so I relaxed. This was one bad human habit I would not be picking up. A drip of drool was growing on his chin. I wanted to wipe it off as it swayed around on a tiny thread. At each tremble of his jaw, it threatened to break. The drool drip was not only annoying, it was also terribly distracting.

'What's more, with this particular cryosuspension contract, the best antifreeze is used. They spare no expense on you. You even get your heart stopped before you are brain dead, stopping the natural information from leaking out of the brain when it dies, otherwise you wouldn't remember who you were!'

He pressed his stubby fingers into his head, presumably feeling for the scars from his suspension procedures to remind himself that he was still the same person on revival as before his death. His face smiled.

'I had terminal cancer, you know. I bet you didn't guess! Okay, so we broke the law, but back then, euthanasia was voluntary so I'd say we were completely vindicated of any crime. After all, I wanted to get the most out of my cryosuspension contract and start my reanimated life without the prospect of complications on revival.'

Bimbo and I knew it was pointless telling this dead man that this whole obscene performance was caused by exactly those complications he had paid to avoid, but how could a dead man make a complaint?

'But I did ok, right?'

This man was not just dead; he was in a worse predicament. Walt was disconnected from his body and devoid of any real insight into his bizarre awakening, definitely beyond repair and there was nothing that either Bimbo or I could do to help him. I wondered how long he could last in this state.

We watched Walt recite an inexhaustible list of suggestions for us to follow. He wanted us to prepare him for a body upgrade and suggested that we use neurochemical enhancers, neural-computer integration, intelligence intensifiers, genetic engineering and nanotechnology to achieve the best results. We were to spare no technique for expense; the cryosuspension company would pay. Walt was going to get his money's worth!

Walt's speech faltered again. The black dots in his white eyeballs flickered and a look of horror spread over his melting features.

Bimbo reacted quickly, charging Walt's body with supramaximal direct cardioversion shocks. I was so horrified by the dissolving man that I was completely unable to intervene. Bimbo was furiously plunging its piezoelectric charger into the organic goo that was once his body. A dreadful pair of blue lips pouted at Bimbo who was making final desperate attempts to bring Walt back to life.

'Bimbo! Bimbo! Stop it! Leave the poor creature, your piezoelectric charges are frying his flesh!'

Bimbo would not stop giving the steaming puddle its undivided attention.

'Bimbo, stop, will you? I can't bear this any more. It's pointless, he's beyond revival.'

Walt was no more than a nasty pool of brown liquid dripping like treacle onto the floor. Whilst the distressed Bimbo looked at the remains of its disastrous resuscitation attempt, I collected a sample of Walt's fluid in a container for analysis before it evaporated.

psychic combat

The Hopper and the Peeper had secured excellent places for the next *Abductee* broadcast on the psychic network.

There was great excitement in the Collective Consciousness and a sense of occasion. The ratings for *Abductee* were higher than for any other programme in the history of the psychic network and Grays were flocking to the Anatomy Channel. Some dipped into the content of other programmes hoping to find an alternative form of entertainment, but they were generally disappointed, as there was nothing to rival *Abductee*.

The Chronicler had become a cult figure. It was seen as a genuine champion of the species because its encounters promised to reveal whether the rumours regarding human encounters with Grays were just stories, or prove that they were real. Each programme brought the Chronicler's fans closer and closer to the truth and there was the added thrill of wondering if the daring Gray might even touch the humans, compelling viewing for the thrill-seeking audience.

As the Peeper studied an information node which gave the latest summary and breakdown score of the encounters, it could hear the excited chatter of colleagues full of expectation. Looking at the Encounter Record posted on the biggest available display, the Chronicler was threatening tactile advances and scoring points of psychic dexterity that completely outclassed the humans. A promotional clip suddenly appeared. The Chronicler was warming up, twirling its probe and boldly asserted its confidence in the forthcoming encounter with its next human challenger.

'I'm in the best all-round condition of my life and I'm going to put the human beings in their place! Make up your own mind, are they fact or fiction?' it challenged its audience as it performed one of its legendary forward somersaults.

The colleagues cheered. They loved this extraordinarily triumphalist approach to the abduction experiments. Each episode presented a new challenge and fans studied every moment of these encounters, exchanging views on the apparent authenticity of each human contender and the Chronicler's success in revealing their nature. So far, the Chronicler was the undefeated champion of the species and its successful disclosures were therefore their own.

In all the excitement, the Peeper was trying to focus in on a few individual conversations to compare its private opinions with theirs on the current challenge. Some colleagues were claiming that the Chronicler would discover the truth behind all the mysteries of Gray culture and deliver the species from the End of Time. Another group was less apocalyptic in their speculations and recounted the details of their favourite encounters.

The Peeper was fascinated by their conjectures and joined in uninvited, until it became quite exhausted by the conversation.

The Peeper had never seen such an occasion. Everyone was in a festive mood and it would never have guessed that the strange image that it had accidentally come across on the Anatomy Channel could ever have led to such a phenomenon.

'Do you have a good enough view?' asked the Hopper.

'Yes, thanks, I have a lovely view and am completely thrilled by the atmosphere. The enthusiasm is contagious, isn't it!' joyfully replied the Peeper who had never been to a live event before.

The Hopper swelled with pride and stopped worrying about the Peeper's impression of the occasion.

The Peeper busied itself studying every detail of the occasion. 'Hey, what's happening over there?' it asked the Hopper.

The psychic bodies of two colleagues were mock sparring and then hugging one another tightly. There was now even a name for this intimate jousting, 'Psychic Shadow Boxing'. Only a short while ago, Underground Intelligence would have put a stop to this breach in conduct, but now everyone was getting physical, even in the psychic network! Pride in physical prowess was the new thing and there was very little that the Underground Intelligence officers could do about it.

The festive atmosphere was infectious and the chanting crowd was making a sine-wave pattern by sequentially increasing the intensity of their psychic auras whilst they were waiting for events to unfold. The multicoloured ripples spread through the audience, into the corridors of the Anatomy Channel and outwards into the public networks where other colleagues who had not specifically uploaded to watch the latest episode of *Abductee* joined in.

Suddenly, the colleagues hushed their chatter and the coloured ripple broke up into thousands of disorganised psychic energy particles. The encounter was about to start. A huge circular mouth filled the screen and the Hopper and the Peeper found themselves chanting with the crowd.

'Probe it! Probe it! Probe it!'

chronicle entry

robots

Venus-2 was a model specimen of human anatomy spoiled only by a red, gaping, toothless O for a mouth so that she seemed perpetually surprised, but she was not made of human flesh, she was an illusion. I suspected that, despite her virtual embodiment, she was of human origin. My impression was not based on any real analysis; it was more an instinctive feeling. As I watched her, I was certain that there was a vital essence shining from her eyes that could not have been contrived. I wondered where her real body was.

'Does that question interest you?' she suddenly demanded of me.

Could she read my thoughts? I resented her direct approach, as I preferred to begin the experimental interview myself, as a matter of protocol.

'Yes, indeed.'

'Can you elaborate on that?'

'Because I think it is important for me to know who you are, if we are going to understand each other.'

'Do any other reasons not come to mind?'

'Well, I think wanting to know more about you is a good enough reason to start a conversation.'

Her eyeballs rolled around, calculating her reply. Her face suddenly assumed a pitiable expression, pathetic and vulnerable.

'Can you elaborate on that?'

There was something very strange about her use of language. I felt that I was going around in circles with this interview.

'You are talking nonsense!'

'Does it please you to believe I am talking nonsense?'

'No, it annoys me!'

'You are being a bit negative.'

'Of course, I asked you a direct question and you gave me an evasive response.'

'Do you wish to ask me something?'

I was losing the thread of what she was getting at and felt she was either very stupid or playing games with me.

'Please talk sensibly to me!'

'Can you elaborate on that?'

'Cannot you talk sense to me? Do you even know what sense is?'

'Oh, I know what sense is!'

'Then what is it?'

'Does that question interest you?'

I was now getting angry at her stupid answers.

'Not in the slightest! The question that interests me is who you are, why you are appearing as an electronic image in this place and where your body is!'

'Can you elaborate on that?'

'I can, but you can't! Or you won't!'

'Do you wish to?'

Rubbish again!

Then, I realised. Venus-2 was providing me with no new information nor insights into her circumstances. After starting with an open question, she simply turned my questions around to appear conversational. I was not talking to a human at all, but some sort of language programme. The idea of pursuing any kind of interviews or examination with Venus-2 suddenly seemed pointless.

I needed to dig deeper and uncover the underlying human intelligence centres behind the language software, if any existed at all. I was now thoroughly convinced that Venus-2 had once been completely human, but the natural thought centres in her were buried under some sort of computer language software. I suspected that all she needed was a shock to override this control programme, so that I could discover her true identity. So, with the typical recklessness I have shown of late, I discharged a volley of piezoelectric current aiming to reconnect the image with the core of her existence.

Venus-2's image flickered and, for a moment, I thought it would be extinguished. Then her voice temporarily wavered, but grew stronger with each sentence that she uttered. Her conversation gradually became more fluent and soon she spoke with the voice of reason.

'You wanted to know where my real body was. Well, you are looking at a virtual image. The metal that embodies my human vital essence, my soul or whatever you call that substance that makes us alive, is many light years away from us. Where are we?'

'I thought you would know!'

'My calculations indicate that we are in another dimension of spacetime, but I do not compute a particular coordinate for this location. Maybe once I would have been able to tell you using deductive reasoning but, as you know, I am not made of flesh. I am a gynoid, an artificial female, but I was once a human.'

'What happened?'

Venus-2's countenance was even more haunting than usual, exuding nostalgia.

'When I was a young human, I had wanted to be an astronaut. In order to secure one of the few prestigious navigator training places in deep space travel, I used hormone injections and metabolites to make my body bigger, more efficient and stronger than other competitors, but I was still not satisfied. So I indulged in more and more extreme body interventions.'

She spoke softly and slowly as though her past deeds could still cause her further injury.

'Yes, I had extensive surgery, mind implants and biochemical re-engineering. In fact, there was very little of my original biological design left after I had volunteered for every new available technique to improve my athletic abilities. But still my performance did not seem perfect enough.'

'In what way?'

'Well,' she blinked a few times at alpha brainwave frequency, 'I could not admit defeat. I could not accept the fact that my biology was going to prevent me from getting what I thought I wanted and so I was prepared to undergo anything, just so that I could be the very best astronaut ever. In fact, once I had started having upgrades to my body, I began to enjoy the process of suffering that each new technique

brought with it. Then, after I had been accepted on the deep-space training course, a fellow student offered me a hormone to boost my performance.'

'What did it do?'

'This particular hormone was able to greatly increase the power in my body and, although I found it difficult to sleep as the tension in my tissues rose, the gains greatly outweighed the side-effects. Exercises that I previously found hard going were now no longer a challenge. It was like the whole world had been freed of gravitational force and I was almost weightless.'

Venus-2's expression saddened.

'My increased strength did not last long, as I started to sustain injuries. My muscles were too strong for the tendons that attached them to my skeleton. First, I tore my Achilles tendon, and then my biceps tendon. They were only the first in a series of many injuries that I suffered until, tragically, the hormone masculinised my body.'

Venus-2's head bowed without letting her gaze move from me and she slowly placed her hands on her groin, rocking backwards and forwards very gently.

'I can show you what was done to me.'

She revealed an irregular gash between her legs. I moved forward and saw the serrated edge of a female circumcision and the open, sore clitoral stump. Why had this abomination not been corrected? Had the memories that had carved out that awful wound disfigured her self-esteem so greatly that she was unable to free herself of this reminder?

'My genitals became enlarged and coarse hair grew over my body. I had extensive laser treatment on my face and chest to remove it, but there was nothing I could do about the masculinisation of my genitals. The hormone was pumping out testosterone and the only way I could save my body from destruction was by totally replacing it.'

'So, what happened to you?'

'Under the influence of the hormone, my body was changing so rapidly that I was in danger of tearing myself apart. Although I had stopped taking the hormone, it seemed to be continuously active and there was no antidote. My female skeleton was simply not big enough to handle the force of my enhanced muscles. Even the smallest movements, such as breathing or coughing, created pressures that

compressed my organs. I was going to die. For the very first time, I longed for my old body. I searched everywhere, but even the major body-technology corporations could not help me. Finally, I came across a pirate body-dealer called Christian. He told me about the twentieth-century theories of Professor Hans Moravec who claimed that humans were only transient evolutionary creatures who would be replaced by completely artificial creatures, or robots. More importantly, he also persuaded me that he had made some progress in achieving a method of achieving total body "upload" and so he could release my entire personality into an artificial vessel.

'So, you wanted to exchange your damaged body for an artificial new one?'

'Yes. Some people told me that this was a form of death but Christian claimed that the human body could be treated like a machine and simply have its failing parts replaced, perhaps indefinitely. I did not need to age, deteriorate, or suffer fatigue. He offered me help and asked me to consider a body upgrade as being the start to my new, improved life. Once my new body was fully uploaded, I could finally continue my training as an astronaut and there would be no natural human that could rival me.'

Venus-2 was staring at some distant point, reliving the moments in which she decided to surrender her human body for her life and her ambition.

'The operation was risky, since the available technology and techniques to create a completely artificial body were still experimental, but I felt I had no option. Christian reassured me that there would always be the opportunity to upgrade my body with new body components. I then went into deep freeze and was cryogenically suspended. Before I went under the big chill, Christian taught me a maxim to keep my memory intact and I repeated the dictum until my vocal cords were frozen. He told me to say, "I am in control of my future".'

Venus-2 blanked for a moment and resumed her conversation, suppressing a great deal of anger. Her voice was sharp and clear.

'For some reason that I have never been able to discover, the operation was aborted, my frozen body was confiscated and the undamaged organs sold off for profit. At a later stage, some unfamiliar

character revived me, perhaps he was a technician. Oh, I don't know, but whoever he was, he thought it was appropriate to bestow me with a beautiful female body and the face of an erotic doll.'

Her voice was icy, if not malevolent, and her virtual body glowed with energy.

'And, since I looked like a sex-slave, that's the function I was expected to fulfil. My original personality had not been altered in any way so I was forced to watch myself be an erotic gynoid for all time!'

I went to touch her image with my probe to analyse her, but she caught the life probe in her grip and did not let go.

'. . . Don't put your probe near me! Don't you think that I have been through enough already?'

I was shocked. She was in a highly agitated state and very unstable. In an instant, a powerful current surged down the shaft of the probe and into my body. Her energy had intensified and I could not make myself let go of the probe. As her lethal energy flowed from her body into mine, my viewpoint on the encounter had changed and I was looking down on the action from a distant perspective.

I could see Venus-2 trying to pull me into the body of her electronic image and I watched myself become helpless with pain, or was it pleasure? I may have even tried to shout down to myself, but could not intervene as the currents she was discharging into my body through my probe were destroying my own piezoelectric circuits. I was convulsing uncontrollably in alternating waves of agony and ecstasy and saw my body being absorbed into her virtual image. Soon, I could no longer distinguish my body from hers; our eyes, limbs and face seemed to belong to one creature. Was I becoming more like a human or she more like a Gray? Who was who?

As I realised I was disappearing completely, I knew that there was only one possible way of stopping her and so, without caring about the consequences, I summoned all my psychic energy to broadcast a distress signal to the Collective Consciousness.

psychic combat result

The psychic combat had lived up to the Peeper's and the Hopper's expectations. They cheered as the Chronicler interviewed the wide-mouthed Venus-2, exposing her artificial nature with its cunning interview technique. They gasped and drew back as she revealed the brutal gash between her legs. However, as the gynoid grasped the Chronicler's probe, they found themselves willing the Chronicler to beat her off and, as they realised her great strength, they started to fight her with their psychic bodies alongside the Chronicler, as did all the other spectators.

Nothing happened for a few dreadful moments but, as the colleagues realised that the Chronicler was not only losing the fight, it could also be extinguished by the angry gynoid, they responded by helping. In a mutual surge of willpower, they combined their psychic energy to participate on the Chronicler's behalf and reclaim it from defeat.

Venus-2 shrieked, desperate to hang on to the Chronicler, but she was no match for the growing anger and combined psychic power of the species. Her electrical energy eddied and went into hyperspin. She released the Chronicler, but the colleagues had tasted triumph and were not yet finished. They attacked Venus-2's virtual image with volleys of psychic energy. She shrieked for mercy as her signal began to break up, only further uniting the Grays in their cause, their combined energy ripping her eddies apart until she disappeared.

Triumphant and confident, the colleagues started to embrace

one another. The Hopper and the Peeper were thoroughly exhausted by all the excitement and quite depleted of their energy. However, their psychic bodies glowed happiness at each other and they downloaded without the need for dialogue to express their pleasure. The Peeper was thoroughly convinced that one day, if it worked hard enough, it could become a champion of the species, just like the Chronicler.

On the Anatomy Channel, the Chronicler's devotees started to post requests for future encounters, demanding increasingly combative episodes of *Abductee* and, as the exhausted Chronicler scanned its fan mail, it started to realise that the strange encounters were becoming increasingly risky. What once had been an exciting adventure was now based on a grim reality.

chronicle entry

wrinkles

Bimbo looks different every time I see it. Its skin had been smooth and blemish-free when I first vitalised it from the incubator, but now it has little lines of expression on its face. Strangely, it is rather proud of these marks and tells me that they say something about its character.

'It's a human characteristic.'

'What is?'

'Ageing!' Bimbo looked at me suspiciously as it knew I was already disapproving of the movements made by its facial lines.

'Human?' Bimbo's increasing identification with the alien race had begun to upset me. 'What makes you think you are human? You are a hybrid. Don't underestimate my part in your conception and upbringing, you arrogant and ungrateful accident!'

Bimbo spun around and glared at me, its little facial lines giving it a ferocious expression.

'How dare you speak to me like that! I am whatever I choose to be and, accidental as my conception may have been, I am the wiser one for it, you narrow-minded, self-important old Gray.'

I could not bear Bimbo's superior attitude and so I refused to be drawn into further hurtful exchanges. I watched Bimbo stalk triumphantly out of the experimental chamber and away into the time-spill's endless corridors beyond the reach of my psychic sensors, taunting me with rejection.

body conscious

After the live spectacle, the Peeper knew what it wanted to do. It wanted to be a champion of the species, just like the Chronicler. It wanted to use the power in its natural physical body to excel. It wanted to make a unique contribution to Gray culture. It wanted to be someone!

The Peeper looked at its skinny body, large head and dark eyes in a reflective surface and thought of the stocky, muscular bodies of the humans. If it were going to be a champion of the species, then it would need to develop the full potential of its crystalline body. It would have to be stronger. It would have to exercise and think of a training programme for its own personal self-development.

It could not rely on its mining duties to provide the necessary stimulus that would get results, because the colleagues were very keen to conserve energy and minimise physical exertion. Those who worked in the mines simply did what they had to without pushing themselves to the limit. When they were exhausted by moderate exercise, they recharged themselves at the Creature Crystal nodes and went back to work. If a task were very energy-intensive, supervisors would simply instruct more workers to assist the others.

No one thought of increasing the strength of their crystalline body, because the psychic body was regarded as being so superior that any downtime not dedicated to improving it was considered pointless.

This made the Peeper excited. It was about to set another new fashion. How would its silica gels respond to exercise? What sort of exercises should it do? How often should it exert itself?

The Peeper looked at its crystalline body again. It wanted more power in its upper body, its legs, its neck: in fact, it wanted to increase its overall size absolutely everywhere. So it uploaded onto the Anatomy Channel and recorded everything that had ever been broadcast on the anatomy of Grays. The Peeper was delighted to note that the Chronicler had carried out most of the work on the Grays' anatomy. Therefore it took even greater pleasure than it had anticipated in studying how its body was powered by the piezoelectricity that ran in the great conduction tracts and how it was given energy through the strength of its silica gels.

As it studied more about its anatomy, the Peeper realised that it would have to take in large amounts of silica salts, consume huge amounts of water to hydrate the new gels and activate its piezoelectric circuits to their maximum capacity.

Soon, it had worked out a whole development programme that included regular silica nutrition by connecting its body to the Creature Crystals at downtime to fully recharge its piezoelectric energy, taking water baths and exercising very hard indeed. It kept the details of its routine secret, but its companions started to notice that it was more efficient at the silica rock face.

'Hey, Peeper!' remarked the Screwer, 'you're getting big . . .!'

The Peeper did not reply. It really did not want to indulge the Screwer's attentions, as this colleague always tried to set you up before it knocked you down. The Screwer, growing impatient at the silence, delivered its spiteful put-down punch line, 'and ugly!'

At this, the Twister and the Nutter giggled. The Peeper realised that, if it let the Screwer make derogatory remarks now, it was only setting a precedent for further humiliation when its physical development became even more pronounced. So, it put down its pick and lifted the Screwer high into the air with one hand. It then spun the arrogant colleague violently around by its skinny neck until it was screaming for mercy. The speed of the rotation had caused the water in the Screwer's gels to come out of colloidal suspension and, when the Peeper let it fall, the Screwer was left lying helpless on the ground.

The Twister and the Nutter giggled uncomfortably at the floundering Gray and crept closer to the Peeper's workface to ingratiate themselves, hoping that it had not taken offence at their behaviour, too.

contest

Posted on the Anatomy Channel by an anonymous devotee.

Abductee fans are fully aware that the Chronicler already has an impressive track record of manipulating human beings into submission and, although it has used rather controversial tactics to win, it has had rather an easy run of late.

'Until I prove myself against these beings and outsmart the best of them, I don't want to be called a legend because I don't believe I am,' admitted the Chronicler. 'I may be destined to be a legend, I may be destined to become a great champion of the species, but at this moment in time, I prefer colleagues to recognise me for my experimental skills in biology, my talent and the amount of times I've held the human beings to account. I do not want to be known just for my entrances in the abduction chambers. I'm not grumbling about it, I simply want to be recognised for the other things I bring out of these encounters. I honestly feel that the next contest is going to be full of surprises and I may have to use a few new techniques, but I'm not going to predict anything. The human being may act provocatively or I may provoke a reaction from it. Maybe I'll have to call on the species again but I don't think so. I'm a fast learner and we'll just have to see if they really have got what it takes to outwit me.'

chronicle entry

cyborgs

I have not seen Bimbo for a while. It is preoccupied with exploring the eternal corridors of the time-spill and has generally avoided participating in the experiments, preferring to communicate with the preborn creatures in the incubators.

My encounters with humans are progressing with great speed. The latest humans I have met are more complex than the androids like Venus-2, in that they are part-flesh and part-metal. Although some of the creatures still consider themselves as humans, most of them call themselves 'cyborgs'.

Cyborgs seem to be highly adaptable, socially adept, politically mobile and sexually flirtatious individuals.

I was surprised by Bimbo's appearance. Perhaps I noticed the difference because I had not seen it recently. Bimbo has changed and not for the better. A horrible tuft of velvety hair sprouts from its head and its limbs look longer and thicker than I recall. Its movements are more controlled, and I never see it bounce about any more. Those lines it started to develop around its face are growing more furrowed and longer and I have noticed some crosshatched lines on the backs of its hands. Although it is getting ugly, it is now wiser and more knowledgeable about human nature than I am.

Bimbo and I are competing for the attentions of a charming and playful cyborg called Morph whose eyes continuously change their shape and colour.

'How did you do that?' asked Bimbo, staring at her face from an uncomfortably close position.

'Do what?' Morph pulled back from Bimbo's penetrating stare.

'Your eyes changed whilst you were talking, just a few moments ago!'

'Oh, that, I do not know. I cannot directly influence my transitions. They happen because my biology is in constant metamorphosis.'

She adopted a new posture and her body language altered. I wanted to know more about the relationship between Morph's looks and her behaviour.

'Does your personality change with your appearance?' I enquired.

Morph was more than happy to speculate on her constantly changing appearance and mannerisms. I hoped she was not going to turn out to be another Venus-2 and tucked my experimental probe out of the way, beyond her reach.

'I am not aware of any changes. You must tell me about them. It is difficult to see myself from the outside. I know I have had modifications to my body that allow me to adapt readily to new environments. Do I seem very different from what I seemed to be just a moment ago to you?'

I made an ambivalent gesture, but Bimbo was not so reserved in its uninvited second opinion.

'Of course you do, you change continuously! It is infuriating since I have to compensate for your psychic patterns. I keep getting a time-lag between my interpretations of your thought patterns and your physical form.'

'How interesting!' beamed Morph. 'So, which changes first, my body or my thought patterns?'

'Your character changes first and then your body adjusts.' Morph was looking at Bimbo now with a soft, dark expression through violet irises. Bimbo continued, reading her mind.

'Your thoughts are always out of phase with the rest of your biology. Someone should try and fix that.'

'Thank you, but not today!' protested Morph as Bimbo drew far too close to her. 'I've had enough of people interfering with my biology, that's how I have developed such an unstable identity in the first place.'

'What have you had done?' I asked and realised that I found the idea of a human body being interfered with strangely exciting.

'Ah, almost all procedures that introduce mechanical implants into the body have been tried out on me and I have just had my internal physiology redesigned to improve my athletic performance. I could have opted for additional sensory organs and communications devices to be attached to my sensory system but, so far, I've resisted the temptation.'

'What do you mean "additional"?' I asked, trying not to let her detect the enthusiasm in my voice.

'Oh, extra ears, digital eyes, supersonic vibrators, thought antennae and supernumerary limbs are the most fashionable appendages.'

'What? People permanently attach strange objects to themselves? Why would anyone want to do that for?' The growing number of lines on Bimbo's face made it difficult to conceal its disapproval.

Bimbo was horrified at the idea of forcing any sort of mutation, artificial or natural, upon a healthy body. Being a hybrid, it could not understand why anyone would not want to be a perfect specimen of a species. Morph was lucky that Bimbo had not met Venus-2 or there would have been little chance of such pleasantries exchanged between them, as Venus-2's bad character would have further prejudiced its reaction to Morph's willingness to mutate.

'Oh, that's easy. If you wear your extra prosthesis on the outside of your body, everyone else can admire it and see how improved you are. It's such a vain thing to do, but aesthetically compelling! Don't you think so?'

I certainly agreed with her. Physical modification of the body simply to create variety was an exciting idea, but Bimbo was thoroughly offended and was becoming highly irritable.

'Could you sort out your conversational phases, please?' it interjected, 'The time delay between what you are thinking and what you are saying is confusing me. Are you sure you don't want me to try and fix your biological rhythms?'

Despite Morph's reluctance, Bimbo's incessant complaining that it had difficulty following her conversations persuaded her to finally agree to a number of small adjustments in her brain. Although she did not welcome our suggestion of taking the nasal approach to her language areas, I promised that my probe would not hurt her, and once the synchronising implant was in place, she would not be able to feel it. In return, we promised the intervention would ensure that her thought patterns would run in phase with her changing cyborg anatomy.

During the operation, Bimbo and I were able to take tissue samples. It was evident that her cyborg cells were chimeras, part animal, part synthetic and part human. Each component was seamlessly intermingled with the next.

Sometimes the human genome containing cells would predominate, and at other times, the synthetic components were most active. We watched the ebb and flow of different populations of cellular components with fascination, gripped by the dynamism of her microcellular anatomy.

We discovered further intriguing properties from her cell lines in that the human cells were immortal. They did not die after a short time outside the body substance, but continued to thrive as autonomous colonies. Bimbo was condemning of Morph's physical make-up, again claiming that her immortal cells were against her nature.

'Human cells are prone to errors by design,' Bimbo pronounced as the display characterised Morph's highly-engineered twisted strands of biological code, 'it appears that death is part of human life even before these creatures are actually ever born and Morph has had her dying sequences inactivated.'

'Well, changing your genetic programme to live longer sounds like a perfectly reasonable modification to make. What could possibly be wrong with that?'

'I don't know, but something about it is not right.'

'Bimbo, you are just being difficult. You have disapproved of Morph from the moment you met her. I believe you want to be the only hybrid around here!'

'No, that's not it at all! Call it an instinct, but she's not all right. She is not all right at all!'

I did not believe Bimbo's observations. Things had become personal in the experimental chamber again.

I have finally had a few moments to study Morph's tissue samples removed during the gastro-intestinal experiment. Most have been upgraded by genetic engineering and contain a large number of inclusion bodies. These inclusion bodies are additional strands of DNA that code for an extra sequence of nucleic acid. As these DNA fragments are so compact, I have been unable to characterise the sequence. In any event, the cells with these extra pieces of genetic code do not appear to be growing or dividing efficiently in cell culture, due to the additional nucleic material that is obstructing the replication mechanisms.

I have decided to culture these cells over an accelerated time period to see what happens to them.

Morph's cultured cells have all turned into cancers.

Morph noticed the lump first. It was hard, painless and loosely attached to the connective tissue under her flesh. We measured and examined it with interest. The cells are cancerous.

Morph is now completely covered with these unsightly lumps and made very uncomfortable by the sheer number of them. She is pale, has lost her glow and become withdrawn.

I have sampled her tissues again and all of her cells are now filled with large inclusion bodies. The DNA inside them is so compact that there is no room for any cytoplasm. They are dying because they cannot produce energy to live.

Finally, Morph's flesh stopped working and we observed her artificial organs continue to pump, stimulate and secrete matter into decomposing organic tissue. Of course, her flesh could not respond and there was no chance of reviving her.

'In a way, I suppose cell death is the antidote to cancer,' mused Bimbo looking thoughtfully at Morph's remains. 'There is a purpose behind all this programmed dying after all.'

chronicle entry

human plants

I have found a fine golden dust that has settled everywhere. It rises again with the smallest convection currents and turbulence, exploding in little mushroom clouds whenever I pass. I do not know how long it has been here because the grains are almost invisible under the harsh lighting and I only really noticed them when I saw fine smoke clouds creep along the floor of the experimental chamber behind me as I walked about.

I have collected samples of this dust.

Bimbo worries me.

It is now horribly wrinkled and finds difficulty in moving. Every action is laborious and painful to watch. It has recently developed a shuffling, off-balance gait and it has begun twiddling imaginary balls of stuff between its fingers. There appears to be no apparent reason for this ritual.

Moreover, its emotional intelligence is dwindling. Once, it would have disapproved of my intimacy with some of the humans, but now it no longer passes spontaneous comments or observations. Fortunately, Bimbo does not appear to have suffered intellectually and, if I can bear the slow pace at which we settle into a conversation, it has developed a profound wisdom in human affairs.

Nevertheless, these changes are really bothering me, so I am avoiding Bimbo. No, I am not, I am ignoring it!

I have banished Bimbo from the experimental chambers, as its finger fidgeting during my investigations is too distracting.

The golden dust showers are a welcome interruption. Billows of dancing, sparkling clouds have appeared from nowhere and are shimmying through the experimental chamber. Every object is spectacularly transformed when the dust clouds come, including Bimbo who is now back again. It looks like a golden statue and is, for once, quite beautiful.

Under the microscope, the golden dust particles appear to be cells. Each contains an unstable nucleus and is coated with a tough fibrous coat. The DNA is not fully human and I have found many odd sections of genetic material that could be from another species.

The particles appear to be absorbing moisture from the atmosphere and I think they are germinating spores, but they will need closer examination.

Bimbo likes to sit motionless beside me as I conduct my experiments and I have let it return to my side since I feel sorry for it and it is no longer finger-rolling. I am concerned that all it is able to do now is observe me, as its body has become so weak and rigid that even the smallest movement does not appear to be possible. I am tempted to retract the hoods over its eyes and pin them back, so that the folds of skin do not obscure its vision.

I have managed to observe some of the germinating particles under low magnification. They are even more scintillating under the intensified light than in the chamber, as it emphasises their dancing qualities. Each particle has sprouted a tiny, spring-loaded tendril that thrashes about wildly, making sharp cracking sounds. They beckon to one another and embrace in their search for an anchor or partner to cling to.

I can tell by the brightness in its eyes that Bimbo enjoys watching the germinating spores almost as much as I do. I am going to have to do something about those baggy folds of skin. I hate the way they flop over Bimbo's eyes.

Some of the germinating spores have sprouted and greatly increased in size. They are golden orbs, big enough to hold in the palm of one hand. Those that have sprouted have produced twisting tentacles that grope about like fingers.

Some of the orbs have intertwined with one another and have organised themselves in a ring. From a distance, the round central body appears to be maturing, pinching in at the waist and adopting an upright posture. As we watch their speedy evolution, they turn into child-like humans whose stubby fingers hold each other's hands and we hear them laughing.

The child-like golden humans have rapidly elongated and matured into multicoloured, elegant adult humans. They continue to embrace one another in their ring-shaped arrangements and from this magic circle of roots and tendrils, each creature gazes in turn at the others.

Bimbo has become much more animated since the spores have 'grown up' and is determined to take tottering steps towards them. I have had to steady it to stop it toppling over, but am encouraged by its current progress.

Bimbo told me that it is trying to speak orally with these beautiful, entwined humans. I am sad for Bimbo because even its face is tense and its words do not come. I am relieved that its psychic powers are still holding strong.

'They are talking!'

Bimbo's staccato speech surprised me. It was looking at one particular ring of multicoloured human bodies, curled tenderly around each other. All I could hear was the squeaking of cellulose fingers rubbing against one another. Where they touched, they exchanged syrupy secretions.

'Listen.'

I was unable to tune into the frequency that Bimbo was picking up and shook my head.

'They are human plants!'

Bimbo was animated, and wanted to tell me what these strange creatures were saying.

'They are very friendly . . . [pause] . . . They all seem to be in love with one another . . . [pause] . . . Can you feel the energy?'

It was true. Although I was not directly experiencing their intimate conversations, I could certainly feel the radiance they spread around.

'These human plants have found the perfect balance . . . [pause] . . . being at one with the natural world . . . [pause] . . . They have combined the advantages of terrestrial plants with animal qualities . . . [pause] . . . to overcome the challenges of energy, time, food and metabolic activity . . . [pause] . . . particularly during space travel.'

'How do you speak to them, Bimbo?'

'It's easy! [pause] . . . They are highly sensitive creatures . . . [pause] . . . They have extremely well-developed senses . . . [pause] . . . and are able to "see", "taste", "hear", "smell" and "touch" . . . [pause] . . . but they access different frequencies to natural humans.'

'But although they grow very rapidly, they hardly move at all. They do not do anything, do they? So what is the point of having these highly developed sensory abilities?'

Bimbo giggled, as if it were enjoying a private joke with the human plants and then became silent again. Despite several attempts to find out more about these enigmatic creatures by trying to flatter Bimbo, I was blanked and left to my own devices.

Bimbo sat almost motionless close to the ring of human plants and, from time to time, it giggled.

I have managed to tune into the psychic frequencies of the human plants and no longer need Bimbo to interpret for me, although it is always close by watching us. Bimbo finds moving around painful and its limbs are now so rigid that its joints are permanently bent up. Occasionally, I detect a psychic impression that suggests Bimbo is in distress, but it remains uncomplaining and observant of the human plants.

The human plants sit together in the experimental chamber seemingly in awe of one another, radiating tranquillity whilst exchanging inaudible secrets. They are using some strange communication frequencies that I cannot pick up with my psychic sensors and I can only imagine the details of their conversations. Perhaps they are discussing the secrets of elemental forces and the erotic sensibilities of life.

At other times, the human plants are silent, quietly absorbing the ambient radiation and positioning themselves strategically under the powerful lighting of this place from which they draw energy. They seem to have a healing effect on Bimbo who manages regularly to alter its position, despite its increasing physical stiffness, in order to enjoy their beneficial effects.

They are disarming, confusing and enchanting. Sometimes, they sing to us.

Angel Berry is a brilliant blue-eyed, lithe male human plant with elaborate facial hair. His beard is a variety of sprouting facial fibres. His green whiskers curl into green corkscrew twists; on his chin is a brilliant red, pointed goatee and his cheeks are framed with black walrus sideburns. He says that his beard changes most rapidly during fasts when the plant hair filaments grow faster.

Although Angel Berry has a digestive system like humans, it is a vestigial structure. Angel does not eat at all. He is a 'breatharian'.

'Why don't you eat?'

'I have trained my body to metabolise in a different way. I think that food is full of toxins. If food is supposed to be so good for you, why does the body try to get rid of it? We are not rubbish bins! So, why should we fill our body with junk?

'Actually, I do not see the attraction in eating. Grays use piezoelectric energy. Do you think that all humans could stop eating?'

'No, not all humans are capable of making the transition to breatharianism, but it has worked for me. It is the secret to health, happiness and long life, what all humans are looking for.'

'Are all of you human plants breatharian?'

'Not all. Some of us feed on the substances that we secrete; others absorb simple sugars and a few of us feed on decaying organic matter. Most of us are not even interested in food. We do not make it a central part of our social lives the way that natural humans do, but I am convinced that "fasting" in general is good for one's constitution, and for staying in shape or losing weight, just to purify the body.'

'Aren't you denying yourself pleasure? I know that humans enjoy their food!'

Angel laughed. A huge multicoloured smile radiated across his face and the tendrils of his whiskers twirled with delight.

'Dear creature, I will let you into a personal secret. Food is not pleasure, it is a base function that has no spiritual qualities. It gratifies the lower centres of human desire, but I am more interested in those pursuits that satisfy the higher centres and, believe me, I do know what pleasure is.'

His enthusiasm was contagious and I was eager to discover his pleasure principle.

'I enjoy much better sex than most people do. I have found that great happiness, as well as exceptional mental clarity and even increased sex drive, comes from combining the ritual with fasting. A breatharian can ejaculate and make love ten times better than someone who eats habitually. A breatharian human plant will experience this pleasure five hundredfold more than natural humans would. Not only is our perception of time different, but we sustain our orgasms much longer than those with organic flesh as the stiff cellulose walls around every cell in our body help us stay rigid for a very long period. We are irresistible by nature, exuding potent pheromones that have an instant aphrodisiac effect on all that come into close contact with us, and our glands secrete sex substances like nectar. Humans even make pilgrimages to find us and join in our love rituals. Everything that we produce during the sexual act is precious and full of pleasure-yielding molecules. When I make love, I keep my sperm pollen seed to heighten my pleasure and save sexual energy. If I do ejaculate, then I'll eat my own sperm and recycle it.'

'But I thought you didn't eat.'

'I don't, I swill it around in my mouth until it gets absorbed.'

With that, Angel beamed at me under a blue tendril of upper lip hair and licked his pouting lips. It was only then that I noticed the milky sap swilling around in his mouth. The musk-smelling sticky fluid rolled around on the surface of his tongue and glistened on the surface of his teeth.

'Gaaaaaaaaaaaaah! See, I have not spilt a drop. It lasts for ages. Do you want some?'

When the oxygen concentration of an environment is low, human plants can produce a metabolic waste product they call alcohol during something that they call the 'fermentation ritual'.

Bimbo, having eventually moved to join the ring, has been sampling some alcohol and this has changed its conduct. Instead of sitting rigidly, as its weak physical constitution has previously demanded, it is able to move about quite freely. In fact, I would describe its conduct as disinhibited and uncharacteristically exhibitionist. I have even seen it shouting, singing and embracing others in the company of its fermenting companions. It seems to occupy a world of its own and ignores me. With its captive audience, its confidence is restored and I have noticed that, whenever Bimbo has been indulging in this alcoholic substance, it tells me to 'loosen up' before it collapses into fits of laughter!

I am worried about the influence that these human plants are having on Bimbo. I am really not jealous about its intimate associations with the human plants, although Bimbo does not believe me. I am simply concerned about Bimbo's health, as in its current fragile condition it should be taking greater care of itself.

Bimbo says I worry too much and finds my concern for its welfare hilarious. At other times, Bimbo is very quiet and just groans, as if in great pain, and is only able to produce very weak psychic impressions. If it manages to speak, it asks for water. When I see Bimbo in such a state, I hardly recognise it as the same Bimbo I released from the incubator. Its progressive frailty and this silly behaviour have alienated it from me.

I want the old Bimbo back.

Some human plants produce clouds of dust or smoke from their lips when they are communicating in the ring. They appear to be burning on the inside. The smell of this smoke is sometimes fruity and, at other times, it is musky. I get a feeling that these creatures are doing something illicit.

Joel Berry is a statuesque human plant of noble poise and is one of the smoking varieties of human plant. His facial hair is not wild like

Angel Berry's, but carefully coiled and he has a long mane of silver tendrils that tumble from his crown to the floor.

'So you are curious to know how we came to be this way?'

I found it difficult to watch his brilliant eyes as he spoke, for his face was always partially concealed by a smoke cloud and he was so tall it was almost impossible to communicate comfortably with him when he was standing. Seeing my discomfort, he squatted down, an action that seemed to take several hours but I was prepared to wait.

'Our ancestors, humans and plants, had totally different biologies and we were created more by accident than by design. We were humans first and acquired our first plant tissues later as artificial organs. Plant cells could be cultured inside the human body and provide a cellulose matrix over which human tissue could be encouraged to grow. These cultures produced a fine network of cells that was similar to human connective tissue and which started to thicken the bodily cellular matter over the course of many years.'

I could see how firm and woody Joel Berry's skin was and watched his hands stretch and grow into a dignified gesture.

'The humans that incorporated plant tissues into their bodies became more beautiful, graceful and cheerful than natural humans. Human plants enjoyed the sunlight because their skin was protected against radiation damage by photosensitive plant pigments and the firm cellulose networks in their skin prevented wrinkling. Human plants were known for their beautiful array of coloured skins, ranging from greens to deep browns depending on the pigments.'

I had noticed that Joel's stately posture was partly caused by his upwardly-turned chin that was searching for light.

'Did the alternative metabolism and anatomy make you human plants so highly sexual?' I could not resist this question any longer, being intrigued by how slowly the human plants moved and wondering how this related to their obvious potency and exuberant sexuality.

'Not really. The first human plants could propagate themselves from grafted pieces of tissue from amputated organs. Sexuality came later, when the human plants produced flowering gonads.'

'How does that work?'

'Promiscuity, my dear, promiscuity!'

Joel blew a huge smoke cloud that tumbled like a waterfall from his lips. I tried not to let him see that the particles were settling on my skin and making me tingle all over in the most pleasant manner.

'Really?'

'Of course, promiscuity is the key to the success of the flowering human plants; we rely on other creatures such as insects to carry our fertile spores, so we must seduce as many creatures as possible if we are to multiply. Male flowering human plants must rub up against another creature in order to persuade them to carry their pollen to the female human plant. For that reason, you will find that male flowering human plants have erotic, alluring personalities and exciting, promiscuous sexual practices.'

I could confirm that the male flowering human plants I had met were very sexual and most enticing, but I wondered where the females were.

'The female?' Joel started to stand up again, making me feel uncomfortable.

'We have only one in our group! Why don't you try and find her?'

It is a vegetable orgy and the female of the species, Esther Berry, is right at its centre. The bodies of the human plants are seamlessly intertwining, connecting, repositioning and exchanging fluids. Heads are buried in limbs. Limbs are wrapped around torsos. Genitals are heavy, in full bloom and laden with sex cells.

Angel Berry has its facial tendrils entwined in Esther Berry's limb petals and Joel Berry is stroking the ripening genitals of the lovers to facilitate their coupling. Others are coiled in, around and out of one another in the most provocative of positions, displaying stamens, stigmas, styles and ovaries that are bursting with juices. The entwining lovers move together as one great fertile beast, slowly undulating and singing reedy, ecstatic songs. The brilliance of their colours is dazzling. The air is perfumed and stifling. Body fluids are condensing on all surfaces. The entire chamber seems to be drawing on the same sustained breath.

The sexuality is contagious. I no longer sense any distance between the human plants and myself. Angel Berry's tendrils are encircling Bimbo's body, whilst Joel Berry is dripping honeyed extract from an oozing tendril on Bimbo's wrinkled skin. Bimbo's eyes are unfocused. I am unable to read its psychic impressions in the overpowering lullaby of the human plant circle. We are both under their spell. There are no longer any discrete sensations, just ecstasy.

I can see sound. Is this an optical illusion? Bimbo is rolling its fingertips together again in that obsessive, neurotic way that I hate and producing long, thin sound objects. Esther Berry smiles, takes one between her lips, and lowers it to her swollen sex organs where she masturbates herself with it. Then, languidly she alternates between puffing on the slender object, and returning it to her succulent, flowering genitals.

I feel tendrils around me. I do not know whom they belong to. I am very close to Bimbo now and I am so very, very happy.

Bimbo and I are reunited. We are exchanging psychic images instead of vocalisations, which is a sign that we are hiding nothing from each other.

The human plants seem be rejoicing at our reunion. They are brighter, fuller and more sociable than before. They are singing new songs and making strange music. They have decorated their bodies with golden fibres studded with small resin jewels. Angel Berry has grown bright red orbs at the tips of his corkscrewing whiskers. He is shouting with great enthusiasm about creatures that he calls 'ants'.

'These little ants are great artistes! They make little black patterns just like my whiskers.' He stretches his facial hair into a long, straight tendril and let it snap back so that the red droplets quivered. 'The secret of the little ants is all in their collective mind. They are so clever and amusing, aren't they? They tickle the funny bone, they creepy-crawl over the flesh and they are very good lovers. Oh, yes, I love these ants, I love to put ants in my pants!'

I think this must be a post-coital joke or ritual of some sort referring to the role that Bimbo and I might have played in the ceremony. Perhaps we remind him of the ants, whatever they are, but I cannot be certain and he looks so silly singing the song that I cannot take offence.

Esther Berry has a swollen abdomen.

'I'm pregnant!' she beamed. Her full red lips were unusually attractive. I focused on the swollen cushions, for the first time regarding the mouth as an organ of beauty. Then she laughed, slowly turning her face away from my astonished gaze.

'The fertility ritual was successful.' She was laughing again.

'You and Bimbo have been vital to our mating ritual. You are our honoured "mobile penises". Thank you for your assistance.'

I was bewildered. Was I going to be a parent again?

'What happens now?'

'We wait for the embryonic spores in my belly to ripen. Here, feel them. You helped to sow them with your "errant virility" and they will soon ripen. Go on, you can touch them!'

When I ran my hands over her belly, I could feel the bumps made by the embryonic spores that pressed tightly against her skin, as if impatient, eager to escape.

I am horrified to learn that Bimbo, despite its impaired mobility, has been by far the more active of the two of us in the fertility ritual.

I am keeping vigil on Esther Berry's transformation. Bimbo is extremely cooperative and we share the watch over Esther Berry's swollen abdominal area that is rapidly becoming redder, thinner and tighter. We also take turns to stroke the surface of the swelling, listening to the tympanic sounds of her skin and chatting to Esther Berry about how she feels.

Esther is radiant, her lips full and beautiful. Bimbo and I cannot bear to be away from her. The emotional radiance she brings with her pregnancy is contagious.

Curiously, Angel, Joel and the other male human plants seem to be becoming weaker and withering away. This is not our main concern and our observations are now focused on the expanding Esther who continues to amaze us with displays, visions and insights into the secrets of fertility.

Esther's glowing body continues to distend.

Bimbo says that it cannot wait to belong to a real family at last.

The other human plants are fading, becoming darkened vestigial appendages of the human plant circle.

There is silence in the chamber, Esther is dead. I am devastated.

I have been looking to Bimbo for an explanation, but it cannot communicate with me.

Joel and Angel Berry have become dark, twisted, statuesque stumps of fibre. Strangely, the expressions carved on their faces convey tranquillity. I have taken these sturdy sculptures and arranged them around the experimental chamber so that I can think of the happy times we had together.

We have spent a long time in silence.

Bimbo has spoken for the first time since Esther's death.

'I touched her abdomen . . . [pause] . . . Honestly, I was only listening for signs of life inside the capsule . . . [pause] . . . when her magnificent red belly suddenly split open.'

'Was she in pain?'

'No, she smiled! . . . [pause] . . . I did not know what to do!'

'Did you try and revive her?'

'I tried everything, but she was lifeless . . . [pause] . . . All that was left was a brown wizened shell . . . [pause] . . . where her beautiful, pregnant belly had once been . . . [pause] . . . I was worse than useless . . . [pause] . . . If only I could have saved her.'

It looked at me despairingly, appearing to be much older and frailer than ever before.

'What about her embryonic spores?'

'Only one . . . [pause] . . . Can you believe that? . . . [pause] . . . Only one.'

'But there were so many.'

'They were all shrivelled up and stony . . . [pause] . . . Only one survived!'

'Where is it now? Bimbo, where have you put Esther's offspring?'

'I don't know . . . [pause] . . . It's gone.'

'Gone? Where has it gone? Why did you let it go?'

'I didn't, I mean . . . [pause] . . . I couldn't stop it! . . . [pause] . . . It was so fast.'

'What happened, Bimbo?'

I was shaking the fragile creature in anger now.

'As her belly split open . . . [pause] . . . I heard a metallic sound . . . [pause] . . . a pure tone ringing and growing louder with every moment . . . [pause] . . . Her flesh peeled back . . . [pause] Inside, there were hundreds of dead little black spores . . . [pause] . . . shrivelled and useless in the pit of her stomach . . . [pause] . . . They were dead, too! . . . [pause] . . . All dead . . . [pause] . . . Except for one large silver cigar-like spore . . . [pause] it looked like it did not belong there . . . [pause] . . . I watched, stunned, as it slowly rose out of her . . . [pause] . . . and then it shot into the experimental chamber . . . [pause] . . . with such velocity that I could not follow it . . . [pause] . . . nor see where it went.'

'Where is the silver spore, Bimbo?'

'I do not know . . . [pause] . . . Why did she have to die?'

'We must try and find the spore, Bimbo!'

'It's all my fault . . . [pause] . . . I should have saved her!'

We both consoled each other promising that we would recover the missing spore but, truthfully, we knew that Esther's offspring was as lost to us as she was.

spore

The strange, silver cigar-shaped spore had torn itself from Esther Berry's belly.

It was not a natural birth, but a freakish pregnancy that had been conceived in the strangest of places, by the oddest of methods and with the most peculiar group of genitors. It was not an ordinary birth, and in any other situation might well have been aborted, but the Time Toroid was not an ordinary place. Even within the vast expanse of the idiosyncratic universe the Time Toroid was a rare entity, so it was able to sustain the most unlikely of encounters and nurture the most improbable unions.

Besides, the spore desperately wanted to be alive and would stop at nothing to ripen into independence.

In some ways, the silver spore was already a mature entity, but it was a mistake. The plant humans had chosen their 'mobile penises' badly, picking an impotent Gray and a hybrid with ambitions to be human to vitalise their seed. As the Chronicler and Bimbo rubbed themselves against the plant humans, their deficiencies rubbed off with the pollen and contaminated Esther Berry's precious seed.

So the silver spore grew in Esther Berry's belly alongside thousands of other embryonic spores. The silver spore was fully aware of the responsibility that was invested in it by its creators and could not allow the other spores to get in the way of the expectations that encumbered it. Mercilessly it strangled their ambitions and siphoned off the sustenance of the other embryonic bodies with which it shared a womb.

Some of its siblings panicked, realising that they were under attack. They grew as fast as they could, trying to catch up with the rapid development of the silver spore and hoping to compete with it. They pressed against the belly of Esther Berry, begging for release, but their mother was not ripe enough to yield to them and so they blackened and withered. Those embryonic spores that were oblivious to the advanced maturity of the silver spore died too, but more slowly from gradual neglect. The silver spore felt no remorse at the mass murder of its mongrel siblings. Quite the contrary. The thrill of its dreadful betrayal only spurred its growth along faster, with the hope of reaching maturity before it was found out. Soon, the silver spore reached escape velocity and, in a split second, it added matricide to its list of transgressions, perforating the belly of the succulent Esther Berry, lubricating its shell with her juices.

Bimbo could have stopped the malignant entity from contaminating the universe with its badness, but for selfish reproductive reasons only human beings truly understand, Bimbo let the silver spore go.

fight for life

Posted on the Anatomy Channel by an anonymous devotee.

The Chronicler is facing the biggest contest in its career and will spare no tactics to conquer its prospective challenger, Janus. In a promotional preview on the Anatomy Channel, the Chronicler seemed in good spirits and on excellent form.

'I haven't come this far for nothing,' insisted the champion of the species. 'Janus appears to be, if you like, the perfect human being. He has not shown any of the usual human weaknesses, but I might just crack him.'

When asked about the challenger, the Chronicler said it was expecting a tough contest.

'I reckon he's going to be hostile from the start but, like most humans, I expect he will tire in the middle of the encounter. It's the same with all humans, no matter what mood or shape they're in. But Janus is a cut above the others. I think I've got to be very careful when I challenge him.'

chronicle entry

viruses

Janus has materialised with immaculate timing. He is sexually ripe, pumped full of steroids, glued together by grafts and driven by technology. Although I initially feared that he would be aggressive, judging by his size and appearance, I have since realised that there is something different about Janus, although we have not yet spoken.

Janus is watching me obediently and his beauty has absorbed me, promising fresh sexual encounters. I have memorised the precise details of his body. His hair is raven black with grey-sprinkled stubble that highlights his temples and frames the side of his face. A translucent skin protects his maroon muscle grafts and I like watching them diving and surfacing with every action he makes.

I cannot stop thinking about him.

I must mention his eyes. They are almond-shaped and slope upwards, framed under his straight black brows. His irises change kaleidoscopically from azure blue, to yellow, green, violet, chocolate brown and graphite, spinning in dizzy chaos patterns punctuated by huge pupillary vortices.

Janus has allowed me to approach him without any resistance. He says nothing whilst I thoroughly examine him with my probe. He just stares obediently at me.

Despite his great muscular bulk and broad stature, he appears to be coy and I find this quality alluring. Although he does not actually speak, he tries to communicate with me, continually practising making words and he looks like he is kissing the air. When he is tired of pretend speech, his lips relax and turn upwards at the edges.

His psychic images change too rapidly for me to follow them entirely. They are full of multicoloured swirls and mathematical formulae. Although I am not sure what these strange psychic fractals actually mean, I think we understand one another.

Janus preoccupies me. His flesh, his face, his mannerisms direct my thoughts. I imagine teaching him how to say his name.

'Janus, Janus.'

I still cannot stop myself thinking about Janus and my fantasies are becoming outlandish. I am tempted to make direct physical contact and thrust myself upon him, but I also want him to encourage me.

Janus has started to speak to me. I am deeply disappointed, as his speech is both hideous to observe and to listen to.

He starts by sucking excess saliva from between the recesses of his teeth. He then blows the gaps clean again, making a frothy hiss before blowing out a long slow breath that ends with his greeting.

'S'nice to sssssssssssssee youse . . . Yesssssssssssss!'

His words are so full of spit and dental slobber that I have to avoid looking at him. I think of this awful drool as 'conversational spraying'. Talking to Janus is a complete waste of time, since I cannot bear the prospect of being spat at just for the further torment of enduring his small talk. He always seems to be clearing his throat and the sound of his bubbling oral secretions destroys my lust for him.

I have noticed an annoying gap between his front teeth that sometimes makes him whistle inconsiderately. Janus most definitely does not excite me any more, despite his perfect physique. In fact, since he has begun to speak, he has become a sexual damp squid. I have noticed how soft and spongy his flesh is, how limp his gestures are and how much he dribbles.

I have started talking in drawn-out monologues and keeping my distance from him, to stop him trying to talk to me. During my lengthy dissertations on life, philosophy and the universe, Janus waits for me to finish with a polite, patient expression waiting for the moment I have finished speaking. Then he instantly attempts to make dialogue. If I cannot ignore him because he is following me, I just glare at him disapprovingly. I want him to go away.

Janus senses that I am no longer interested in examining him intimately. It has taken him an amazingly long time to come to this conclusion, given that I have been doing my utmost to be spiteful at every occasion. He is either very slow with his comprehension skills or emotionally vacant.

He has asked if we could be 'friends', but since we have never said anything of any value to one another, I told him I did not really think so. I do not know why he is so eager to please and befriend me when I am acting extremely rudely, but he takes all my insults with incredible grace and tolerance.

'Yessssssss, I sssssssssssee.'

If he 'sees' so much in my persistent put-downs then he should take the hint, leave me alone and go elsewhere.

'Yessssssss, we all need privassssssssssssssssee!'

I take some of my derogatory remarks about Janus back. Although he is stubborn, he is not stupid. He is trying to rekindle my attentions by stripteasing for me from a distance. He seems to have finally worked out that I find his conversation appalling and keeps his distance without trying to talk to me, so that I can admire and lust after him again.

I made the mistake of succumbing to Janus' striptease.

I was watching him pose down, rhythmically swaying his hips, tracing a finger around the contours of his chest, belly and groin. The strong, graceful movements started me thinking about probing his flesh with my investigative instruments and lubricating his skin with conductive gels. I was already imagining sharing body currents when a psychic image jarred in my thoughts, interrupting the seduction. I drew back and looked at the gyrating Janus in horror. There was something corrupt about his flesh. I replayed the psychic impression to discover what it was about Janus that did not make sense. There! I felt it again, so I replayed the image to make sure that the anomaly was really there. Instead of the hard body that I imagined he was offering me, the psychic analysis betrayed that his body was pliant and his drool was rotten.

I am convinced that Janus contains a malignant substance. I must be careful.

His desire to seduce me is now extremely problematic. I think he is trying to force himself upon me but, for some reason, he needs my cooperation. Perhaps this is because his body is so unwholesome.

Every time he sees me, he flexes his muscles. Then he turns his back to me and lifts his buttocks with the palms of his hands, gently massaging them in circular motions. He drops his head downwards and looks at me from between his legs, smiling sweetly and drooling. Then he takes one of his fingers and runs it around his anus, looking at me quizzically.

I cannot even look at him any more.

Yes, it was once alluring. Yes, it used to excite me, but no, no way can I persuade myself that there is any personal benefit in having sex with this sweaty-fleshed dribbler. Not even to get rid of him. I want to rewind and erase all memories I have of this deeply disturbing character.

I have made a mistake and I have now changed my mind.

Janus will not give in. He is trying a different approach to win my attention. I still do not know why he is so persistent; I am finding this whole situation not only embarrassing but also menacing.

We have struck a bargain. After a long argumentative debate, Janus has agreed that I can sample his tissues on condition that I do not ignore him. He was reluctant for me to use a probe, preferring that I touched him directly, but when I threatened to withdraw my side of the bargain, he drooled reluctant approval.

I want to discover why Janus is so bizarre and I have prepared the tiny femto-needle attachment of my probe to take samples of flesh. Whilst I am close to this disgusting creature, I may as well confirm my prejudices about him and use some of the specimen for a formal genetic analysis of the sequences that encode his personality profile.

The femto-needle analysis confirms that Janus is a cyborg entity, but has an abnormal quantity of excess information carried in its electronic and biological codes. I am not sure what information the extra data encodes, but it is everywhere and I think it is infectious.

Janus' personality profile has given me more cause for concern. The patterns are unintelligible and he continues to make excessive and outrageously promiscuous approaches, despite my persistent rejections. I am convinced he has an ulterior motive for seducing me.

I need to find Bimbo.

Sometimes I feel bad about only seeking Bimbo when I need help.

Bimbo is rapidly deteriorating. Although it is not possible for it to become any more rigid, the lustre from its eyes has dimmed and the hoods have partially slipped over them again. I do not think it is worth pinning them back. Notably, though, Bimbo's intellect is fading, as I thought. When it is asked a question, its answers are rambling. However, it still has some pertinent insights to offer and, amidst its advancing dementia, its moments of wisdom are few but precious.

'What do you make of this profile?' I asked, holding the hoods up from its eyes to help it study the data.

Bimbo studied Janus' personality traces for a long time. I thought it had fallen asleep, so I prodded it. Bimbo grunted and continued to stare at the display.

'Sense and non-sense,' it finally remarked, after a lengthy pause.

I was not sure if it was referring to its own physical state of health or Janus' results, since it has a strange sense of humour and continues to communicate on the new psychic energy frequency that it seems to prefer.

'Bimbo, I do believe you are quite senile!'

I was determined that Bimbo was going to help me, so I folded its tiny, fragile body in my arms and carried it over to Janus. Maybe Bimbo would be able to make sense of the being if it encountered the vile creature directly and, if not, at least I would be able to keep my eye on them both.

Janus seemed startled to find the two of us. He must have taken my solitude for granted and did not greet me with his usual unwelcome drooling. I propped Bimbo up on a bench where it focused on Janus with an intimidating intensity.

'S'nice to sssssssssssssssee youse . . . Yesssssssssssss!' Janus initially looked at me and then at Bimbo.

Janus tried to focus his attention on me, but he seemed distracted. I wondered if he was actually distressed by Bimbo's presence. I tried to make psychic contact with Bimbo to explain the situation, but it already seemed to be unusually focused and was obviously psychically scanning Janus. Janus appeared to be ignoring Bimbo and started to approach me, gyrating his hips in an irritatingly seductive manner. Suddenly, I felt an urgent psychic impression from Bimbo forcing me to listen to it.

'Janus is a virus . . . [pause] . . . Be careful . . . [pause] . . . He is a shape-shifter . . . [pause] . . . No more than a shell . . . [pause] . . . Pure data . . . [pause] . . . He is full of sense and non-sense codes!'

The clarity and fluency of Bimbo's warning stunned me. Despite its psychic impressions being interrupted by pauses, its overall thought transfer was much faster and made better sense that it had done of late. In spite of its appearance, Bimbo was on form. Not only that, I realised that it had never been senile. 'Sense and non-sense codes', of course! That was what it had been trying to tell me earlier. Janus was inherently corrupt.

'How can he be? He looks so real!'

'He's lethal! . . . [pause] . . . There are viral life forms in all humans . . . [pause] . . . Some of them are harmless . . . [pause] . . . others are deadly.'

'What are you saying? Is Janus human or not?'

'Yes and no . . . [pause] . . . The virus is a great shape-shifter . . . [pause] . . . existing in many different forms . . . [pause] . . . benign, virulent, DNA . . . [pause] . . . RNA, digital, electromagnetic and quantum . . . [pause] . . . A virus is rogue information . . . [pause] . . . that has to replicate itself . . . [pause] . . . but lacks the machinery to do so . . . [pause] . . . It is a parasite . . . [pause] . . . Janus looks human . . . [pause] . . . but that is because . . . [pause] . . . he has already infected a human body . . . [pause] . . .

Janus is a virus by nature . . . [pause] . . . and needs to gain entry . . . [pause] . . . to invade and control another host system.'

'Entry to a host?'

'In this case . . . [pause] . . . call it a "relationship" . . . [pause] . . . Some viruses form cooperative alliances with their hosts . . . [pause] . . . others have moderate effects . . . [pause] . . . and a few are lethal . . . [pause] . . . Within minutes of contact . . . [pause] . . . Janus is looking for a relationship with you . . . [pause] . . . in order to control you . . . [pause] . . . He will stop at nothing . . . [pause] . . . until you make intimate contact with him . . . [pause] . . . and then he will replicate himself . . . [pause] . . . using your own biological machinery . . . [pause] . . . to accomplish this.'

I looked over at Janus, trying to convince myself he was capable of such deviousness but, in spite of myself, found him strangely irresistible. Even the loathing and hatred I had harboured only moments ago for his drooling, adoration and tolerance did not distract me from admiring his perfect body and succumbing to the desire to make intimate contact with him. His energy was overpowering.

Janus' eyes were streaming fractals and the technicoloured filaments began to creep outwards over his skin.

'Be careful . . . [pause] . . . he's virulent!' hissed Bimbo, helplessly.

I could not take my eyes off him now. I was hypnotised. His willpower was infecting my mind and he was gaining control over me. The vortices of Janus' pupils fixed my gaze and I could not look away.

Bimbo rocked neurotically in its aged and rigid body, trying to come to my aid, but could do nothing to stop me approaching Janus.

'It is a virus . . . [pause] . . . a parasite . . . [pause] . . . It wants to take over your body . . . [pause] . . . It will infect you . . . [pause] . . . and you will die!' Bimbo's psychic impression was so strong and desperate that it almost formed a wall between the seducer and me, but I could not be stopped. I broke though Bimbo's barrier of psychic energy. Swept along by desire, I moved towards Janus, spinning out the eternity of the precious moment before we embraced.

Suddenly, I doubled over with pain. Something was eating my insides. Waves of nausea surged through me, my belly split open and fluid squirted out, hitting Janus full on. I was now fully aware of my predicament. What had I done?

Janus glowered angrily, covered in my abdominal vomit, and retaliated, knocking me to the floor and pinning me down in a fierce embrace that was sheer violence, not an act of passion. The waves of pain surged through my body again more powerfully than before and my split insides were leaking silica gel everywhere. I was losing energy rapidly.

'I want to get inside you!' he drooled.

I was conscious of being 'raped' and yet I just let him do it. I saw my innards swimming around me on the floor and thought this would be the last sight that I ever remembered. Then Janus struck me across the face, spitting venomously, frustrated by a sudden impotence.

'What have you done to me? What the hell are you?' Janus demanded.

Exhausted, humiliated and broken, I could not reply. Janus' anger was overwhelming, striking my belly and face again with an incredible force. He accused me of being an inorganic impostor and an impossible host body.

'Sssssssssssssssssssssssshit!'

Then Bimbo was upon us, attacking Janus, somehow preventing him from extracting the dwindling life force from my body. How had Bimbo managed to move? Janus turned his attention from me to Bimbo. His face lightened and his eyes smiled.

'Sssssssssssssss, what hasssssssssssss we here?'

Bimbo's ebony eyes were moist with fluid, like human tears. The hoods stared open so that Janus had a clear view of Bimbo's terror. The poor creature was instantly inert again and put up no more resistance or fighting. Janus simply closed in on it and entered Bimbo's body.

For one spectacular moment, Bimbo blossomed. Its features were full of colour and then in the next instant it changed, becoming more like Janus until the two body images completely merged. Strangely, it was not Janus' muscle-bound body that emerged triumphantly from the struggle, but Bimbo's elegant and revitalised form.

At first, I thought that Bimbo was going to get up and help me, having vanquished the foe. I needed someone to help me to my feet as

I was a pathetic sight, clutching my still splitting abdominal skin, groping at the silica gel around me, damaged and mortified. I felt too weak and crippled to think about anyone but myself or contemplate revenge.

'Bimbo, help me!'

Wondering what was taking Bimbo so long in communicating with me, I looked over and was horrified to see that my fortune had changed again. Bimbo was shrivelled and motionless once more. Its limbs were tightly folded and I noticed that its belly was swollen.

Bimbo did not move nor did it make any acknowledgement of my call. It looked so peaceful, just like when I first saw it in the incubator as a preborn. That seems such a long, long time ago.

sacrifice

With hindsight, Bimbo need not have been so brave, as the Chronicler had no discrete cells for Janus' viral particles to infect. The Chronicler's substance was just a mass of silica gels and tracts and so the viral particles could not take hold of it. They twisted furiously around, groping desperately for some structure to cling to and tearing up the Chronicler's internal gel matrix in desperation. Bimbo's hybrid human cells, however, were a perfect host for the virus, that needed to find a recipient before its viral seeds withered and died.

As Bimbo thrust itself between the Chronicler and Janus, the viral particles were attracted towards its human cells. When Bimbo and Janus touched, the virus leapt from its impotent Gray host into the fertile biology of the hybrid. As Bimbo struggled with Janus, it felt the virus creep into its body, weakening its energy and using its cellular machinery to create more copies of itself. However, Bimbo did not surrender. Using its last surge of psychic energy, it forced the virus into a metabolic hyperspin, so that the cloning became defective and every cell that it touched turned cancerous. Janus struggled to survive; its virulence was so fierce that it was rapidly burning out. It fought to gain control of every cell line Bimbo possessed and went for the stem cells that makes the sex cells. However, Bimbo was ahead of Janus, driving every cell into accelerated growth and, as Janus chased it for a receptive cell to overthrow, Bimbo became riddled with cancer.

Janus was defeated, but left a host of little monstrous cancer-born creatures inside the victorious Bimbo as its final insult.

Bimbo was not dead. It was drifting out of its cancer-filled body and was floating into a long tunnel. At first, it felt pain and sorrow for the Chronicler and remorse at any hurt it might have caused. Bimbo continued to float further along the tunnel walls that now seemed to be made up of moving images. It was no longer grieving for its companion, but was very comfortable and could think clearly with no distractions.

Then Bimbo heard a calming voice that it instinctively trusted.

'Everything will be all right, Bimbo. Come to me, I'll help you!'

At the end of the tunnel was Svar, looking as fresh as the day that they first parted. Svar brought Bimbo to the end of the tunnel and asked it to look into the inky blackness.

'The mirror sector, Bimbo, remember? Do you want to come with me?'

Bimbo gasped in awe. There was no past, present or future here. Suddenly, the nature of the universe and its own destiny were clear.

'What about the others, Svar? We can't leave them behind!'

'They'll find their own way, Bimbo. You must think of your own future now.'

Svar pointed into the blackness at a huge, floating, white obelisk. As Bimbo looked at it more closely, it saw that it was a giant puzzle in the process of being solved and that its surface was moving.

'Another piece of the mirror sector, Bimbo, but this time you can see it. You can be a part of it, too.'

As Bimbo watched the puzzle being rearranged, it realised that the choice it would make would influence the position of the pieces.

Bimbo thought of the preborns in the incubators that would miss all this. It thought of the Chronicler that it had left in pain and terror in the experimental chamber and felt profoundly sad.

Then Bimbo turned to Svar and looked deep into the mirror sector, feeling the pull of eternity in it.

'Let's go!'

chronicle entry

cancer

Somehow, I managed to pull myself together. I must have struggled on my own for some time and I do not remember much about how I restored my body.

I do remember the pain and I remember Bimbo's silence.

Bimbo is lifeless and its swollen belly makes it look unbearably ugly. I find it difficult to believe that this creature is the same one as the lively black-eyed being that leapt from the incubator. I could not endure being disfigured this way, so I cut it open with my laser scalpel to reduce the swelling. Inside, I was surprised to find a smaller version of Bimbo. It was peaceful, curled up like a preborn, but imperfectly formed. Its head was flat, making the eyes seem ridiculously large. The stillborn had its own abdominal swelling that I also dissected with my laser.

Inside the belly of the flat-headed version of Bimbo was a similar creature, even more deformed, with a single eye and flipper limbs. The flipper-beast was also carrying an even more diminished, monstrous version of Bimbo inside it and this mutant was also pregnant with another monster, that bore another and so on. As I cut open these abortuses, there seemed to be an infinite number of crippled Bimbos inside every swollen abdomen. Each creature was smaller and even more deformed than the one before.

I have been examining the Bimbo mutants. All of them are cancerous. Janus' lethal codes must have caused its tissues to malfunction and left this abominable legacy of mocking mutants.

Maybe I can restore its body on my native planet where Grays do not die. I need to take Bimbo to the mines where I can repair and restore life to its damaged body.

chronicle entry

pain

I blame human biology.

Back on Rune 66 there is no death; we are recycled, reassigned and made wholesome again by the planet's vitalising ecosystem. There is no beginning and no end to our existence. Even when we come-into-being, we are simply continuing a journey that was started a long time ago and, when we are recycled, we will continue on a new assignment.

At least, that is what we are told and, in this particular situation, it is what I wish to believe in. I do not really believe that Bimbo has 'gone' and, despite its lifeless body before me, I reject the notion of death.

Human biology has contaminated Bimbo's flesh. It should never have suffered this dreadful cancer. Bimbo was not wholly human. In fact, I consider it more as a Gray and hope that it can be reanimated whole again. I must be able to restore Bimbo to life, treating its deanimation in the same way as the Grays'. I will feed its remains to a Silica Worm and wait for the great beast to expel Bimbo's remains as a new preborn crystalline body. Once Bimbo's form has been restored, I will be able to revitalise it at a Creature Crystal node.

I must find an opencast birthing mine to perform this experiment and so, rather than wait to return to Rune 66 in a haphazard manner which is the usual way, I have to impose my will upon the idiosyncratic nature of the Time Toroid. I must overcome the gravity of this place and summon all my strength to take Bimbo home with me.

The Creature Crystals are chattering and piezoelectric warmth is oozing into my body. Have they revitalised me? Somehow, I managed to leave the experimental chamber by force of will. Maybe the Creature Crystals played a part in my return as we are interconnected species. Are they aware of my alien encounters?

For the first time, I was with Bimbo in my own dwelling.

I studied Bimbo's remains under the fluorescent light of the Creature Crystals, checking to see that they were complete after the transfer from the time-spill to Rune 66, and then I started to document them.

Although the body still appeared to be whole, the once glistening, ebony eyes were dull and indigo. These lifeless ovoids had retracted into its skull and its oral aperture hung open in a tiny o, as if it was about to speak. Bimbo was decaying so rapidly that every observation I made remarked on another change in its appearance, so that it was impossible to make an accurate record of its anatomy. I needed to take its remains at once to the metropolitan mines and feed them to a Silica Worm before it vaporised.

Bimbo's frail body felt peculiarly heavy. I attributed this to the gravitational differences between Rune 66 and the experimental chamber. It was not easy, but somehow I travelled to a suitable opencast pit without detection.

I waited for a change in downtime shift and, as the workers swapped duties, I took the crumbling Bimbo and dropped it in front of a hungry-looking Silica Worm. To aid the digestive process I stamped on Bimbo, crushing its head into splinters. As its dull eyes appeared to stare quizzically at me, I hammered my grief into the ground.

When I had completely pulverised Bimbo's remains, I swept the particles towards the mouth of the Silica Worm that was already sniffing around for silica sustenance and raced away to watch.

Immediately, the Silica Worm made an unpleasant, piercing shriek that rooted me to the spot. Before I had time to turn and marvel at the twists and contortions of the suffering beast, I was grabbed by a number of workers. They pinned me to the ground whilst a supervisor started shouting instructions.

'Shoveller, Hacker and Picker, take care of that Silica Worm! I want a full report by the next downtime period. Get to it!'

Then the officious colleague looked at me.

'So, what kind of Gray do we have here and what have you been doing to the species preborns?'

I was about to protest and make some elaborate excuse professing my innocence, but thought better of it. I was in serious trouble and had to think very carefully before I confessed to anything. The supervisor drew its face uncomfortably close and scanned my psychic impressions which, mercifully, I had blocked out.

'Blanking, eh? Well, let's see how long that lasts. Underground Intelligence are already on their way!'

defeat

Posted on the Anatomy Channel by an anonymous devotee.

The Chronicler's spectacular defeat by the human challenger, Janus, must be one of the biggest shocks of all time to its devotees. Though it seems unbelievable, I wonder how many pairs of eyes turned upward as the Chronicler fell flat on its face during that infamous encounter? I know mine did, just for a second.

What now prevents *Abductee* from cataclysmic decline is the heroism that the Chronicler's name still represents. Its performance, agility, wit and action-at-all-costs style has indeed imprinted the Chronicler's name into the memories of a generation of *Abductee* fans and made it generally acclaimed as the champion of the species. But now the Chronicler has been beaten, dethroned and injured. In all honesty, the lifeline by which its popularity has been won is now severed. Colleagues are tuning in to other programmes, exploring other channels and finding other pursuits to amuse themselves. The *Abductee* programme is becoming a lonely graveyard of nostalgia.

conspiracy

The Chronicler was charged with the serious crime of disturbance of the planet's equilibrium, the penalty for which was reassignment. All that stood between its future reincarnation and its present misery was the systematic interrogation, humiliation and ultimate deanimation that would take place in the Sensate Senate.

The trial by thirteen selected senators, all Psychic Grays, required the accused to stand alone in the tall, centrally-placed defendant's seat in the Judicial Chamber. First, the senators would prepare their verdict in advance of the trial in a pre-trial committee meeting. Then the defendant made its own case to the court. Finally, an official prosecutor appointed by the senators concluded with a list of accusations. The trial ended with a sentence and penalty which were the same as the ones that the senators had decided on before the show trial had begun.

The Chronicler's crime was regarded as a wilful attack on not just the Grays, but on all the species of Rune 66 and, in this particular case, the Chronicler was alleged to have executed its assault using 'cancer' as its weapon.

Until this particular trial, the concept had never existed in Gray culture.

Grays are great conspiracy theorists. They have a craving for gossip and trivia that outweighs their desire for facts. As they did not understand the admittedly confused confessions from the Chronicler, the Underground Intelligence officers invented their own version of events and began an abominable rumour that would reach the Collective Consciousness and the senators before the trial ever took place.

They said that the Chronicler was crazy. They said that its programme was shaming the Collective Consciousness and took it off the psychic network. They said that the Chronicler contaminated preborns by feeding cancer into the bodies of the Silica Worms. They said that that this was only the first part of a plan to pollute the entire species with monstrous mutants. They said that these monsters would be sightless. They said that the Chronicler was the agent of cancer and that, if any colleagues were to touch it, they would become sightless, cancerous monsters, too. They said that the Chronicler was stopped only moments before it succeeded in executing its plan.

in and out

The Chronicler refused to feel humiliated in its retention cell.

The pending trial was of little interest to it at this time, as it felt strangely buoyant. This was both a literal and metaphorical sensation. The Chronicler was genuinely contented. It had accepted that it would be reassigned and so its mood lifted. Curiously, too, it felt that its psychic body had loosened itself from its crystalline gel matrix and was ready to float off at any second. This was such a weird and delightful feeling that the Chronicler realised that it could no longer feel sad. Despite its misfortunes, it would make the same decisions again and its only regret was that it was unable to keep its diary up to date.

The Chronicler thought how bland, uneventful and pointless the lives of ordinary colleagues were. Surely, it was better to live an adventure-filled life and experience something meaningful for a short while, than to endure a lengthy, bland existence. Yes, although it was sitting alone with only the barren granite walls for companionship, it had been lucky. It had been privileged to experience the Time Toroid. It had found and lost its own offspring and had met the humans.

Yet, suddenly, experience alone was not a sufficient platitude. The Chronicler grew indignant that it was misunderstood and that its so-called crime, although grave, had been an accident. Whatever happened at the trial was beyond its power to influence, but it wanted a fair hearing. Before the Chronicler was reassigned, its last wish was that it wanted justice. It knew by convention and instinct that it was already pronounced guilty, but what could it do?

As the Chronicler was reflecting on its predicament, wondering how it was going to fight its way out of the trial intact, its visual sensors failed briefly, without warning. The Chronicler was terrified. It stared as intensely as it could with its eyes wide open and noticed a movement in one sector of its coarsely-defined visual field. Using its psychic vision to help it, a swarm of tiny cigar-shaped objects appeared that started to grow. As they became larger and more intrusive, they hovered annoyingly close to the Chronicler's head and it tried to swat them away. Taking advantage of the Chronicler's imperfect senses, the spiteful swarm retaliated, discharging a stinging volley of projectiles. The Chronicler threw itself on the floor, hoping that they would disappear. Soon, the stinging stopped and when it looked up again, the phantoms had disappeared and its vision was restored to normal.

Perhaps, thought the Chronicler, it was mad after all. Perhaps those memories that it held of life on Rune 66, like this moment now, were just windows of lucidity in its breakdown. Maybe all the encounters with the strange experimental chamber, its hybrid offspring and the weird aliens were nothing but manifestations of psychotic decay.

The Chronicler no longer felt accountable to the species. It was an alien in its own community and a freak among its own species. Assuming the identity of an outsider, its confidence grew. It would have to be heard. It could not just accept its role as a villain and scapegoat.

The once-champion of the species would not surrender to destiny quite so easily, and resolved to give the jury a fight.

One that they would always remember.

senators

The Sensate Senators' duty was to protect the integrity of the species, for which they served a term of office. They unanimously condemned the Chronicler's crime.

The Grabber was acting as Chief Justice in the Chronicler's case. In a pre-trial consultation, it signalled the twelve other senators and bade them take their positions around the domed floor in the Great Committee Hall positioned directly over the Judicial Chamber. They would adopt this same configuration when the trial itself began. The Grabber led the way, taking its place at the apex of the dome positioned directly over the defendant's seat and then read out the seating order for the twelve appointed senators that sat equidistantly about a round table.

'The Diplomat, The Ungrateful, The Manipulator, The Opportunist, The Hero, The Enthusiast, The Ancient, The Upstart, The Academic, The Groveller, The User and The Charmer.'

The senators took their places with a dignified and grave air, enjoying their self-importance and looking forward to passing sentence on the Chronicler. Naturally, none of the senators was supposed to be aware of the charges, but the rumours of the great cancer plot spread by Undeground Intelligence had already reached them.

The Grabber, observing that they were all settled, began the judicial pre-trial ritual.

'Today's briefing is to prepare you for a heinous case that is most bizarre. The case of the Chronicler is one of the most disturbing I have ever encountered. The official indictment is for disturbance of the planet's equilibrium, where the accused was found poisoning Silica Worms.'

The senators murmured disapproval.

'That is not all. According to Underground Intelligence, this poison is called "cancer" and was intended to destroy the species by introducing mutants amongst us.'

Psychic clicks expressing outrage were exchanged.

'The mutants would be psychically weak, sightless and physically deformed. It appears that the Chronicler intended to spread cancer throughout the entire species and had already set up an indoctrinating programme called *Abductee*, in which it persuaded feeble-minded colleagues to touch one another. Underground Intelligence claim that this cancer is spread by physical contact and the whole plot is the work of a deranged and dangerous mind.'

The Ancient gestured that it wished to ask a question.

'How does this cancer work? Is there a cure?'

The Grabber looked a little uncomfortable.

'It's a secret weapon. We do not fully know, but we have it on good authority that it is disfiguring and incurable.'

They all nodded, without questioning the source of the information. Indeed, no one asked if any Grays had actually contracted the illness, or how the agent had been detected in the first place. In fact, no one asked any important questions at all. It would have been too time-consuming. The answer to the first question would have revealed that, although mutants were found inside the Silica Worm, no colleagues had been infected. The second question would have revealed that cancer in the preborns was only diagnosed from the jumbled psychic memories that were floating around in the Chronicler's mind when it was under examination by Underground Intelligence. However, these details would have only complicated the issues and, as no one really understood these technical matters, the senators were more than happy to pass over them and get to the nub of the trial.

'Naturally, I do not want to prejudice the outcome of this trial, but the Chronicler is a dangerous and deluded psychopath that protests it is the victim of alien forces. It is totally remorseless. Can we let such a creature free in our society?'

The senators clicked angrily and the Opportunist spoke.

'In my experience, such a dreadful creature could hardly be considered a colleague, surely it does not deserve a trial and should be reassigned immediately.'

The User, suddenly incensed, agreed, crying 'Immediate reassignment!' and hammering its fist on the side of its seat. 'Immediate reassignment!'

Suddenly, all the senators were moved to support this gesture, expressing their outrage.

'Senators, senators, not so hasty! We are principled colleagues and it is in our constitution to ensure that justice shall be done.'

The Manipulator interjected.

'The Collective Consciousness cannot be denied this trial. It will show how deluded this colleague is and that deviants will not be tolerated!'

The Hero had another agenda to fulfil in the trial.

'Yes, this must be a high-profile affair, as I have received many complaints from some of the more eminent Psychic Grays that there is far too much physicality going on in the metropolis. In convicting this criminal, we must also demonstrate how dangerous the physical implications of its activities have been, too. We must put a stop to this perverse conduct. Perhaps we should spread the message that contact spreads cancer. This deviant behaviour must be stamped out.'

They started banging the sides of their chairs again.

The Grabber gestured to restore order but, since the senators were making so much noise, it could not be heard, so it had to wait until they reluctantly settled down. The Grabber rose to its feet.

'There is only one complication. The Chronicler has insisted that it will remain silent for the entire duration of its allocated defence period, a span of one hour. Apparently, this is in protest that this hearing is unfair and prejudiced. This is outrageous behaviour, especially when all colleagues are fully aware that the rule of the Sensate Senate is absolute.'

The senators all rose to their feet and started calling for the Chronicler's instant reassignment.

'Patience, patience!' shouted the Grabber. 'You will have your chance to cast your vote and make your own judgements on the fate of this vile creature in due course. However, before you prepare yourselves for the trial itself, I will show you final evidence that may persuade you of the extremely dangerous nature of the character we are dealing with. These extracts on the psychic screen here are from its perverse programme, *Abductee*.'

The Grabber extended its arm and used its silica crystal amplifier to produce a three-dimensional holo-movie out of thin air.

'Note the combative style of interview here. Look at the body language, it's very aggressive and notice the intimate nature of the experimental procedure. Surely, there can now be no doubt that this is the work of a deranged mind. Notice also how the audience is invited to participate in these monstrous activities and encouraged to touch each other. This is disgusting! Clear proof that the creature has no remorse. Finally, look at the monstrosity of the creatures that the defendant chooses to interact with. It has no aesthetic sense and no responsibility towards its colleagues. Senators, we are dealing with a very dangerous psychopath here. This is the profile of a potential mass destroyer.'

The senators were obediently silent, swearing revenge for the attack on the integrity of the species. The Grabber sensed the gravity of the others and proceeded to the final part of the pre-trial procedure.

'Senators, I have now only to introduce you to the prosecution. After the Chronicler has presented its abominable silence, we will then have the great fortune to listen to the allegations made by the Star Commander, a colleague of perfect psychic integrity, that will confirm its opinion of the latent psychopathic nature of the defendant.'

There were murmurs of relief all round.

'However, it is time for you all to go and make your preparations for this case. Think carefully, for it is not just the Chronicler's fate but the destiny of the Grays that is in your hands.'

on trial

The Chronicler sat on the defendant's seat in the Judicial Chamber, waiting for the psychic interrogation to begin. What was the point of this ritual, when it had already been analysed, judged and sentenced?

The Chronicler steadied itself, having briefly lost its balance because its visual sensors had temporarily failed again. After sitting motionless for a lengthy period, the Chronicler noticed that its entire body was anaesthetised and that its perception of time was altered, as if it had been frozen in a single eternal moment.

Recognising these as the familiar symptoms that preceded its abduction into the Time Toroid, the Chronicler hoped that the powerful cosmic entity would take control of its life. In the meantime, the Chronicler decided that its best strategy would be to ensure that the senators' hour of silence was as awful as its own. So it remained agonisingly silent and intended to continue its silence until it was forced one way or another to leave the defendant's seat.

prosecution

countdown 8

Waiting alone in the Prosecution Gallery that overlooked the defendant's seat in the Judicial Chamber, the Star Commander grew impatient. Although it had felt perversely honoured that the senators had chosen it to provide a character reference for the deviant seated in the defendant's seat, it could not help but be irritated by the Chronicler's protest of silence. There were routine Aerial Intelligence duties to attend to and surveillance missions to conduct. This protest was mere time-wasting tactics on behalf of the accused colleague and the Star Commander wanted to return to its various assignments. To be perfectly honest, it thought to itself, with some careful psychic cloaking in case the senators overheard it, it could have done without this unexpected honour.

countdown 5

Never before had silence sounded so loud! The Star Commander wished that the Chronicler would tone it down. Still, the Chronicler had only a few more countdown minutes to complete its soundless protest and, despite the futility, the Star Commander admitted that the silence was effective. Indeed, it had developed a dull pain in its psychic sensors from the awful silence that was amplified by the acoustics of the Judicial Chamber.

The granite sphere and amethyst defendant's seat were perfect conductors of psychic frequencies and the position of the defendant was at the centre of the sphere. Everything that the defendant thought was therefore transmitted with equal intensity to all observers around the perimeter of the Judicial Chamber, but all they were getting was psychic white noise that disoriented them.

countdown 4

The Star Commander looked down at the Chronicler, stubbornly broadcasting its silent protest and had to look again. Was it imagining things? The Chronicler's outline seemed to be a little indistinct.

The Star Commander checked its visual sensors and rewound its visual memory traces. Yes, the Chronicler's image did appear to be pixellating and melting away. This was absurd. The Star Commander cross-referenced its visual memory traces with its psychic memory. It had never come across anything like this before. The psychic impression it had captured of the Chronicler was unsteady, too, with flickering and some nasty grainy patterns surrounding its body. Could these be plasma balls or were they glitches?

countdown 2

The Star Commander looked back into the Judicial Chamber. This time, it was certain that the Chronicler's image looked very faint, but the power of its protest of silence had not diminished: it was still unbearable. The Star Commander now knew that something was very wrong.

countdown 1

The Star Commander raced through the corridors that led into the Judicial Chamber but, by the time it reached the bottom of the amethyst shaft that supported the defendant's seat, the Chronicler was no more than a pixellated ghost, silent and motionless.

countdown 0

When the Star Commander reached the top of the column, the Chronicler had completely disappeared.

mission to search

The Grabber was thinking about calling for an emergency ruling to reach a verdict without waiting for the character reference from the Star Commander who had been expected to state the prosecution case. He hoped that a guilty vote would be passed immediately, but the Chronicler had outwitted them all.

Most of the other senators were still reeling after enduring the hour of enforced silence the Chronicler had imposed on them. The psychic white noise from the defendant had disorientated and confused them so much that it was not until countdown zero that the senators realised that the defendant had gone.

The Upstart was the first to announce the extraordinary event.

'The Chronicler has disappeared!'

Shock waves spread around the circle.

The Hero was outraged, as it was ultimately responsible for the defence of the species. It needed to be seen to take swift and effective action in front of the other senators. If the Chronicler had escaped, it could be forced to resign.

Outrage and commotion ensued as the senators made various pledges to bring the Chronicler to book for its crimes, but they were not thinking as sharply as usual, since they were still reeling from the psychic damage they had suffered during the protest of silence.

The Hero was already calculating a search plan. Its psychic senses had fully recovered and it was scanning the Judicial Chamber for clues.

'Your honour, I think we should send our good commander to look for the accused. It's already examining the defendant's seat for evidence.'

The Grabber placed its hands together and filled the silent Judicial Chamber with its booming psychic aura, causing the Star Commander to automatically salute with a double-breasted arm-strike.

'Commander, you are required immediately.'

The Star Commander reflected on its mission objectives to search for the Chronicler, having already decided that it would begin with a full scan of the psychic network. However, although it had made an extensive scan of the Collective Consciousness and thoroughly interviewed the Underground Intelligence patrols, there was nothing to betray the Chronicler's presence. Even the *Abductee* site was deserted, as if the usual fans had expected their champion to abandon them.

Growing very concerned at the implications for the species of such an unusual event, the Star Commander decided to conduct a thorough search of its dwelling. What had taken place in the Judicial Chamber, right in front of its own senses and how had the Chronicler been able to disappear in full view of the senatorial jury, seemingly without a trace?

search

Although it had begun its search for the Chronicler immediately, the Star Commander developed an eerie feeling that this particular investigation was long overdue. Perhaps any evidence to suggest the Chronicler's whereabouts had already gone, just like the Chronicler itself.

Outside the Chronicler's residence, the Star Commander switched on its psychic memory recorders to document its findings. It hammered at the entrance of the dwelling, as if it was expecting someone to answer. An eggshell fracture appeared in the wall as the Star Commander pounded the lock to smithereens and burst inside.

Crystal grey splinters from the break-in littered the floor, glittering under the ultra violet lighting of the first chamber of the spartan dwelling and the Star Commander carefully avoided recording this wanton damage in its psychic memory recorders. It panned around, stopping at strategic moments to review the manoeuvre in psychic playback and editing out potentially incriminating shots.

The dwelling was a conventional arrangement with four chambers. Unusually, two of these opened out to and overhung an underground Creature Crystal network that had been cultivated to form a garden. As the Star Commander scanned the dwelling, it noticed a desk and large stone chair in front of a laboratory bench. The experimental tools had been carefully arranged and there were various wall markings giving references to certain chemical reactions. A neat pile of biological samples was arranged to the right and a tall container of jelly-like substance stood to the left. Placed perfectly centrally was a bright, silver experimental probe that winked a spot of light from its tip, the only sign of activity.

The chair slowly spun around as if guided by a remote force, revealing wafer-thin sheets of silica bound in lithium thread resting on its seat.

The Star Commander studied the odd object without touching it. Perhaps it was contaminated with cancer dust. The Star Commander did not trust this strange and absent colleague to have left a document like this without some ulterior motive for its discovery. After a thorough psychic scan and some detailed memory recordings, the Star Commander decided to touch the document and on opening it, realised that it was a diary.

There was something weird about the whole situation. Almost as if it had been stage-managed. The Star Commander had only experienced such an eerie feeling once before in its current lifetime and that was when Rune 66 had briefly 'wobbled'. The Spotter and the Observer had later explained that this was due to some distant cosmic event that caused the planet to move out of its natural orbital position and this had caused a time-shift.

Was it experiencing a time-shift? The Star Commander refocused on the task in hand and tried to overcome its disorientation.

time patrol

The Star Commander put the Chronicler's diary aside and pondered on the strange series of events that had led to its discovery. Although it had not been able to retrieve the missing colleague, the diary's contents disclosed that the strange Time Toroid was at the centre of these events.

Before it could begin to make a report for the senators, the Star Commander knew that its search would not be complete without a successful visit to the Time Toroid. This time, it must gain access to the entity and confront the troublesome humans or prove that the Chronicler was indeed deluded, leaving its disappearance an unsolved mystery.

To explore this unfathomable cosmic entity, the Star Commander realised that it would have to recruit the most loyal and psychically agile Aerial Intelligence officers to help it assess the Time Toroid and so it would have to choose carefully.

Unusually, all its officers were off-duty. Even more surprisingly, they were spending this downtime on the planet surface, apparently taking advantage of the calm skies. As the Star Commander approached, it could see that the officers were in the midst of a recreational pursuit and, without making its presence known, decided to watch them.

'Who is in goal for the Stripes this time?' shouted a bossy Star Fleet One officer who had assumed an organisational role in the game.

'Chequers Number Twelve, will you get to it? You are letting the side down!' This officer was waving its skinny arms about in a dangerous manner and focusing its huge black eyes on a rather distracted colleague that seemed to be preoccupied with some detail of the game.

'Hang on! Someone has moved the meteorite markers, this one was nearer than it is now, just a few moments ago!'

Intense glares were exchanged between the opposing teams that had set up a local psychic network to act as the boundaries to the pitch. As usual, there were three teams playing at once and each team was inaudibly accusing the others of cheating. The Stripes, the Stars and the Chequers teams had been allocated their members randomly by the bossy officer that was still giving orders.

At kick-off, Stars Number Four raced straight towards the Stripes' goal, rather artlessly but enthusiastically punting a honeycombed spherical meteorite straight at the Stripes goalie. Meanwhile, the Chequers team was obstructing the Stripes players from intervening by forming a wall between them and the speedy striker. The meteorite bounced gracefully on the pitch and slowly curled towards the Stripes' goalie that had begun fussing over the position of its own goalpost. There was a groan from the Stripes players as the meteorite passed over the goalie's bowed head, scoring the first goal of the match.

'Referee!' Stripes Number Twelve protested indignantly to the organising officer who had also assumed the role of match adjudicator. Meanwhile, its Stripes colleagues huddled together, conspiring how to concede fewer goals. Should they sack their own goalie?

The Star Commander admired the hexagonal pitch with its three goals and was rather enjoying the game of three-sided football. Although it had never indulged in this rather conspiratorial sport, it rather approved of the basic rules. The aim of the match was not to score the most goals, but to concede the least. Goals were conceded when the ball passed between the goal markers not more than a head above the goalie. This was an exercise in cooperative behaviour with one side persuading another to join in a campaign against the third.

'Bring the ball back to kick-off!' bellowed Stripes Number Eight. It was furious at being so easily deceived by the treacherous Stars players.

Soon the score was 1–2–1 to the Stars, Stripes and Chequers teams. Despite the inattentive goalie, the Stripes proved to be the most successful of the three teams. Stripes Number Twelve was looking to be player of the match, as it had somehow discovered how to confuse both the Stars and Chequers players by promising an alliance with each of them in turn and would not take no for an answer.

Chequers Number Seven became emotionally dysfunctional three-quarters of the way through the match as it had taken all the tactics used against it in the game as personal affronts. It became so emotionally crippled that it sat on the pitch rocking backwards and forwards unable to console itself, wracked by feelings of betrayal by its colleagues.

'Don't take it all to heart, you idiot!' snapped Chequers Number Two. 'It's just a game, toughen up!' prompting Chequers Number Seven to rock harder and faster than before.

'Just a game?' screamed Stars Number Eight, refusing to give in to the Stripes and incensed at the suggestion that the game was somehow trivial or even futile. 'I play to win and hope that you do, too!' Psychic blows between the two colleagues were quickly followed up with a few physical jousts. Their supporting team members cheered the battling colleagues onwards, as their spindly limbs struggled against the air, trying to make an impact on one another.

This affray only upset the sensitive Chequers Number Seven player even more and it huddled itself in a tight ball of misery, preventing the progress of the game.

Rather irritated by the delay, the Star Commander decided that this was a good time to interrupt the game. As soon as they saw the Star Commander approach, the officers stood to attention, wondering if they had been watched.

'Many of you are needed on an urgent, top secret mission. We will access Far Space to conduct a surveillance mission on a strange entity that may be a giant time-spill that I believe is a Time Toroid. The purpose of our mission is to get inside it. Any questions?'

'Yes, sir! Sir! How do we get to it, sir?'

'I have already prepared details of the route from my reconnaissance missions and I have been able to successfully return more than a dozen times. There will be no problem in reaching the Time Toroid. Once we are within its range, we will need to be prepared for anything. It is constantly changing and very powerful.'

'We will launch Star Fleet One. We must get as close to it as possible and a whole squadron will be deployed. Those who are dispatched will need all their psychic energy resources to enter the Time Toroid. Any more questions?'

'Sir! You said you had not been inside, sir. What are the chances of us making it?'

'It is a very dangerous situation, but I am sure we shall be successful. Any more questions?'

An unsettling silence followed whilst the Star Commander scanned the auras of the attentive officers, who were beginning to feel very ill at ease. However, they were promptly dismissed and set about preparing Star Fleet One for the launch. The gravity of the mission was slowly dawning on them, but their anxiety did not last long as they realised the possibilities for adventure and heroic deeds. Soon, they were excited and eager to rise to the challenge of the impenetrable Time Toroid and the mission preparations were swiftly completed.

The Star Commander took the controls from the centre of the spacecraft and adopted the formal navigational posture, standing upright with its arms folded across its chest. It bowed its head, relaying a psychic beam from its eyes that connected every officer with one another so that the ship and its crew were a united body of psychic energy. Star Fleet One was now prepared for take-off.

Panel crystals sparkled, piezoelectric currents started to flow and the spacecraft rose vertically off the irregular, meteorite-scarred surface of the planet, leaving a long amethyst-coloured trail behind it.

Starcom One confirmed the mission destination with the Star Commander: the Time Toroid.

teamwork

Star Fleet One squadron felt the gravitational pull of the Time Toroid as they left the safety of Near Space and ventured into the uncharted realm of Far Space.

It was magnificent.

As they drew nearer, they could see the surface details of the turbulent transparent body of the Time Toroid. It was fizzing with activity. From its swirling surface, time flares spat showers of time droplets only to drag them back into its body as they tried to reach escape velocity, the speed needed to break free of the Time Toroid's gravitational pull. The continuous rise and fall of charged time particles created powerful time winds that battered the circling spacecraft.

They were in the presence of nothing less than a new phenomenon. The preliminary observations indicated that the Time Toroid was a source of pure time energy! This was legendary matter, believed to be the substance of eternal life.

The Star Commander had taken Star Fleet One into a safe orbit, although it was still difficult to hold the spacecraft steady, as time winds and volleys of escaping time droplets periodically challenged them.

The psychic surveillance scans revealed that the core was made up of densely-packed, high-velocity time particles and the Star Commander followed their journey to the surface, noticing that they moved in stable frequencies with a highly regular structure. These standing waves had a unique configuration; they seemed to be hollow, like long, interconnected corridors wrapped around each other, without beginning or end.

Starcom Two had been silent in its flight cocoon since take-off and had made a remarkable discovery.

'Sir, the Time Toroid appears to be made up of heavy, slow isomers of time!'

Starcom Two had the Star Commander's full attention.

'This time isomer is very much like the time that we already know, but it carries much more energy than our native time particles. This variant of time is very long-lived and does not decay like ordinary time, so that it appears to run down very slowly.'

The Star Commander did not reply, but acknowledged the report with a double-breasted arm-strike across its chest. What would be the effect of this energy-rich time on living beings? Would a mission to penetrate the surface of this entity be a one-way journey?

'How are we going to get inside, sir?' Starcom Seven had not ceased feeling anxious about the mission. 'Do we have sufficient psychic power to enter the Time Toroid and return to base?'

The Star Commander glared over at the officer.

'Of course, we are going in! Starcoms One to Eight at the ready. Your mission is to enter the Time Toroid and report your findings. You will maintain contact with base at all times.'

The Star Fleet One officers uncurled from their flight positions and moved forward equidistant to the Star Commander who established a connection between itself and the psychic bodies of each officer, creating a safety harness between them and the spacecraft.

'Officers, stand at the ready. Eyes towards target. Establish psychic lock on the target. Adopt surveillance postures.'

Starcom Eight psyched itself up for the mission, erasing any previous thoughts from its memory circuits that it might not return. Its mind was blank for an instant, becoming a receptacle only for details of the mission. It would carry no psychic baggage.

Starcom Two had made infinite calculations about the rotational period of the Time Toroid and had therefore judged a phased entry to be the safest course of action. The time isomer of the target oscillated between a prolate shape that was like a cigar and an oblate one, like a pancake. Momentarily, the Time Toroid was configured in a spherical in-between shape. Starcom Two calculated that this was the optimum moment of penetration.

'Go for it!'

The remaining officers watched the psychic auras of Starcoms One to Eight streaming away from the spacecraft. Soon, they were no more than disappearing specks of psychic matter approaching the Time Toroid. The ensuing silence was unnerving. For what seemed to be an eternity, the remaining crew heard nothing and, then, they heard Starcom Seven sobbing. It was in trouble.

Almost without delay, Starcom Seven's psychic aura was back on the spaceship's flight deck. It was in shock. Starcom Thirty-Seven disembarked from its flight cocoon to recharge the damaged officer's rapidly fading psychic energy and reported that the officer had been ejected by a gust of time wind. The violent eruption had hurled Starcom Seven's psychic body away from the surface of the Time Toroid, expelling it like a time droplet back to the ship.

However, it was now safe and the squadron paid attention to the other seven officers who appeared to have succeeded in entering the Time Toroid. Strangely, their psychic auras had disappeared without trace, despite the Star Commander's psychic reinforcement and express orders to remain in contact.

Although the Star Fleet One crew could not see what was happening to the remaining seven Starcom officers, they grew anxious as they felt the umbilical psychic connections to the spacecraft snap. The auras of these seven officers plunged into the time-memory crust of the Time Toroid and the sea of time-particles rapidly swallowed them up whole. They were battered by the powerful time-current and sucked towards the core by vortices that led to the chamber and corridors constituting the habitable region of the Time Toroid.

Starcom Two had made a perfect entry through the time-memory crust, using its phasing strategy, and it now found itself inside the Time Toroid's corridors. What on earth was this place?

Under the brilliant diffuse light, it could make out countless rows of draped experimental tables. Drawing back the covering of one of them, it gasped. Beneath the cloth lay a naked body that was instantly recognisable as being human from the rumours on the psychic networks of Rune 66 and, more recently, from the Chronicler's broadcasts. So, these aliens really did exist after all! Starcom Two formed a clear recognition signal, like a flare, and released it in the direction of Star Fleet One. However, there was no reply. It decided to change position, hoping that it was just in an area with poor psychic reception, and started to move in one direction along the corridor, releasing psychic flares as it moved. Was there any way out of this place?

Soon, Starcom Two was shouting at itself, delivering increasingly frantic psychic distress signals. Surely, someone must have heard it by now. Why had there been no contact and no rescue signal? Was that its own voice again or was it a reply from Star Fleet One? Starcom Two listened intensely to the sounds of echoes. How long could it continue like this before it drove itself mad?

Starcoms Four, Five, Six and Eight had adopted a quadrilateral configuration for penetration of the Time Toroid. Starcom Eight was spearheading the formation and made towards the core of the Time Toroid, bracing itself as its psychic body penetrated the time crust.

'Do not uncouple your psychic fields, whatever happens!' insisted Starcom Eight, assuming command. 'I think we have just lost contact with the Star Commander. We must keep this formation until we have completed our mission.'

Their progress started to slow down in the time substance itself. The heavy time isomers gripped their bodies, threatening to drown the four officers in a time-freeze, but together they were strong. Finally, they found their way into the complex of eternal corridors.

Starcom Three had suffered a turbulent passage. It instantly tried to return to the spacecraft on penetration of the time-memory crust, but found that it had lost the psychic connection. Trying to remain composed, it started to push through the swirls of time-particles that pitted its skin, and it was only then that it realised it had been badly burnt. Starcom Three tried to keep moving, but it was weak. The entity seemed to be feeding on its psychic energy. Gradually, it started to fade away until it was unable to think at all, losing all sense of its original mission. It forgot its identity and began to relax until it was simply floating in the time-particles, unable to escape and unable to communicate.

Starcom One was completely out of phase with the time substance. It had plunged into the clear time-particles with a huge splash and was instantly sucked into the bright core of the Time Toroid.

Starcom One moved slowly inside the internal corridors. It had been traumatised during penetration of the time-memory crust and suffered first-degree time-friction burns. In its mind's eye, it was aware of only two things, the light and the stiffness of its psychic body that was starting to feel very heavy. The slow isomers of time had completely penetrated its psychic body and, as they took their full effect, Starcom One simply stopped.

Back on Star Fleet One, the bodies of the seven missing officers remained still and devitalised, whilst only Starcom Seven showed any signs of psychic activity and the Star Commander feared that its psychic integrity had been irreversibly damaged.

star gazing

The Star Commander looked back towards the Time Toroid, hoping to find signs of the seven missing Starcom officers, but it detected no sign of psychic life. It studied the lifeless crystalline shells which had once contained their psychic bodies and silently paid its respects. The Star Commander did not take the loss of its officers casually, but a further mission was a serious risk and there was little chance that the missing officers could be rescued.

The Star Commander reviewed the psychic impressions that Starcom Seven had suppressed from the others during the return flight. Although its psychic energy was still very weak, Starcom Seven could not conceal its disordered thoughts from the Star Commander. Studying the silent account, the Star Commander examined the trauma sustained by the officer during its forced ejection by the time-wind. The injuries to its psychic body were unlike anything that the Star Commander had encountered before; its aura was perforated by slow isomers of time and deeply scarred by residual fragments that were still diffusing through it.

To prevent the other officers discovering the extent of its dysfunction and so avoid potential alarm, the Star Commander had reluctantly ordered the decommissioning of Starcom Seven.

During a psychic interview with Starcom Seven shortly after the ill-fated mission that the Star Commander was using in its report to the Sensate Senate, the extent of the officer's trauma was revealed. During this interview, Starcom Seven confessed that it would be impossible to return as a fully operational officer to Star Fleet squadron duties.

'I am falling apart. I just cannot face anyone. I spend most of my time in my dwelling alone in the basement. I know the other officers have tried to tell me that they understand what I went through and will help me get back on my feet, but I get so uncomfortable talking to them. I can't tell them what happened, as I can't find the right way to say it. I feel a failure and want to get away. Sometimes, I get really angry over nothing and have violent psychic outbursts. I don't know why I do this because I feel ashamed of myself afterwards. Sometimes, my head plays tricks on me. I think I am back at the surface of the Time Toroid and that I am about to be ripped apart. These feelings come creeping inside me all the time. It's so hard to push them back and I think that it is getting gradually worse. I don't want to go there any more. I just want to be left alone. I can't go back to squadron duties because I cannot concentrate on anything, but I would still like to be a part of the team because I'm lonely and frightened. I don't want to be left alone, but I cannot stay around others. I know what is happening to me will frighten them, too. Why am I like this? What happened and why did it happen to me?'

Starcom Seven was crippled and would certainly need to be reassigned. This was a great pity because, of all its Star Fleet One officers, Starcom Seven had possessed the most natural instinct for doing the right thing in perilous situations and had therefore been the best mission scout the Star Commander had ever worked with.

The mysterious Time Toroid had already taken one casualty and made seven officers unaccounted for, which was too great a price to pay for the sketchy information they had gleaned. Its nature remained as elusive as ever and it was almost certain that more Aerial Intelligence losses would result until some other way of gathering information was discovered.

The Chronicler's disappearance still remained a mystery.

indignation

The Spotter and the Observer were surprised and then annoyed that their observatory had drawn the attention of a number of enthusiastic colleagues. Apparently, their eclipse programme, unimaginatively called *Eclipse* on the Meteorology Channel, had gained great popularity, especially now that *Abductee* had been officially withdrawn from the psychic network.

Eclipse reflected an increasing concern that was spreading throughout the Collective Consciousness: that the End of Time was coming.

Some colleagues understood the End of Time as an expression to convey change in their culture, for there had certainly been a lot of that about recently, but others preferred to treat the expression more literally. These colleagues relished the propagation of conspiracy theories and were viewing the broadcast of *Eclipse* as a source of fresh evidence that the End of Time was going to happen and that the extinction of the species was imminent.

The Spotter and the Observer began to feel uncomfortable with the number of uninvited colleagues who had traced the source of the information back to the real world. Many fans had camped outside the observatory and were shouting questions to the meteorologists from outside.

'I can't concentrate with all these interruptions!' moaned the Observer, so they built a secret retreat in the metropolis in which they could indirectly watch the eclipse without being pestered by the conspiracy theory enthusiasts.

curiosity

'Hey, Peeper! Are you coming?' The Hopper put its head around the entrance to the downtime recreation recess to check where its colleague was.

'Yeah, come on, Peeper. It's going to be a real occasion and, would you believe it, even the supervisor is coming,' added the Digger.

The Peeper had certainly felt the growing excitement. The day of the extraordinary eclipse predicted by the Spotter and the Observer had finally arrived. Although the Peeper had been tempted all morning to peek at the celestial events, the timing clashed with its daily workout.

'No, I don't think so,' replied the Peeper, in spite of its mounting curiosity.

'Whyever not?' wondered the Hopper out loud. 'Wasn't it you who said that you would definitely . . .'

'I know,' snapped the Peeper, feeling pressurised rather than persuaded, 'but I've got my workout to do. I've not had a chance all day to get into my routine. Everyone has been running about like crazy and this whole eclipse thing has been such a distraction!'

'You take that exercise stuff so seriously, it can't be good for you,' warned the Digger. 'It's going to be your downfall, mark my words!'

'Look, this is important to me,' retorted the Peeper. 'Right now it is more important than looking at an eclipse and I'd like some peace and quiet to get on with my workout.'

'But this is no ordinary eclipse,' reminded the Digger. 'They say it's one of the signs of the End of Time. I think that your excessive exercising is more likely to wipe you out than the eclipse is. We are obviously not designed for physical exertion, you know, just look at us, with our naturally skinny arms and legs and thin bodies.'

The Digger started walking in a precarious manner, swinging its feet in wide circles before it placed one in front of the other and threatening to topple over at any moment. The Sucker, who had just joined them, whistled at the Digger's pose, complimenting it on its fabulous litheness. The Digger, pleased with the attention, stopped its catwalk strut and continued to show off.

'What do you need all that extra bulk for, Peeper? You think you are strong, but you just get to do more work. Have you ever thought you might be the victim of a conspiracy that wants us all to make our bodies more powerful, so we all get to work longer and harder and have fewer downtimes?'

'The thought never crossed my mind,' the Peeper replied curtly.

'Then maybe you ought to get using that big psychic muscle behind your eyes and work it out for yourself. Too much working out and not enough working-it-out, I'd say.'

The Peeper sprang to its feet at the insult and the Sucker leapt to the Digger's defence.

'Hey, Peeper, it's just a joke! I tell you what, I'll give you a first-hand account of the eclipse myself, in glorious psychic multi-colour. Now let's all go away and leave the Peeper to its workout. We'll take it easy and have some fun!'

The Peeper was relieved when the colleagues departed. It double-checked to ensure that no one had returned and, when it was absolutely certain that it was alone, it focused its psychic body on activating its crystalline gel and started to pump.

'One, two, three, four, five (strain) . . . six (pain) . . . seven (gain) . . . eight (do it again!)'

skywatching

They had said it was unprecedented, but omitted to say how beautiful it would be.

It was one thing to talk about the celestial event, speculating on how the three moons Neo, Homo, and Retro had been pulled back into alignment and another to witness the uncanny splendour of the phenomenon.

Many curious Grays that were on downtime breaks stopped what they were doing to go and watch the unprecedented eclipse. Others that were working saw the departure of their colleagues and persuaded their supervisors to grant them leave. The excitement of the spectacle spread rapidly through the networks and by word of mouth. Few were left untouched by the occasion. Even the sceptics and workaholics found ways of persuading themselves to go outside to skywatch.

When the sky started to turn a little more violet as the partial eclipse approached, the first psychic impressions were transmitted to the broadcast networks.

The images were spellbinding and soon thousands of colleagues were calling to each other. As they congregated in their masses under the disappearing sun, they formed a collective psychic wave that resonated beyond the limits of the established psychic networks. This uncommon state of mutual thought was known as the Call of the Species.

As the three moons glided towards the sun, they appeared to take tiny 'bites' out of it. The delicate veils of cloud that framed the spectacle only added mysticism to the astonishing drama that had begun to unfold. As time progressed, the bites-out-of-the-sun became more apparent. The pace seemed to quicken and the light changed. The temperature started to plunge and a cold, icy wind crossed the surface of the planet. The spectators shivered and fell silent, captivated by the eerie events. As the shadows of the moons coalesced, the darkness intensified, deepening in its purple hue. Suddenly the sky blackened, a moment that made every spectator quiver with dreadful awe, leaving only a tiny sliver of sun glowing in the sky, with thin ribbons of transparent cloud trailing across it. When the eclipse reached totality, there was a reverent gasp and a sudden, spontaneous burst of applause rose from the throng of spectators. Even the Creature Crystals responded to the premature darkness by radiating out light from the burrows, so the planetary surface sparkled and glittered like a night sky.

As the colleagues gazed skyward in total amazement, they witnessed the strange, white aura of the solar corona radiating across the sky as an awe-inspiring halo of fire. More twinkling lights appeared, created by the disorientated Creature Crystals and then, on the far distant horizon, a streak of light came towards them, intensifying in colour from pink through to apricot, orange and finally red, spreading across the sky at a phenomenal rate. Within seconds, the darkness had vanished and the air started getting noticeably warmer, but the colleagues were still standing looking skyward on the surface of the planet. They did not return to their duties for they were completely unaware that the sunlight had returned and, despite the returning ambient warmth, they believed they were still looking at the totality. In their mind's eye, they were staring into total darkness.

impatience

The Peeper had finished its workout a long time ago and was waiting for the return of its colleagues. Downtime was over and yet no one had returned to start work. Surely, the eclipse could not have taken that long? The Peeper was at a loss as to what to do with this unexpected extra time. It normally planned its daily schedule meticulously, not wasting a moment, and so it was in a dilemma. Should it do another workout, experiment with some new exercises or go and look for its colleagues?

Eventually, after having done two further workouts and bettered its personal best for a psychically-assisted dead-lift, the Peeper decided to venture onto the surface to see what was happening.

The spectacle that confronted it was deeply disturbing. As far as it could see, the whole species was standing with their heads upturned to the sky in broad daylight.

'Hey, what are you all looking at?' cried the Peeper.

Its search for an explanation was not met with any reply. In frustration, it roughly grabbed hold of one of the skywatchers and noticed that its eyes were not the usual jet-black colour but milky-white. The Peeper was appalled by the appearance of this colleague, but was even more surprised that the white-eyed Gray had not objected to being touched. In desperation, it turned to another colleague for help and another and another, finding to its horror that all of them had unresponsive white visual sensors and were quite unabashed by the Peeper's touch.

What had happened? The Peeper cried out for someone to help, but the colleagues stayed still, blindly skywatching. When the Peeper tried to establish a mental connection with them, it realised that they were in psychic shock. How could it make contact with these silent Grays? Breaking the time-honoured taboo again, the Peeper tapped some of the colleagues on the shoulder and found they responded to its tactile approach by squeezing its hand reassuringly. Unfortunately, the Peeper could not strike up a conversation using body language, but it was relieved that the colleagues were at least responsive in some sensory modalities.

Maybe the psychic networks could account for this dreadful spectacle but, when the Peeper uploaded on the nearest node, it found that the network was derelict. In the hope of finding out what was going on, the Peeper made its way to the News Channel. The last entries reflected the collective enthusiasm for the eclipse and reinforced the Call of the Species, persuading all colleagues to come and celebrate. It was only then that the Peeper understood what was the matter.

'Oh no, the colleagues don't realise they are blind. They still think that the eclipse is happening!'

The Peeper rushed out to look for its mining colleagues and it was able to identify the familiar forms of the Hopper, the Digger and the Screwer from the rest of the crowd. They had found a place near the Spotter and the Observer's observatory and were staring upwards along with the rest of the species, towards where the eclipse must once have been.

After fighting its way through the crowds, bumping into white-eyed, skywatching Grays, the Peeper touched the Digger on the shoulders. Despite its sensory paralysis, the powerful touch of the Peeper immediately identified it to its colleagues.

'Hey, Peeper,' shouted the Digger 'you made it after all!'

The Peeper embraced its mining colleagues and they found great reassurance in touching one another.

Gradually, the spectators started to recover a little from the psychic shock they had initially experienced. The Peeper and its mining colleagues started to communicate with others, to tell them that the eclipse had passed and that they and all the other colleagues on the planet's surface appeared to have been blinded by it.

As the tragic news spread amongst the white-eyed Grays, they instinctively started hugging those colleagues that were standing next to them. The tactile messages spread and emotions rose as the skywatching colleagues gradually came to the grim understanding that they would never see the sky or understand their world in the same way again.

Their distress greatly moved the Peeper. It could only deal with its mining colleagues for the time being, so it led them back inside to the downtime area in the mine where they had last said goodbye to each other.

Outside, hundred of thousands of white-eyed Grays openly mourned their loss of sight and fumbled blindly around, hoping that someone would guide them safely home.

sensory crisis

'Honourable members of the Senate, I need to interrupt you with an observation that may be of great significance!' announced the Grabber.

The senators looked up abruptly as the psychic frequency the Grabber was using was reserved for emergencies.

'What is it?' enquired the Opportunist.

'The Collective Consciousness is in psychic shock.' The Grabber extended its hand with the silica crystal amplifiers and drew up a screen showing a number of distribution maps.

The senators looked on aghast. Everywhere around the metropolis and even out in the outskirts were very low points of psychic activity. This suggested that either a mass migration of colleagues off the surface of the planet had taken place or almost no one was thinking.

'Is it a hysterical phenomenon?' asked the Ancient.

'It's difficult to characterise,' replied the Grabber. 'I suggest that everyone uploads and finds out what is going on in the networks for themselves.'

'It's creepy,' declared the Ungrateful, staring at the Grabber's patchy map, 'as if everyone has suddenly vanished.'

'I've just got word from the Star Commander,' reported the Hero. 'The Chronicler's dwelling has been successfully infiltrated and a diary has been found. It's on its way right now!'

The Grabber appeared almost irritated by the update.

'Yes, yes, yes! Very good, but I think we now have an emergency situation. The crisis of the species is far more serious than the Chronicler's escape, the diary can wait. If the psychic traffic is at a standstill, then at least our reputations will not suffer for the time being. We will attend to the problem of the Chronicler, once this much more serious crisis has been resolved.'

There was a general murmur of consternation at this unexpected pronouncement. The Hero saluted with a double-breasted arm-strike, indicating that the Grabber's authority as Chief Justice was being respected. However, its assertive gesture served to remind everyone present that the Hero was the real expert in intelligence affairs and that it was not happy at being overruled.

'Your honour, the two may be related,' conjectured the Enthusiast whose appointment to the Sensate Senate was due more to its charm than any service it had offered the community.

'Enough!' The Grabber raised its hands above its head and stood to its feet, drawing the energy from the senator's psychic circle into its central position.

'Until we find out what is going on, there will be no attention paid to the problem of the Chronicler crisis. Do you understand?'

'But, what if the Chronicler has released its cancer particles?'

'Then we are too late and it has beaten us, but can we please stop all this speculating? Yes, it is bad timing that the Chronicler has disappeared but, as the Hero has pointed out, we will soon be in possession of the diary and then we shall be able to trace the Chronicler's whereabouts. Right now, we have an emergency situation, as I said. We need to establish what has caused the psychic paralysis. I fear something extremely serious has happened. Are there any further questions or objections?' But no one voiced their concerns as it would only waste more of the Grabber's valuable time.

The Groveller tapped its hand impatiently on the side of its chair, waiting for the emergency session to finish. It hated ingratiating itself with its colleagues and only did so when it needed their support. From the configuration of the psychic activity distribution, maps that the Grabber had presented, it looked like it would be lucky to find any colleagues at all. This was going to be a useless exercise, but it resigned itself to the task and uploaded with the others.

action

The Peeper went to the place that was the centre of Gray intelligence, the Sensate Senate. If anyone knew what was happening, the senators would.

It was worried that it had been able to enter the atrium unchallenged by Underground Intelligence officers and, as it descended the amethyst spiral staircase that led to the judicial chambers, it started to wonder if it was the only sighted colleague left. Approaching the grand entrance to the Great Committee Hall, it started scanning for signs of activity and was relieved to sense powerful psychic frequencies. There was a council in session.

It stood hesitantly at the entrance, listening to the senators talking and found itself trembling, fearing that an Underground Intelligence officer would seize it at any moment, but it was determined to interrupt at an opportune moment and so it tuned into the discussion that was going on.

'Nothing out there,' the Manipulator sighed, 'it's all very puzzling.'

'I noticed that you were the first to return,' grumbled the Ancient. 'Just exactly what investigations did you make?'

'None that were any less effective than yours, Ancient!' came the sharp retort. 'You haven't exactly solved the mystery yourself. Your sloth is not impressive. I am quick because I am an efficient agent.'

'Talking about time wasting,' observed the Ungrateful, 'just where is the Groveller and what is keeping it? We need a full Senators' Council to ratify a new course of action.'

The Grabber had remained silent, listening to the frustration of its senators and growing very concerned by the lack of progress. It held up its hand for their silence.

'Is there anyone who has anything positive to contribute?'

The Peeper chose this moment to enter the chamber and introduce itself to the senators.

'I do!'

The senators turned to study the strange anatomy of this colleague. It was obviously a miner, but what an abnormally powerful body it had! Didn't they destroy mutants the moment they came-into-being any more?

The Grabber beckoned.

'Introduce yourself! What are you doing here and what do you know?'

'The Peeper, your honour,' bowing its head in respect, 'I'm a miner and I have just witnessed a catastrophe for our species.'

The Peeper wondered just how detailed it needed to be. It realised that some of the senators were looking at its anatomy disapprovingly, so thought it best to keep its account concise and to the point. There was no need to make an emotional appeal; it would detract from the gravity of the situation.

'My mining colleagues that had been granted supervised leave to watch the eclipse for a few minutes during downtime did not return by the end of the recess. So, I went to look for them. Senators, when I stepped onto the planet's surface I saw literally thousands of colleagues, my associates among them, staring up at the sky. When I went to find out why they were still looking at the sun when the eclipse had long passed, I realised that every one of them was visually blind and in a state of psychic shock.'

'Everyone?' echoed the Grabber

'Every last one of them, your honour!'

There were murmurs and then gasps amongst the senators, their concern and bewilderment growing to a crescendo.

'Your honour,' continued the Peeper, 'I managed to escort my associates to a place of safety, but all the other colleagues left on the surface of the planet are just beginning to realise that they are blind and are very frightened. They are starting to behave in a destructive and disorderly manner. I am here because I am unable to take every Gray safely home on my own. I do not know of any other colleagues that have preserved their sight and I am hoping that you would be able to assist me. All these blind colleagues must be brought to a place of safety where the extent of their sensory paralysis can be assessed and they can obtain any help that can be offered.'

The Grabber looked very concerned.

'What can you tell us about the nature of this sensory paralysis, Peeper? Is it permanent or did it look like some of the colleagues were recovering?'

'Your honour, that sort of question is beyond my assignment capabilities to answer. Some of them were able to respond to psychic signals, although initially they had been in a state of shock. So, it appears that some degree of recovery may be possible. However, to what extent their injuries have damaged them, I cannot answer. I am a Crystalline Gray by nature and consider myself a colleague of action rather than knowledge.'

'This miner may not be able to offer the insights that we will need to mount an effective restorative programme but *I* have made some important findings!' No one had noticed the Groveller's return. On downloading and taking its place at the round table it had been rather annoyed to find the Peeper, clearly only a Crystalline Gray, at the centre of attention. However, as the Groveller listened to the Peeper, it realised that the physically over-developed miner was not devious enough to claim credit for a rescue mission and could even prove a very important ally.

The Grabber waved its hand, bidding the Groveller to keep speaking.

'I have made contact with two sighted meteorologists that were updating their report on the Meteorology Channel. They were easy to find as they were the sole source of psychic activity in that region of the psychic network. I downloaded at a nearby node and found myself in their observatory.'

'Had they seen the eclipse?' wondered the Manipulator aloud.

'Yes, they appear to have escaped the deleterious effects of the eclipse by observing the phenomenon using indirect means and are already analysing the nature of the condition reported to us by the Peeper just now. Initial analyses have suggested that the damage sustained by the spectators could have been due to an anomalous form of radiation, but it will take time to confirm this.'

'Radiation damage during an eclipse,' the Ancient mused. 'I don't believe that's ever happened before.'

'It seems that nothing about this eclipse has been usual,' continued the Groveller. 'However, they are dedicated colleagues and I am sure they will be of great use in discovering what we shall need to do in order to start a rehabilitation programme.'

'What if it is not possible to rehabilitate these damaged colleagues?' the Ungrateful speculated.

'I think it would be wrong to jump to immediate conclusions,' snapped the Groveller, hoping to impress its good intentions upon the Peeper to win its confidence. 'Let's do first things first. I think we should give this miner immediate assistance in bringing the blind colleagues home. Now that the meteorologists may have established the cause of the psychic paralysis, we can continue to search for sighted colleagues in places where some individuals might not have been able to watch the eclipse. We need to build up a rescue team.'

The Grabber nodded.

'That's an excellent plan, Groveller. You go with this miner and evaluate this terrible situation yourself. Hero, you make a reconnaissance, with all the sighted intelligence officers under your command, to find out how many visually intact Grays remain. These colleagues will form the core of our emergency and rehabilitation teams. Ancient, I want you to go down to the opencast silica mines and oversee the coming-into-being of new colleagues with the Academic and ensure that the Silica Worms have enough sustenance to make new preborns that are sighted. We need to muster as many colleagues as possible to do this task. The rest of you will join me in Council. We have some very serious issues to consider whilst these preliminary steps are being taken.'

The Groveller rose and walked over to the Peeper, saluting its bravery with a double-breasted salute. This had the desired effect on the miner's self-esteem. As they left the Sensate Senate, the Peeper walked with pride in the company of the senator and told it everything it needed to know and much, much more about the whole event. It also unwisely revealed too much of its personal history to the ambitious senator before they reached the surface but, by this time, the Groveller already knew it had the Peeper exactly where it wanted.

rescue

It was far more bizarre and upsetting than the Groveller had imagined.

'Their eyes are white!' gasped the Groveller, 'they can't see a thing!'

Many thousands of colleagues were crawling around the pitted surface of the planet, groping at one another and uttering distress signals.

A growing number of white-eyed Grays were joining a chain of colleagues which had formed somewhere close to the middle of the crowd. They linked to their neighbours by holding hands. The leader of this group had just risen to its feet when the Groveller spotted them. Those that were touching it also stood up from their crouched postures, growing in confidence and creating a ripple of vertical movement. As the chain of colleagues stood hand-to-shoulder with one another and started to walk, those white-eyed Grays still fumbling around on the ground reached out towards them, feeling for the end of the chain. The Grovellor flinched at this breaking of the strong taboo on touching each other, but in the circumstances there was nothing he could do.

The leader of the chain of white-eyed Grays seemed to be walking towards the entrance of a burrow. But, just as the shuffling chain of colleagues seemed destined to reach the safety of firm walls in the metropolis, the leader stumbled over another sightless colleague who was thrashing about in fits of violent terror.

The Peeper and the Grovellor watched helplessly as a wave of white-eyed Grays fell backwards, in slow motion, with the leader sent toppling by the terrified, sightless Gray clinging on tightly to its leg. It turned and began to strike the perpetrator of its apparent assault. The Groveller cringed as it imagined the thin limbs of the now ex-leader, snapping under the furious blows, and looked away.

However, outbreaks of disorder were taking place throughout the terrified crowd, the highly charged emotions of the sightless Grays making them react unpredictably to the slightest provocations or accidents.

The Grabber turned to the Peeper that was assessing another characteristic of the situation. A few colleagues were standing quite motionlessly, despite the chaos around them, waiting for the sun to return. They were still unaware that they had become blind. Which of them was going to break the news to these colleagues?

Then, one terrified worker that was running about on its feet, in no particular direction, suddenly embarked on a direct collision course for the Groveller. As it hurtled towards the senator, the Peeper stopped it, catching the terrified Gray in its arms and using its physical strength to boost a psychic impression of comforting into it.

'Hey, it's going to be all right. Help is here!'

The worker started hugging the Peeper which responded with what the Groveller considered to be indecently intimate gestures, but this tactility seemed to have the desired effect. The Groveller shuddered at the embrace, sickened by its double hatred of the white-eyes and the tactility of the occasion. However, the Groveller was impressed by the Peeper's instinctive handling of the situation as the worker quickly calmed down and looked towards the Peeper with its useless visual sensors for guidance.

The Groveller turned away, as it had already seen too much.

It realised that it was unable to share this tender moment or even to gaze reassuringly into the whiteness of the unfortunate colleague's radiation-damaged eyes to add its own message of comfort.

triage

'Members of the Sensate Senate, I am sure you are aware of the gravity of the situation. Our culture has been greatly damaged by the tragedy that has happened to those colleagues that observed the unprecedented and injurious eclipse.' The Grabber was holding out both its arms and the senators noticed that it was using two silica crystal amplifiers to conduct this meeting.

'I have here a documentary psychic holo-movie that the Groveller has just transmitted back from the surface of the planet only a short distance from the metropolis. I must warn you now that some of you may find these images disturbing, but it is vital that you pay close attention, since our subsequent decisions will be influenced by the contents.'

As the Grabber crossed the crystals over its chest, a large three-dimensional projection appeared. The senators had prepared themselves for a distressing report, but the reality of the situation stunned them into silence. The normally dry and uneventful wasteland was literally crawling with Grays. They were grovelling on the ground, groping at anything that passed them, cuddling one another, uttering shrieks of abandonment and calling for help. Then a particularly unstable individual turned to look straight at the audience, its eyes white and blind!

The Manipulator click-clicked its fingertips together in distress at the sudden revelation and turned its back on the documentary.

'I can't bear it, it's so horrible! So . . . debauched!'

'Just look at their eyes!' cried the Ungrateful, unable to restrain itself from comment.

'They are hideous,' added the Diplomat, 'I can hardly bear to watch this!' but it was transfixed to the appalling vision anyway.

'They remind me of those monsters, those humans,' added the Enthusiast, who was well known to be a fan of the *Abductee* programme and often watched it 'for laughs', a practice that was disapproved of by the other senators. 'When I first saw their eyes I too got a shock, but humans have tiny little pinpoint dots in their eyes, whereas these colleagues' eyes are completely white. I must say, though, it looks uncanny on a Gray.'

'Look at them, they are actually touching one another. Gross! Gross! Gross!' protested the Manipulator.

'Perhaps it is one of the signs of the End of Time,' remarked the User, who was always open to shifting perspectives on any affair and, just like many other academics that preferred to think of this event as a metaphorical one, was now open to the possibility of it being a real occurrence.

'Well, whatever your feelings may be,' observed the Opportunist, 'no one seemed to be in pain. These colleagues are just in shock: they are not constitutionally corrupted, they are still ordinary Grays that are just not used to existing without their natural senses. Their broaching of our cultural conventions that you find so disgusting, Manipulator, is not wilful, they are simply trying to use other senses to understand what has happened to them!'

'I don't care,' protested the Manipulator. 'It's a disgusting thing to do, grappling about with one another. Even if I were visually-impaired, I would never stoop so low.'

'How are we going to deal with this catastrophe?' asked the Ungrateful. 'We've got to get rid of them before they defile the species.'

The Grabber froze the documentary psychic holo-movie at a place where two distressed colleagues were embracing.

'Are you proposing a mass reassignment programme?' The

Grabber's tone was deliberate, as if it had been waiting for one of the senators to raise this issue.

The Ungrateful, having had its conjectures eloquently phrased for it, realised that this was exactly what it intended.

'Well, we can't just let them live like that, can we? What sort of existence would that be?'

'Exactly, poor things, what a shame this has happened! We must put their suffering to an end as soon as we can,' cajoled the Manipulator.

'Are not you forgetting one small but important detail?' sighed the Opportunist. 'These "poor things" keep our metropolis running. From a purely practical perspective, we do not have enough sighted colleagues to deanimate these visually-impaired colleagues and, even if we did, how long do you think it would take? Months? A year? How do we get their cooperation? Oh, and in the meantime, how do we keep the others busy working?'

The Manipulator was irritated at being challenged in this way.

'Oh, I do not know. I just want these white-eyed Grays out of my sight. Moreover, I suggest that they are kept out of the sight of the preborns that will be coming-into-being. We certainly do not want to raise our new colleagues into a tactile society!'

'Perhaps we could rehabilitate them,' the Opportunist suggested with an icily corrective tone.

'Rehabilitate them!' laughed the Enthusiast. 'How do you intend to do that? These colleagues would need constant supervision. You have already told us that there are insufficient sighted colleagues to carry out reassignment. Well, Opportunist, correct me if I am wrong, but reassignment would restore these colleagues to full working function rather quickly, whereas rehabilitation would keep them in an impaired state requiring perpetual input. Where is the foresight in that, if you'll forgive the pun!'

'You are forgetting that these colleagues will be able to adapt and learn how to cope with their impairments. It is possible that they would even have a happy alternative lifestyle,' retorted the Opportunist.

'I agree,' added the User, shifting its perspective on the argument. 'In any event, mass reassignment would remove most of our workforce and cannot be done without provoking the greatest inefficiency in our system, let alone the controversy it would provoke. For example, who would we reassign, what timing would we use and how would we tell them?'

'Yes,' added the Upstart, 'the standard protocol either requires a colleague to be so malfunctioning that they volunteer their reassignment or have committed some constitutional offence for which it is forcibly reassigned. It seems to me that we would either have to persuade every affected colleague that it is desirable to be reassigned or pass a law decreeing that white-eyed sensory paralysis is a constitutional offence. I can't see either working, to be honest with you.'

'I can see a solution.' Everyone turned to look at the Groveller. It had a disturbing habit of slipping into meetings unnoticed, but it tended to offer useful solutions to difficult issues so the senators were instantly curious. 'But I don't know if you'll approve, let alone like it. It involves the Peeper.'

The Grabber motioned the senators to be silent, as their murmuring was distracting.

'We rehabilitate the white-eyed Grays whilst we implement a progressive reassignment programme. That way we allay the fears of colleagues that may have adapted and are reluctant to be deanimated. They will cooperate with us and work for us whilst they are waiting reassignment. It will be written into the design of the rehabilitation protocol. We will need to re-educate the culture to make it work and, to do that, the species will need a new hero. That is where the Peeper comes in.'

'Oh, that's great, Groveller!' said the Opportunist tartly. 'You saw how passionate it was about its associates. Do you really think that it will cooperate with a progressive and subversive reassignment programme? It's more likely to start a revolution on behalf of the white-eyed workers against us!'

'That's the clever part.' The Groveller had everyone's attention now. 'We allow the Peeper to take responsibility for rehabilitation in its own way. I have seen it out there and it has the ability to communicate with the workers. It would be able to win their confidence and so they would do whatever it says. This is something that I could not do and I have a much stronger psychic body than it does. Once the Peeper feels it is making progress with rehabilitation, we then appoint it to the Senate and remove it from the field.'

There was protest at the very idea of a Crystalline Gray becoming a senator, but the Grabber insisted on silence.

'Once the Peeper has been made a senator, we start the progressive deanimation programme. Naturally, we will not tell it anything about this. It will continue to believe that its own rehabilitation programme is being followed, while we leave the task of deanimating the white-eyed colleagues to the Star Commander. The Star Commander will not need any persuasion to cooperate, after all, it has already appointed itself as protector of the psychic integrity of the species. What mission could be worthier than reassigning thousands of potentially impaired and overly tactile Grays? Within a very short space of time after its appointment to the Senate, our culture will be populated by fully functional colleagues and there will be no white-eyed Grays left.'

'Oh, Groveller, that's so cunning, it's brilliant!' squealed the User, whose overall opinion had changed yet again.

'Well, I still think it's all disgusting,' grumbled the Manipulator. 'These degenerates need to be eradicated now. I cannot see any reason why we cannot be honest about this!'

'That is because you are not a real politician like the Groveller!' chimed in the User. 'This way we get our own way with everything, despite being heavily outnumbered. We get the white-eyed Grays effectively to agree to be deanimated by embarking on the rehabilitation programme in which they occupy themselves pleasantly until their time comes and it is nothing to do with us. There will be no objection, no revolution and, in fact, the process will be thoroughly enjoyable. I love it!'

The senators began to debate the issue. Most were dubious about the case for protecting these defective colleagues in defence of the integrity of the species, but a few considered a mass deanimation programme to be a rather draconian solution to the situation. The argument was brief, however, since the preservation of so-called 'degenerates' was ultimately indefensible. The Groveller's plan was easily voted through and the Grabber brought the session to a close.

cure

'I need to bring an unfinished issue to the attention of the Senate,' declared the Hero. 'The Star Commander has finished its analysis of the Chronicler's diary and its report is in the final stages of completion.'

The Grabber indicated that the Hero should resume its seat.

'Hero, it is deeply regrettable that your great commander has spent so much time on this document. Indeed, we should have resolved this matter earlier but, as you are aware, other far more serious matters distracted us. As far as I am concerned, the case of the Chronicler is finished and should never be raised again. There is much change in the behaviour of the colleagues with the advent of the white-eyes and the issues that the Chronicler's case raises would just complicate an already delicate situation. The diary and the report should be immediately destroyed.'

'But your honour . . .' The Hero was demoralised. The Star Commander had been rather excited about the contents of the diary and had indicated, off the record, that the diary contained some extraordinary revelations. The Hero was looking forward to reading the report itself.

'Be quiet, Hero. We do not want to know the outcome of the commander's findings, as it will only serve to fuel conjecture. If there were any significant findings in the report, then the diary would only serve to bring this appalling affair to the Collective Consciousness again. If the report is fruitless, then we have lost nothing. The report must be suppressed at all costs or we will have a crisis in confidence on our hands.'

The Grabber was insistent.

'I forbid you to pursue this issue further and, furthermore, we will strike this conversation from the record.'

The Hero returned to its seat, disappointed in the Grabber's ruling, but accepted its decision and, at that moment, the Chronicler's case was effectively erased from the memory of the Collective Consciousness.

agenda

The Hero wondered how best to break the disappointing news to the Star Commander. It was a great shame that the same senators that had placed great faith in its expertise were now withdrawing its services. In honour of its legendary reputation of psychic strength, the Hero decided that a visit to its duty office would be the most fitting way of addressing the Star Commander.

'What can I do for you, senator? This is a most unexpected visit. I have not yet completed my report on the Chronicler case.' It paused, 'Is there something wrong?' The Star Commander stood to attention, giving a double-breasted arm-strike in salute.

'That is exactly why I have come, Star Commander.' The Hero was serious and direct with its news. 'The Chronicler Case is being dropped.'

'Dropped? What do you mean, that it is to be postponed?'

'Indefinitely.'

'But that is outrageous! This deviant has already posed a significant risk to the physical and psychic purity of the species. How can the case be dropped? Surely, I am to complete my report on the diary at least. I am convinced that, once the senators are presented with the evidence, they will change their minds.'

The Star Commander had hoped to link the growing number of bizarre events in the metropolis to the strange time-spill that the Chronicler had described in its diary and then mount an official investigation of the Time Toroid.

'Not at all, Star Commander. Nothing will persuade them to pursue this case further. Believe me, I have tried. You are to cease all activities related to the Chronicler case from this moment. Moreover, you are to destroy any evidence that such an individual or case ever existed.'

'But why? Surely, nothing can be more important than protecting the psychic purity of the Grays?'

'Indeed, Star Commander, but I cannot think that the current disaster has escaped your attention. Think of the negative reaction that issues raised by the Chronicler's activities, such as a cancer scare propagated through colleagues touching each other, would have on public order. The white-eyed Grays need to be tactile just to get about!'

The Star Commander looked grave. Of course, it had not overlooked the outcome of the peculiar eclipse. Indeed, its own theory on the events was that the solar event and the strange, blinding radiation were also linked to events in the Time Toroid. But unless it was able to formally present the findings of the Chronicler's diary, it would be impossible to explain its position clearly. It must find a way of reasoning with the senators to make its appeal for a formal hearing of its report.

'But there is no one on the networks any more. No one will be speculating on details of this affair! It is not like the old days when scaremongering and conspiracy theories were rife whenever any abnormal activity occurred.'

'No, but there is a whole generation of rapidly growing sighted colleagues newly assigned to the culture that must not react badly to tactile behaviour, despite its grossly offensive nature. If a rumour is allowed to spread, that touching one another spreads cancer, then to permit contact between colleagues would create a conflict between the white-eyed Grays that need to feel their way around, communicating with tactile gestures, and the customs of sighted colleagues.'

'Senator, with all due respect, I believe that the Chronicler poses a much greater threat to the species than the maintenance of public order. I believe our entire culture is at stake here. Let me finish making the report on the diary and I will prove the seriousness of the case, giving a clear indication of the important links and establishing the reasons behind its conduct.'

'I cannot let you do that, Star Commander. It is beyond my jurisdiction. The Sensate Senate had been most clear about this case. This is an order. I am also personally advising you to stop your work immediately and destroy any evidence that you may have that the Chronicler ever existed, including that thing,' motioned the Hero, pointing towards the Chronicler's diary as it left the duty office.

When a good distance was between them both, the Star Commander allowed itself to think the unthinkable. It had never disobeyed orders but, just this time, the first and only time it ever contradicted a command, it uttered its defiance.

'Not if I can help it! I will complete my report and spare the Chronicler's diary which I believe is the key to discovering what links these catastrophes that threaten all life forms here on Rune 66. The Sensate Senate will hear of my report, in one way or another.'

sightwatching

The Spotter and the Observer had returned to their observatory and drawn the screens across all the portals that overlooked the planet's surface. They simply did not want to see the outside world because, although the blind Grays had been rescued by the heroic efforts of the Peeper and the Groveller, the memories of that dreadful time disturbed them. Despite frantic psychic ablutions to remove this data from their psychic memory recorders, the images of the white-eyed colleagues and the strange, blinding radiation still troubled them.

Instead, they threw themselves further into analysing the strange eclipse and deduced that the source of the abnormal radiation came from somewhere in Far Space, but they did not possess the psychic range to study it in more detail. Only Aerial Intelligence had access to the spaceships that might have provided the meteorologists with the means to overcome this distance, but they declined the Spotter's and Observer's request, since they were making fewer missions owing to the lack of sighted officers.

However, the meteorologists never discovered the cause of the unprecedented and disastrous events, as their analytical talents were genuinely needed elsewhere. The Hero and the Groveller visited their observatory to order them to abandon their meteorological duties and direct their statistical talents towards analysing the damage that the white-eyed Grays had sustained.

The Spotter and the Observer raised no objections as they were obedient to the law of the Sensate Senate but, instead, grumbled constantly about their new work. However, once they began to regard the study of the holes and defects in their colleagues' visual field as being equivalent to mapping the sky, they found their meteorological talents were directly transferable to this task and grew passionate about their work.

In their first set of trial studies, they made the remarkable observation that, as the white-eyed Grays built up the strength of their crystalline bodies, their psychic bodies grew in strength accordingly. They predicted that this might even be increased to the point that, in theory, the white-eyed Grays might even see again!

Within minutes of this revelation, the Sensate Senate was aware of the discovery and was evaluating the implications.

strength to strength

The Peeper and the Groveller had been working together. From the moment they had witnessed the dreadful confusion on the planet's surface following the eclipse, they had mounted an extensive rescue programme with increasing numbers of sighted colleagues who had appeared from all sorts of reclusive places within the metropolis to bring the white-eyed colleagues home.

Not too long afterwards, the first sighted Grays that had just come-into-being under the supervision of the Ancient and the Academic joined in the assignment that was officially supposed to rehabilitate the white-eyed Grays. All the time they were at work, however, these damaged colleagues were really being kept occupied whilst the deanimation chamber was being built.

The Hero and the Groveller received the news from the Spotter and the Observer that it was possible the white-eyed Grays could be restored to full health.

'What did you make of that, then?' asked the Hero of the Groveller as they returned to make their report to the other senators. 'I thought you handled those two very well!'

'Hmm,' replied the Groveller, 'it was necessary to subdue their enthusiasm for their work or the reassignment programme would be at risk.'

'I think that they took your threat to reassign them seriously, though.' The Hero caught hold of its colleague's arm as they approached the entrance to the Sensate Senate.

The Groveller turned to face the Hero, looking deeply into the space behind its psychic sensors, making sure that its reply was unambiguous.

'I *was* being serious.'

Seated in their usual places around the Great Committee Hall's round table, both the Groveller and the Hero recommended that the deanimation programme should be started as soon as the remaining sighted colleagues had been taught what to do. No further mention was made of the possibility that a complete recovery of the white-eyed Grays was possible.

The Peeper worked continuously, never doubting for one moment in the rehabilitation of its unfortunate colleagues, only pausing to replete its powerful body with silica salts and water to give it strength enough to carry, console and instruct the white-eyed workers. Even when the visually-impaired colleagues had all been safely returned to their dwellings, it did not stop working.

Instinctively, the Peeper started to teach the sighted assistants and white-eyed workers the physical exercises that it used itself, so that they could build up their crystalline bodies and consequently increase their psychic powers. When the Peeper was confident that its power techniques had been fully understood, it began devising a sensory programme.

The Peeper remembered the game that it played with its colleagues when *Abductee* was first broadcast and taught the rules to its visually impaired colleagues. Soon, the white-eyed Grays had learned how to use their physical bodies to boost their psychic bodies whilst having fun. There was widespread laughter in the mines and the tunnels and recesses were filled with white-eyed Grays wrestling, wriggling and cuddling each other in games that started to give them greater powers of perception. The white-eyes were growing stronger. The Peeper's game became something that almost compensated for the white-eyed Grays' lack of sight and soon it reached cult status. The Peeper became a hero, just as the Groveller had predicted.

The Manipulator was outraged.

'When are we going to appoint this troublesome do-gooder to the Senate and remove it from mischief-making in the metropolis? Have you seen the orgies that are being endorsed by this misshapen colleague?'

However, the Opportunist had restored its support for the Peeper, having been impressed with the level of happiness in the metropolis.

'You are so narrow-minded! The white-eyes' conduct is doing them and us a great deal of good. We are actually witnessing a great increase in productivity as the blind white-eyed Grays are working harder in the mines than before they ever lost their psychic senses. They seem to be stronger and use their physicality in a very effective way. I don't think we should begin this deanimation programme at all! I would say that we should let the Peeper work in the field for as long as possible and keep the white-eyes working. Besides, they are happy.'

The Manipulator could hardly contain itself. 'This is outrageous! I think these white-eyes are disgusting and their overtly tactile behaviour is an insult to the integrity of the entire species. The sooner we deanimate them the better! What if they grow stronger than we are? What if they force us to become tactile degenerates, too? We are looking at a potential revolution of subordinates. You are a traitor to the species, Opportunist! Have you lost your own psychic integrity?'

The Grabber brought the heated exchange to order.

'Let us not fight amongst ourselves. I understand your point, Opportunist, that the Peeper is doing some very good work, but our original plans to deanimate them still hold. It is delightful that the white-eyes will enjoy their time before deanimation, but we have a duty to restore the order of the species. Therefore, until the white-eyes have been completely reassigned, we should just let the Peeper work in its own way. I don't want to hear any more speculation on its techniques from you, Manipulator. The Peeper has indeed accomplished a great deal and we should be grateful that it is so committed to safeguarding public order.'

The Groveller listened carefully, knowing that none of this would happen without careful guidance. It would have to take matters into its own hands.

cull

The Groveller reviewed the blueprints for the so-called rehabilitation centre and congratulated itself on how well-concealed the deanimation programme was. From a naive perspective, the centre offered all the facilities that could be expected from a centre of excellence, but for those with a more technical understanding of the equipment, there were some interesting anomalies.

'Sorry not to have told you about this construction project earlier, Peeper. It was always a part of the rehabilitation programme, but we did not want to bore you with the details as you have been very busy working with the white-eyed Grays and you've been very difficult to get hold of. There is no need to concern yourself, however, as the senators have already approved it. We are all very grateful for your efforts and I hope that you will be equally enthusiastic about these blueprints, too!'

The Groveller had expected the Peeper to ask a few awkward questions but knew that, as a Crystalline Gray, its intelligence was constitutionally limited. The Peeper looked over the plans that the Groveller produced, using a handheld silica crystal amplifier. It appeared that a new facility was to be built on the outskirts of the metropolis that would accommodate groups of white-eyed Grays. These residences offered gymnasiums to train up the physical body, rich Creature Crystal seams to charge the sensory body and a closed psychic network where colleagues could develop their psychic bodies.

'It looks great, Groveller, but why have you prevented the

white-eyed Grays having access to the public psychic network?' the Peeper enquired and the Groveller looked concerned.

'Peeper, I am glad you raised this serious issue, but we were thinking of the welfare of the colleagues. It's too early to let them back into the Collective Consciousness. They may get frightened or lost. We need to make sure that they are strong enough before we can take that sort of risk with their psychic welfare.'

The Peeper saw the sense in this, though it thought it would be a shame that the colleagues would not be able to communicate with the rest of the Collective Consciousness. Still, it supposed that would be the next stage in the rehabilitation programme. Then it remembered its old associates, how far they had come in their training and knew that they would be enthralled by the challenge of the new programme.

'I know of some white-eyed Grays who would be more than ready for every part of this programme. In fact, I'd like to personally recommend them to you. I'm sure they will set an excellent example!'

'Really?' encouraged the Groveller, 'well, if *you* recommend them, then we shall make sure that they are the very first to go. Would you like me to break the news to them, or will you?'

The Groveller uploaded onto the News Channel in its private office at the Sensate Senate, looking for updates on metropolitan affairs and noticing how much more psychic traffic there seemed to be now that the psychic networks were back in operation. At one node displaying the demographic profile of the species, its personal observation was confirmed. There were indeed many more sighted Grays coming-into-being. The Ancient and the Academic had been working hard and efficiently. Production of the crystalline bodies by the Silica Worms had rapidly increased and there were remarkably few mutants.

The Groveller sat back and reflected on the next step in its action plan. The success of the repopulation programme meant that deanimation of the white-eyed Grays could happen almost immediately. Now, the Star Commander needed to be briefed about its role in the programme.

reunion

The Peeper was delighted to meet up with the Hopper, the Digger and the Screwer again.

It had been so busy saving and rehabilitating the rest of the colleagues that it had not spent any time with these old associates. They had grown strong as white-eyed colleagues and, like many others, had been happily employed in the mines having learned to compensate for their lack of vision in other ways.

The Peeper was only too delighted that it had found an excuse to see them and was doubly thrilled because it was about to deliver very good news about the new rehabilitation centre.

The Hopper placed its hands on its shoulders and gave the Peeper a hug, as it could not find the words or psychic images to express its true feelings.

'We are so delighted you came, Peeper!' laughed the Screwer, its sense of humour drawing off some of the intensity of the emotion that was being exchanged between the two colleagues and lightening the atmosphere. 'We really owe you an apology.'

'Don't be absurd, you have no need to ask pardon from me! Whatever do you want to apologise for?' exclaimed the Peeper.

'Ah, well, call it a point of contention, but we need to settle the score. You were right about your exercises and we were wrong about the eclipse.'

'Forget it,' sighed the Peeper, 'that was a whole existence ago and I have a new challenge for you.'

The white-eyed miners were excited when the Peeper told

them about the Groveller's plans. 'I know you are the right colleagues to test it all out and, when you get back, I would be very interested to know what you make of it.'

They spent the rest of the precious time they had together playing the Peeper's game, cheating as usual and hugging one another, as if they somehow knew that when they parted they would not meet again.

psychic purity

'Commiserations on the Chronicler case, Star Commander,' the Groveller's tone sounded sincere. 'I understand that you made much progress, but I am sure you understand the importance of the Senate's decree regarding the destruction of the diary. I am sure you appreciate that these are difficult times!'

'Yes, sir.'

'I have a proposition for you that you may like to hear. Of course, everything that I reveal to you will be entirely off the record, so I am asking you to switch off your psychic memory circuits before I proceed.' The Groveller paused, waiting for the Star Commander to decide what to do.

The Star Commander preferred to record every conversation from senior figures, so that it could review the contents and ensure it was obeying commands. It was always suspicious of off-the-record conversations as it followed orders to the letter and expected its seniors to honour them. However, something about the Groveller's approach intrigued the Star Commander and it was prepared to entertain the senator's proposal, no matter how irregular it appeared to be.

The Groveller saw the transient spark of blue pass over the Star Commander's visual sensors as it deactivated its psychic memory recorder and relaxed. Although the senators had broadly approved of the project, it was certain that some members would raise objections to a number of details in the deanimation protocol. Once it had secured the Star Commander's cooperation, the Groveller would have completely delegated its responsibility for the deanimation process and would have a senior Gray to blame in the advent of any potential scandal.

'I have been most impressed by your dedication, Star Commander, and I am hoping that you will not let your talents go to waste because of recent unfortunate circumstances. I am hoping that you will put your great experience and many skills into implementing a very important and secret project that will secure the psychic purity of the species.'

The Star Commander listened attentively in the echoless chamber, whilst the Groveller outlined the phased deanimation programme that would operate under the guise of a rehabilitation centre.

'I think you will share my opinion that it offers our species great benefits in the long-term, although the shorter-term aims perhaps appear a little disagreeable. However, the psychic nature of the white-eyed Grays will never be equivalent to the sighted members of the species and, besides, they are overly tactile, a perversity in conduct that must be stopped at the earliest convenience.'

The Star Commander reflected on the request. The proposed assignment did not allow it to command spacecraft, nor would it stretch its psychic body to its limits, but the objectives coincided with the Star Commander's beliefs in improving the psychic integrity of the species. Perhaps, the Star Commander wondered, the Groveller might even reconsider the importance of the Chronicler's case if the Star Commander proved itself a reliable ally. Since it was unable to pursue the Chronicler's case on its own accord, the Star Commander thought that it could at least oversee the covert psychic cleansing programme and raise questions again about how this tragedy could have happened in the first place. It accepted the assignment, but much less enthusiastically than the Groveller had expected.

'I'll be in contact again when we are ready to start the programme!' promised the Groveller. The Star Commander gave a brief double-breasted arm-strike in respectful acknowledgement of the Groveller's personal visit, before it turned to leave. But it had to steady itself for some time before it could function properly again.

In truth, the Star Commander was not at its usual strength. It was suffering transient episodes of psychic breakdown and during these times it would lose perceptual clarity. During the conversation with the Groveller, the Star Commander had been aware that its surroundings were, fleetingly, breaking up. Now that the Groveller had left, it tried to recall the details of the assignment, but the whole picture was not clear. The Star Commander's memory traces were vague in parts and there were discontinuities in what it recalled about the conversation. The Star Commander thought it was a pity that the Groveller had asked it to turn off its psychic memory recorder as this was one occasion where a rerun of the conversation would have been invaluable.

dilemma

The Star Commander had not destroyed the Chronicler's diary, but had read it many times now. It turned to the page where the Chronicler's sense of reality seemed to be breaking up and identified with the symptoms. Could the Star Commander itself be suffering from the very same thing?

The Star Commander was convinced that the Chronicler's disappearance, the calamitous eclipse and the other strange events on Rune 66 were, somehow or other, linked to the Time Toroid.

Since it had secretly compiled its report on the bizarre account of events documented in the Chronicler's diary, the Star Commander had grown rather used to reading it by now and found itself stroking the odd characters for comfort. They no longer seemed quite so perverse and it found itself wishing for the old days when psychic purity was much simpler to patrol and when it had led the squadrons of silver cigar-shaped Star Fleet ships on their reconnaissance missions.

Then the negative symptoms that it had associated with an imminent breakdown in its perception of reality came again, intruding on its escapism. Everything around it appeared to be melting and the atmosphere felt very heavy. The Star Commander tried to move, but it felt as if it was being compressed under a huge weight that was not made of matter but something else. It was choking and everything appeared in monochrome. The Star Commander felt as if its entire surroundings were being swallowed up into its own body which then contracted again into nothing more than a full stop.

'Stop!' shouted the Star Commander, forbidding the assault on its senses to return. Something was very wrong.

The Star Commander instinctively knew that its adversary was something of cosmic dimensions. The more the Star Commander reflected on the events, the more convinced it became that the species was still under threat, not from within its population but from forces outside.

The Star Commander needed to know whether the species was under attack by an alien entity somewhere in the Time Toroid manipulating them all, or whether the tragic events were simply a quirk of cosmic forces that were coincident to this phenomenon, without any intention behind them. If this was the case, then these bizarre and frightening events might pass on their own.

This was an important distinction to make. If the Grays were under attack, then it could not act alone and would therefore have to approach the Sensate Senate and persuade them to let it take out a Star Fleet Mission into Far Space to investigate the Time Toroid again.

This would not be an easy task and it reached for the Chronicler's diary that it had preserved, wondering if there was something important in it that it might have overlooked.

progress

The Peeper was trembling with emotion.

'Are you sure about this?' The Groveller was very happy to oblige it with reassurance.

'Perfectly! The decision is unanimous.'

'What would I have to do if I became a senator?' The Peeper was unsure that it had the mental facilities, experience or wisdom to carry out the enormous responsibilities that the senators were entrusted with, which meant that no Crystalline Gray had ever been appointed before.

'That is easy. You would be required to take full responsibility for the rehabilitation programme. There is no other colleague on the planet who is more qualified to perform this task than you are.'

The Peeper thought carefully about the offer. It had worked exhaustively since the time of the eclipse, first treating and then educating both the white-eyed Grays and their sighted helpers. Many teams were now operating in the metropolis and, although there was still much more work to be done in the field, a managerial role in the programme would offer it a new perspective on the rehabilitation programme. Perhaps it would serve its colleagues better if it could influence events at the centre of the culture and ensure that the rehabilitation exercises were properly implemented throughout the metropolis.

'What exactly would I be required to do?' enquired the Peeper, still wondering if it had misunderstood what it had been told.

'Well, you would have to attend the council sessions at the Sensate Senate and delegate your field duties to others.'

'I see.' The Peeper was now a little unsure that it was ready for such responsibility and was looking for reassurance.

'Listen, Peeper, there is no need to decide now, but come with me and I will give you a proper tour of the Sensate Senate. There is still much you do not know about its chamber and its complexities. Perhaps if I showed you around the place where you could be working in the near future, it might help you decide. You know, even now, I still get a feeling of awe when I stand back and think that I am a senator and I actually work in the Sensate Senate. You know, as a newly come-into-being Gray, I used to walk past its great granite walls and the amethyst crystals that encrusted them and imagine what great beings must reside within the chambers of such a place. Like you, I never thought that I could be a part of it, too. Sometimes I imagine I am that newly come-into-being again and, when I do, I feel that same thrill, that same awe and, Peeper, I must say it is at those times that I feel most alive!'

'I am not sure, senator. My instincts tell me to spend some time alone, reflecting on this matter. I do not want to make a hasty decision. You are always so terribly persuasive and I am still unsure whether this is the right time to leave the field.' The Peeper felt vulnerable. It knew it was being flattered and charmed by the senator but, still, something deep within the Peeper's conscience told it that the appointment was just a little premature.

'Peeper, you are more than capable and ready to be a senator. Any colleague will tell you that! For goodness' sake, the whole Collective Consciousness is begging for you to take this place. It is not my request alone, it is the species that needs you.'

The Peeper wavered again. The Groveller was right. The needs of the species were greater than its own insecurities about how it would cope with such responsibility.

'Senator, you have convinced me. The species is telling me that I must take this new role and I shall have to meet their needs. I will come with you to the Sensate Senate, immediately!'

The Groveller announced the news on the psychic network

and the senators greeted the Peeper with double-breasted arm-strikes as it walked shoulder to shoulder with the Groveller into the Great Committee Hall.

'Welcome, Peeper, I am glad you have decided to join us!' congratulated the Grabber. 'Approach the chair so that the initiation ceremony can begin.'

The Peeper stopped an arm's length from the Grabber, who took its silica crystal amplifiers and projected a holographic sheath around it. The virtual armour was intricately constructed with a tall, spiked helmet that looked like a receiver and jointed plates with inscriptions on them that were fitted to each section of its body from the neck downwards. Around it little fingers of piezoelectric current danced. The Grabber raised one of the silica crystal amplifiers that it held in its hand, placed it on the Peeper's forehead, between its eyes and asked it to repeat the oath of allegiance to the Senate.

'I, the Peeper, promise to serve, protect and advance the purity and strength of the Collective Consciousness. As a servant of the species, I declare that my crystalline and psychic bodies are the instruments of every colleague and that anything that harms the species harms me. I undertake to follow my assignment to the Sensate Senate to the full and work with the other senators to progress our collective ambitions. This I swear in front of these honoured witnesses.'

The Grabber placed the silica crystal amplifier in the Peeper's hand and the other senators rose from their seats.

'We, the governing senators, welcome the Peeper into our Council and will assist and guide it to advance the interests of the Collective Consciousness.'

Then they all started slapping the side of their chairs and clicking loudly.

'Welcome, colleague! Welcome, senator!'

The Peeper swelled with pride. It clutched the silica crystal amplifier, feeling its smooth edges and receiving comfort from its hard physicality. As the congratulations died down, the Grabber motioned silence again.

'Peeper, you have served the species well in this difficult time and I have a special honour to confer upon you. You are already aware of our plans to open a rehabilitation centre, but you will not know that we have decided to name it in your honour. The centre will be called the "Peeper Playground", so that your role in the rehabilitation programme will be forever honoured.'

The Peeper bowed its head appreciatively, secretly feeling that it could have done without this honour and that the name did not really convey a serious place of work, but it did not object since it was genuinely flattered by the gesture.

There were more clicking noises and slapping of chairs and the Peeper walked through its virtual armour to take its position at the round table for the start of the new council session. At the end of the meeting, the Grabber motioned the Groveller and the Hero to stay behind.

'Are we ready to start the deanimation procedure?'

'Yes, your honour!' confirmed the Groveller, 'the finishing touches to the centre were completed a few days ago.'

'The Star Commander has agreed to oversee the project, but I must admit I am a little worried about its competence for the task. It has not been quite itself since the Chronicler case,' added the Hero.

'Do you think this will be an insurmountable problem?' asked the Grabber. 'This project must remain secret at all costs. Our reputations are at stake.'

'I have confidence that the deanimation programme will go according to plan. The Star Commander's role is a token one and, just like the Peeper, it will carry the blame in the event of any failure or scandal,' assured the Groveller. 'In fact, I am expecting the whole programme to be a great success. There are already thousands of white-eyed Grays signed up for the Peeper Playground as the old associates of the Peeper have spread the word. In fact, I believe that every white-eyed Gray is happy to go to the centre. If we act swiftly and with purpose there will be no scandal, as our aims will have been fulfilled before anyone has time to ask questions.'

'Very good!' asserted the Grabber. 'Keep me fully briefed on your progress.'

The Hero and the Groveller gave double-breasted arm-strike salutes and turned to go.

'Hero,' added the Grabber before it left the Great Committee Hall, 'keep a close eye on the Star Commander for me, please. The last thing we need is a disillusioned colleague to head our programme. If it becomes tiresome, I want it decommissioned. Do you understand?'

'Yes, sir.' The Hero snapped its heels together and saluted the Grabber again. It was confident that it would be able to control the situation as it had recruited many newly-born sighted Grays to assist the Star Commander in its work and they were all assigned to report any aberrance in their senior's conduct directly to the Hero. What a brilliant idea of the Groveller's it was to start the colleagues watching one another.

confusion

The Hopper, the Digger and the Screwer were amongst the first white-eyed Grays to arrive at the Peeper Playground.

Despite huge queues to sign up for the rehabilitation camp, their former associate had been as good as its word and ensured that they were included for rehabilitation in the first intake. There was a general air of anticipation outside the Peeper Playground and, as the white-eyes were allowed to pass into the recreation area, they moved together in orderly chains linking shoulder to arm.

'Why do they do that?' asked one sighted newborn. It was delighted to have a supervisory role in this historical event as the opening of the Peeper Playground was widely announced on the psychic networks as a place that would preserve the psychic integrity of the species.

'I think they are gathering collective sensory information,' replied its colleague, having recently been briefed on the white-eyes' unique behaviour patterns by the Star Commander itself.

'Oh,' replied the other, 'but it's disgusting, isn't it?'

'Well, yes and no,' its well-informed colleague retorted. 'You are not allowed to say it is "disgusting", you must refer to everything they do as "unorthodox". That's what the Star Commander says and it knows everything about everything.'

'Well, I don't approve of touching!'

'Nor does the Star Commander. It says that it weakens the psychic purity of the species, but you do not have to approve. You just have to understand why they do it and then it is not threatening. Anyway, these colleagues won't behave so disgracefully in the future as they are all going to undergo an improvement programme. You'd better get used to it around here in the meantime as the Star Commander has already informed us of the arrival of the next group.'

The Digger stopped walking when it reached a smooth knee-high protuberance and sat down on it.

'Hey, check this out, it's a chest expander,' it called over to the Screwer and the Hopper, who were both a little cautious. They had been following the Digger in a shoulder to hand arrangement, the same as they now used to fulfil their mining duties, and could already sense that something was not quite right about the place.

'Here, you take these handles and bring them together with your arms straight. Do not bend at your joints because it makes the exercise too easy. I wonder how you increase the weight to make it a more difficult exercise. I am determined to get some results now that this new centre has been built for us.' The Digger was flapping the handles together, making an irritating noise, but it did not provoke comment from its colleagues as they had sensed the arrival of the Star Commander.

The Digger did not care about the comings and goings of the sighted Grays. It was thrilled to be in a state-of-the-art gymnasium. In a very short while, it became bored by the chest expander and found a piece of recumbent apparatus that required it to stand up against resistance. This was much harder as its legs were still very skinny.

The Star Commander looked down at the entry of the white-eyed Grays from an elevated ramp in the centre of the 'playground', saying nothing, just observing.

The Screwer was unsettled by the Star Commander's dominant psychic presence and had noticed that they were not alone when trying out the apparatus. A very diligent, sighted newly-born Gray had been following them around and taking notes. When it was within arm's reach, the Screwer suddenly grabbed it and asked what it was doing. The startled newborn, who had been briefed that the white-eyes were blind and stupid, told them that it had been assigned to record everything that they were doing. The Screwer only let the squirming colleague go when it felt the newborn had been sufficiently intimidated by forcing it to look at its sightless eyes.

The Digger was now enthusing about another piece of apparatus where it pulled itself up from the ground holding onto a couple of high-reach handles. The Screwer pulled the Hopper close to it, when it was sure that the newborn was just outside its psychic range.

'There is something strange about this place!' whispered the Screwer.

'That's because it's new, Screwer. This has never been done before,' reassured the Hopper.

'No, it's not just new, there is something else about it. Firstly, I do not like that idiot following us and, secondly, I do not think the apparatus is designed to assist us. This place has another purpose. Mark my words, Hopper, something else will happen here.' The Screwer could not relax and decided to avoid raising the suspicions of the vigilant newborn by giving the impression that it was testing out the apparatus. Although it tried to exude an air of composure as it pushed against various resistances, it was acting extremely oddly. The newborn duly made a note of this.

There was a general hush amongst the newborns as a general message relayed that the Star Commander was about to make an announcement.

'Welcome, colleagues, to the Peeper Playground named after your newly-appointed senator, the Peeper, whose role in your rehabilitation has been both remarkable and dedicated.'

There was a cheer from the white-eyed Grays with the mention of the Peeper's name and the Hopper, the Digger, and the Screwer held each other's hands in respect.

The Star Commander continued to outline the objectives of the centre and details of the programme.

'The equipment here has been designed to support your unique constitution. Through the novel devices that are embedded in the exercise machines, you will discover a new dimension to your existence where your abilities may be restored to you.

As you are the first intake of white-eyes, you will be setting the standard for those that follow you and I am hoping for your full cooperation in this pioneering programme.'

During the whole introduction, the unwanted newborn observer distracted the Screwer by continually fidgeting with the apparatus settings.

The Star Commander stepped down after its address and a confident newborn continued, informing the white-eyed colleagues that their sighted assistants were there to assist them with the various pieces of equipment. The newborns would make the appropriate adjustments to the apparatus, so that each white-eyed colleague would be able to test and ultimately improve their sensory abilities, then their physical strength and finally their psychic powers in the Peeper Playground.

The constant fidgeting of the newborn was beginning to anger the Screwer and it wondered if the sighted colleague was actually familiar with the controls.

'I don't like this at all,' it complained to the Hopper, as the newborn persuaded it to connect to the first exercise test on the sensory network.

There was a brief pause in the operation where the white-eyed Grays relaxed, and the supervisory sighted colleagues checked their connections before a silent signal was given for the power to be connected. Instantaneously, the senses of every white-eyed Gray were overridden.

'It hurts!' shouted the Screwer and it started to laugh despairingly before it collapsed.

The Digger and the Hopper shouted for the Peeper to help them, but the system was too powerful and they were rapidly deanimated with all the other white-eyes, but it was not quite over. The newborns proceeded to transfer the devitalised bodies to the resistance machines that were adjusted to exert powerful pressure that crushed their remains. Then groups of newborns worked together to collect their residues for recycling into the opencast mine nearby where every last one of them was fed to the giant Silica Worms.

'Poor things,' said one newborn, 'but at least they are out of their misery now.'

'Yes,' said another. 'Fancy not being able to use your visual sensors. It must really affect the intellect. This assignment gives you a real sense of achievement. Isn't it wonderful to know that, when they are deanimated, revitalized and subsequently reassigned, they will be whole again. What an important task we have been given here.'

'It's quite simple, really, isn't it? I was expecting something much more dramatic or sophisticated,' speculated the first newborn, contemplating its handiwork.

'Me, too, but I am not sure I understand what all the devices are for here. What is the closed psychic network for?'

'I am not entirely sure either, but I would suspect that it will be used to extract any useful or functional psychic bodies from these degenerates. Besides, it will stop them communicating with the Collective Consciousness and upsetting all the other colleagues. I've also noticed that, when they arrive, the gymnasium serves a useful cosmetic function. They cannot tell that they are going to be deanimated by feeling around the equipment set up here. At least, that's my impression. The poor things are not aware of their situation, you see. They are so deluded that they think that they are completely ok. You know, when I spoke to a few of them with my loudest psychic impressions, they really seemed to believe that it was possible to be rehabilitated in their white-eye configuration.'

'That's incredible! It just proves how damaged they are.'

Just then, the Star Commander returned to review the outcome of the first intake of white-eyed Grays. The two contemplative newborns gave a double-breasted arm-strike salute and stood to attention. Their senior walked slowly by them both, musing that the operation was successful. It only stopped when it had paced around the entire Peeper Playground, having checked for any telltale traces of the deanimated white-eyed Grays. When it was convinced there was no evidence to suggest their fate, it issued orders for the next group of colleagues to be deanimated.

The Groveller was watching from the entrance to the Peeper

Playground. It had arrived unannounced and intended to depart without revealing its presence to the Star Commander. There was no need for concern about the Star Commander's conduct, it reported to the Hero; their stooge was playing its part beautifully.

food for thought

The Creature Crystal network was proliferating, owing to the increase in psychic ablutions that were now being performed regularly, if not obsessionally, by the newborns. The Creature Crystals sought after the nourishment from the ablutions of the newborns as they were filled with multisensory material. Indeed, the number of vitalising nodes greatly increased around the open-cast mines where the Silica Worms produced the newborns' crystalline bodies as the Creature Crystals assisted the population increase in the metropolis. The ecology of the planet was evolving.

'Tastes good?'

'Tastes different!'

'What has changed?'

'Well, I suppose the thought is richer. The intellectual aspect is full of sensory information, it's really rather filling.'

'So it's better then?'

'I'm not sure.'

'What's wrong?'

'Well, there is an aftertaste.'

'What kind of aftertaste?'

'Hmmm, something quite bitter, but it passes quite rapidly and yet there is still something there, something lingering but I can't describe it. It's without character.'

'So, which do you prefer, the old ablutions or the new ones?'

'Oh, definitely the new ones!'

peace

The Star Commander looked up at the skies.

They were heavy with meteorite dust scattering the bright, violet light, enough to hide the moons from view. Through the haze, the Star Commander could just tell that the sun was its usual crimson red.

'Someone should have cleared that debris by now,' it grumbled aloud, making a mental note to reprimand the newborn squadron of Ariel Intelligence officers that it had personally drilled in the art of meteorite dust collection during routine sky patrols. However, it was glad to be responsible for Aerial Intelligence once more, now that the crisis in Gray culture had passed.

Life within the metropolis had been uneventful since all the white-eyed Grays had been deanimated. The number of bizarre events happening throughout the metropolis had stopped and the Star Commander was relieved to return to its original duties. It was even beginning to accept that the series of inexplicable events that had signposted a change in their culture from being psychically-based to intensely intellectual may indeed have been no more than a series of coincidences.

Nowadays, it was forbidden, not just taboo, for colleagues to touch one another. The psychic networks were full of horrific programmes on white-eyed Grays, directly linking their tactility to their shocking appearance as a cause-and-effect. Naturally, the newborns took this information to heart and strove to improve their psychic and intellectual bodies to levels that had been previously unheard of in the mines. Still, none rivalled the Star Commander in psychic strength, although there were many pretenders.

The Star Commander inspected the meteorites on the planet's surface, as if it were taking a military drill, noting their markings, their colour, their composition and their position around the craters. Amongst the graveyard of battle-weary meteorites, it felt at peace, weighty and somehow connected to a greater system whose power flowed within its body. Unlike the meteorites, the Star Commander did not feel that its purpose was over.

Since its release from the Peeper Playground duties, it had spent much time reflecting on its situation.

It was happy now. The metropolis was restful and it was able to spend its downtime freely. It mostly spent this time exploring the psychic networks, looking for new information on the profile of the species. It had been encouraged by the newborns whose average intelligence was now forty percent greater than that of the Collective Consciousness at the time the Chronicler was broadcasting *Abductee*.

The current programmes had a mainly documentary focus and the Star Commander was relieved that there were now far fewer gossip nodes. The Star Commander noted that the most popular programmes on the network were so-called 'Psychic Sports'. A whole channel was dedicated to reporting how the most intellectually-gifted colleagues sparred with one another in psychic combat. The winners of these psychic sparrings used psychic tactics to score the greatest number of 'put-downs'. Colleagues could either upload to watch the competitions by remote control or queue for the best view. The Star Commander enjoyed these jousts as it shared in the triumphs of the winners and, in each battle, it saw hope for the future strength of the species.

At the same time as it found reassurance in the activity of the Grays in general, it was personally worried about how long it was going to remain the strongest Psychic Gray, since it was still being disabled by frequent sensory breakdowns which made it confused and frightened. Another, related concern was that the Time

Toroid, although still a long way from Rune 66, was still perceptible in Far Space.

On this brilliant day, as the Star Commander made its usual surveillance of the skies, it suddenly decided to take complete control of its life and make one last mission to the forbidding Time Toroid that remained at the limits of its psychic range, alone.

It looked skywards, projecting its psychic from its crystalline body and feeling it rise from the planet's surface out into Near Space. Soon, it reached the region of Far Space that hosted the Time Toroid. But, instead of holding a steady pathway to its destination, as it had done many times before without the added assistance of a spaceship, the Star Commander started to spin around and around, faster and faster, until it lost consciousness.

being

The Star Commander gradually regained its senses. It did not recognise its surroundings and had the instinctive feeling that something was very wrong.

The intense lighting of the space it found itself in bleached out its vision. However, the Star Commander's position sensors told it that it was recumbent, but it could not feel its crystalline body. Where was it? Regaining control of its psychic sensors, the Star Commander reached out and felt the presence of another being that seemed to be studying it with piercing blue eyes. Despite its alien appearance, there was something very familiar about the creature.

'Welcome, Star Commander!'

The Star Commander was amazed that it spoke its psychic language.

The blue-eyed being read its thoughts.

'Don't be surprised by anything here.'

'Where am I?' the Star Commander wondered.

'You are lying on an table in the experimental chamber of the time-spill that you call the Time Toroid.'

'The Time Toroid! Of course, I am inside at last,' remarked the Star Commander trying to move, but finding itself unable to. Under the piercing blue eyes of the being dissecting its thoughts, the Star Commander summoned its strength.

'What are you?' demanded the Star Commander.

The blue eyes sparkled mischievously.

'I am the ultimate progeny, a Simbeing.'

The Star Commander felt as if it was being toyed with.

'What do you want with me?'

It hoped that whatever the blue-eyed creature had decided to do with it would be over swiftly.

'I want to talk to you.'

The Star Commander did not believe the creature. Those blue eyes were too unsettling and seemed to be a façade for infinite complexities and inconsistencies in its character. This being was untrustworthy.

'What about? You can read my thoughts, so why don't you just scan me and get it over and done with!' snapped the Star Commander, feeling very vulnerable.

The eyes were laughing.

'Relax, Star Commander. I just want your cooperation. You see, I am on a progressive evolutionary mission. I am using the Time Toroid as a vehicle in which I travel throughout the universe. My ambition is to visit all cultures and all species. When I have fully understood each creational being, I shall embrace the best features of each kind, absorbing them into my own form.'

Now the eyes were hungry.

'What do you want with the Grays?'

The being twirled and then skipped slowly around the Star Commander who tried to follow its position. Damn! It still could not move.

'Right now? I want to talk to you, to study you in order to discover which features I wish to adopt. I study many individuals over many generations, so that I obtain a complete picture of the entities with which I wish to hybridise. I find the Grays fascinating. They are a very sophisticated species and I am most curious to understand your psychic abilities further. You have a particularly strong psychic body. What can you do with it?'

The eyes stopped bouncing around and held the Star Commander in their gaze.

'I won't cooperate until I know more about you'.

More laughing in the being's gaze.

'Ah, do not worry about my intentions. All I am interested in for the moment is an in-depth interview with you. Oh, and I also want you to work with me. The way this will happen is that I will return you fully to your life on Rune 66 from time to time. Another thing, I had better warn you now, when you return, your former life will appear strange, distant and obsolete to you. This is a necessary part of the process. I call it "quarantine" because you will feel isolated from your culture. As I said, this is entirely necessary. If you need an analogy, you may think of it as being a "control" in a formal experiment.'

The Star Commander was gradually adjusting to the strange environment and the shock of the experience.

'Are you attacking the Grays?'

If it was going to have its mind manipulated, the Star Commander was determined to have a last window of clarity and find out if this creature was responsible for the strange events on Rune 66.

'Ah, your unsolved riddles. You really are most suspicious, Star Commander!'

The Star Commander would not be patronised nor denied the answers for which it had risked whole squadrons of its Starcom officers.

'Was it you who brought about the eclipse?'

The eyes were laughing again. The being was enjoying itself.

'Not directly, but let us say that a certain amount of collateral damage is inevitable, given the power and range of my experiments. The Time Toroid itself is an entity in its own right. I only use its powers to achieve my aims. I cannot prevent catastrophes; I just exploit the natural forces of the Time Toroid. As you have witnessed for yourself, these are vast and are difficult to harness. Come now, don't be so naive, Star Commander, no advance in history has ever been accident-free and it never will be. Although I regret any harm to innocent beings, it is in the nature of the universe that these minor tragedies happen.'

The Star Commander was incensed.

'*Minor tragedies?* They are not minor to our species. We once had a whole generation of visually impaired colleagues that we had to deanimate because they were degenerates. Do you have any idea what that did to our culture? The whole incident was a catastrophe! The Grays are naturally a "pure" psychic species, but these colleagues were completely damaged by unexplained radiation. Was that your doing? Were you involved in some sort of a so-called progressive evolutionary experiment at the time? I bet you were, and I expect that you had something to do with the inexplicable behaviour and disappearance of the Chronicler and probably the fate of my Starcom officers, too!'

Why could it not free itself from the being's gaze? Surely, there must be a way of overcoming its paralysing powers.

'Now you really are angry, Star Commander. You are usually so marvellously self-composed, yes, I already know a little bit about you. I have been studying you. Didn't you feel the sensory disorientation that happened when I abducted you here for observation? No?'

The Star Commander tried to respond, but outrage at the Simbeing's conduct clouded its reason.

'Don't be so incensed by it all, Star Commander, for you have already told me that you have realised that certain events that have taken place in your culture cannot be natural misfortunes, but are unfortunate casualties. Indeed, it is true that my experiments have been rather widespread and have had serious consequences for your fascinating planet, but I cannot take responsibility for every misfortune that happens in pursuit of my own mission. As I said to you earlier, the Time Toroid has a momentum of its own. I have already studied the Gray that you mentioned, the Chronicler. It is a most gifted and insightful individual. It was born at a moment when your species was at its most balanced and therefore susceptible to my influence. If you reflect on my appearance, you may be able to explain your feelings of familiarity. You think you recognise me, don't you? Well, look closer, what do you see?'

The Star Commander drew closer to the Simbeing. Behind the piercing blue eyes was a psychic body, turbulent and precariously formed. A character profile slowly formed in the Star Commander's psychic vision. Yes, there was something familiar in the shapes that the Star Commander's psychic probing was uncovering. It followed their traces deeper still and stopped when it had clearly identified the essence of a Gray, a very familiar Gray, and one that had recorded its trauma in a bizarre diary.

'The Chronicler! You have absorbed some of its characteristics. It is part of you, this is perverse.'

The Simbeing's whole body laughed.

'Yes, I have already selected those characteristics of the Chronicler that, after a period of experimental observation, I considered most desirable as part of my schedule to fully understand each creational being. A perverse idea to you perhaps, but a delight and a triumph for me! I do think the "new me" is rather good.'

The Star Commander hated being made fun of. 'What did you do to my Starcom officers?' it raged.

'Temper, temper, Star Commander. As I said, I am not responsible for everything. The fate of your Starcom officers is different to that of the Chronicler whose evolutionary leap, I fully admit, was my doing. Your officers were at the mercy of the Time Toroid. Constitutionally, most were not strong enough to survive the abrasive time-substance, unlike the Chronicler and yourself who are made of much tougher stuff. Those that did not perish got trapped. I believe that a couple of them may even have found their way to the mirror sector.'

The Star Commander wondered if there was a way out of the Time Toroid after all.

'The mirror sector?'

Had its Starcom officers escaped? If it could only free itself from the paralysing powers that bound it, the Star Commander vowed to find the mirror sector.

'There is so much for you to learn, Star Commander. The Time Toroid opens onto a new dimension, which is the mirror sector. You will learn more about the Time Toroid and its complexities in due course as you work with me but, for now, I can see that you are overwhelmed.'

The Star Commander noticed that the definition of the experimental chamber had become softer in focus and the lights were brighter. As it tried to protest that it was not in shock and that it wanted to know more, its thoughts began to become muddled. As the Star Commander tried to fight off its increasing state of confusion, the Simbeing bade it goodbye.

'Star Commander, I will now draw our first conversation to a close. It has been most delightful. When your perceptual clarity returns, you will find yourself back on Rune 66 and your memories of this space will be indistinct. As I use you in my various experiments, you will find yourself continually transported, quite unpredictably, between these two existences just like the Chronicler before you was. Good luck, Star Commander. I think I am going to enjoy our work together.'